OFF-TARGET

In an all-too-possible near future, when genetic engineering has become the norm for humans, parents are prepared to take incalculable risks to ensure that their babies are perfect, altering genes that may cause illness, and more . . .

Susan has been trying for a baby for years, and when a one-night stand makes her dream come true, she'll do anything to ensure her husband doesn't find out — including the unthinkable. She believes her secret is safe. For now.

But as governments embark on a genetic arms race and children around the globe start experiencing a host of distressing symptoms, something truly horrendous is unleashed. Because those children have only one thing in common, and people are starting to ask questions . . .

EVE SMITH

OFF-TARGET

Complete and Unabridged

CHARNWOOD
Leicester

First published in Great Britain in 2022 by
Orenda Books
London

First Charnwood Edition
published 2022
by arrangement with
Orenda Books
London

*A catalogue record for this book is available
from the British Library.*

ISBN 978-1-4448-4916-5

For Nuala and Aaron

'*A mother's love for her child is like nothing else in the world.*
It knows no law, no pity, it dares all things and crushes down remorselessly all that stands in its path.'
— Agatha Christie, *The Last Séance*

'*Don't see the genetics revolution as abstract science. This is the story of you and your family and your future, and it is unfolding in front of your eyes.*'
— Jamie Metzl, author of *Hacking Darwin*

I'm just taking my last swig when the doorbell rings.

My hand freezes, glass against lip.

Have they come back early?

Wine sours on my tongue as the early-evening sun dances leaf patterns across the room.

Idiot. I swallow. As if Steve would ring his own bell . . .

Now there's a knock.

Two knocks.

'Delivery!'

I lever myself up and squint at the security cam. A guy in a short-sleeved shirt and navy baseball cap is standing in my porch, clutching a small package. I think of those macabre leaflets in the bin, and my stomach tightens. But he looks legit.

Knowing Steve, it's probably some enhanced wearable. I imagine hurling his new Smart Band against one of the empty squares on the wall.

Then again, it could be for Zurel.

I activate the mic: 'Just a minute.'

I shuffle down the hall, wiping the mascara smears under my eyes.

I should fetch that box down from the spare room and hang all the photos back up. That would show him. As I turn the latch, the thought makes me smile.

The door slams into my face.

I stagger back, cupping my nose.

The man drops the package and barges past, his shirt straining against his chest, as if it can barely contain him. I glimpse a tattoo, the length of his forearm. He scans the lounge and marches upstairs.

Red petals spot the carpet.

I need to run, but my legs won't move.

I hear him thudding around, opening all the doors.

Adrenaline surges, and I rush to the SmartPod, hit the button and steady my voice to give the command.

Feet hurtle down the stairs.

I race for the back door, but a hand grips my shoulder and spins me against the wall.

Black eyes consume a sharp white face.

I point at my bag on the table. 'Money, cards. Take them.'

His mouth twists. There's a ferocity in those eyes: drugs? Booze?

Something else.

'Where. Is. It?'

My phone starts to ring, its playful chirps now obscene.

'I . . . ' I swallow. 'I don't know what you — '

He clamps my neck, stopping my breath like a valve. 'The abomination.' Each syllable, staccato. 'Where is it?'

He leans closer, crushing my arteries. Black discs spin behind my eyes.

And that's when I realise. He's here for Zurel.

I claw at his face, scrabble at his fist, a primal strength eclipsing my fear. The choke releases as he grabs my wrists; breath and blood rush free. His arm wedges into my cheek; there's an inked black cross tapered like a dagger, two words underneath:

Isaiah 64

'Where . . . is . . . it?'

Fingers drill into my neck. The room begins to blur. I hear the ringtone again: faint, like an echo.

My lips make the shape of words. 'Don't . . . know.'

Pain explodes under my ribs. Instinct commands my body to double over, but I am pinned by the throat.

' 'Know that the Lord Himself is God; it is *He* who

has made us, and not we ourselves." His lip curls back in a snarl. "We are the clay, and He is our potter, All of us are the work of His hand' . . . '

Pricks of light detonate in my eyes.

I think of that first scan, her twilight hand lifting in a wave.

He squeezes harder, spit foaming his chin, hot wafts of breath and sweat. 'Children are begotten, not designed. We will purge the rot, and restore Adam's line.'

Darkness swoops. I strain every nerve and muscle to hold on.

I'd give my life for hers, willingly.

But I cannot protect her if I'm dead.

Part One: The Wish

1

A hand seizes me, deep inside. It twists and balls into a fist. The pain radiates up my spine; immobilises me sinew by sinew. I sag over a mustard-brown stain, veined, like a fingerprint. Blood? Vomit? Shit? All are possibilities. A remote fragment of my mind picks over them, before lurching back to safe mode.

A voice swims past.

Sweat streaks my face as the pressure mounts, no space for breath. The hand loosens its grip. I slump over my knees and gasp.

'That's it, love: keep breathing.'

Something cold and wet presses against my forehead. Muscles, ligaments regroup. I open my eyes and see Steve, mopping my cheeks with the gentle precision of a bomb-disposal unit. He kisses my clammy head.

'Clever wife,' he whispers. My heart swells.

Babies *can* save marriages. As well as wreck them.

He scans the purple peaks on the labour tracker. They arc higher and higher, the gaps narrowing in between.

He squeezes my hand. 'You're doing great.'

I used to be such a wimp, but these past months have cured me of that. No epidural. No opioids. I swore to myself the end of this pregnancy would be natural and pain was part of my dues. I guess you could say it's a kind of penance.

A memory ambushes me — of another hospital in another country, where I was not so brave. Labour's

9

so much easier than all the hurt I endured before. At least this agony will end.

'Everything OK, Susan?' Clare, the midwife, looms over me.

I nod.

'Can I take a little look?'

I grunt and manoeuvre myself round like a prize pig, fix my gaze on the vent in the ceiling. There's a primal, metallic smell that must be coming from me.

'Things are moving along nicely. Baby's right in position.'

My body answers with a violent wrench. That one felt different. And, before Clare utters the words, I recognise it: a visceral quickening. Steve senses it too. His grip tightens.

A breeze whips my cheek as Clare darts past. There's a clatter of trays, the glint of light on metal.

'OK, Susan,' chimes Clare. 'Time to push!'

I screw the sheet tight around my fingers. So close, now, so very close.

'Not too quick,' says Clare. 'Nice short breaths . . . '

I try to slow, but a storm within me is propelling her down. In this moment I can do anything: rip through buildings, smash alien ships.

'Steady, Susan! Whoa . . . gently, now . . . OK . . . Stop pushing!'

'A head!' cries Steve. 'I can see her head!'

An intense heat floods my cells.

'I've got the mirror, Susan,' says Clare. 'Do you want to look?'

My throat constricts. Just a tiny prick of fear, like a spindle's.

'Here, let's sit you up a bit.'

A pillow thumps into my back. Clare angles the

10

mirror between my legs as I peer round my belly. At first, all I see is blood. But then I spot her russet coils of hair.

Steve's breath fizzes. 'Can you see her?'

Hot tears spill onto my gown. All those swollen stomachs I've coveted, the endless procedures and fights. And now, like a miracle, she's here.

Clare snaps the mirror shut. 'OK, Mum. I think it's time to meet your daughter.'

My lungs inflate with a surge of air. I push, forcing my own gravity; imagine my blood rushing down my veins, to her.

'Almost there, Susan. That's it, one more should do it . . .'

And out she slips, like a seal pup.

Silence.

And then I hear it: a faltering, phlegmy mewl that builds to a cry.

A fumbling of hands and blanket, a blur of wriggling pink limbs. And she's in my arms.

My eyes race over her. A bubble of saliva graces flawless lips. Two midnight-blue eyes squint at me, blinking back the light.

Clare runs the sensor over her. 'Heart-rate spot on, and the reflexes of a prize-fighter.' She beams at me. 'Congratulations. You have a beautiful, healthy baby!'

Relief sweeps through me, more powerful than any drug. Everything is going to be fine. We will be happy, now, the three of us. It will all have been worth it.

'Would Dad like to cut the cord?' asks Clare, fixing the clamps.

Steve's face has transformed, as if the years have been ironed out. He looks like he did in those photos he keeps in the loft. From before.

11

He takes the scissors and opens the blades. My breath stills. Some fathers in the animal kingdom kill and eat newborns: even their own. Grizzlies are renowned for it. That's why mother bears are so fierce.

It takes Steve a good few cuts before he severs it. The scissors crash into the bowl. I exhale. Now, we are two.

'I'll just take some blood from the cord for the screening.' Clare busies herself with the syringe. 'We'll get the placenta delivered shortly, but right now . . .' She smiles. 'You three have some cuddle time.'

I hold my baby close. She blindly mouths my nipple and latches on. As her tongue presses in, there's a tingling, pulling sensation that I have never known. Milk flows from my breast, like ancient magic.

Steve glides his finger along the sole of her foot. He looks drunk. Giddy. 'I can't believe it.' He shakes his head and grins. 'How could we make something so perfect?'

I fix my gaze on her nose as she suckles. Her fidgeting pink toes.

'You see those dimples?' I stroke her cheek. 'Just like yours.'

The secret snarls: baulking at such audacity. I smother it. Bury it deep in my bones where no one will hear it. Not even me.

Her lips make a smacking sound and we both laugh. Steve is her daddy now. Any test will prove it.

But he wasn't her father.

2

10 months earlier

I pinch the foil pouch between my fingers and, with practised precision, prise it apart. According to the app, my period is twenty-eight hours, seventeen minutes late. That's got to signify something. My heart manages a dull thump, like a half wag of a tail. I have come to loathe this stick. Like Gandalf's staff, it can enthral or terrify; embrace life or obliterate it. My bladder throbs, desperate for release. Still, I hesitate. Because, however miniscule, the possibility exists that I *might* be. It shimmers in my mind like some distant, tropical island: utterly beguiling but impossible to reach.

I suck in a breath and thrust the wand between my legs. My bladder muscles get a touch of stage fright; Jesus, you'd think they'd know the routine by now. I summon some inspiration: pelting cascades at Folly Dolly Falls; waves crashing on Holkham beach. Just two of our abortive 'baby-dancing' weekends. But whatever dance Steve and I were doing wasn't right. Because no baby arrived.

I hear a thud through the door: Steve, shuffling out of bed. Need to move things along.

I give the stick a gentle shake. The app beeps:

Sample valid

Now, the wait.

I used to think three minutes wasn't very long, but pregnancy tests are like black holes: they dilate time, stretching minutes into eternity, hope and fear stringing you out like spaghetti. To counter this, my pregnancy app offers distraction tools. Music. Meditation. Podcasts. I've tried them all. Plus a few others of my own. Like digging my nails into my thighs until they bleed.

Today, I employ a different strategy: counting the seconds backwards, cradling the app in my palm. I get as far as fifty-five when my phone chirps. I take two breaths — I always take two — and enter my PIN.

The fan whirs behind me: the drum roll before the crash.

The results box flashes.

My throat makes a hissing sound, as if I've been punctured.

In some alternative universe, I have peed into life one fuck-off pink tick.

But not this one.

★ ★ ★

'Susan? You alright in there?'

I flex my fingers, draw the skin tight around my eyes.

'Yeah, out in a mo!'

I drag myself up and glimpse my reflection. Test Day face: not pretty. I splash water on my cheeks and take a couple of breaths.

Steve's by the bed. He frowns as I hurry past. I shove my head in the wardrobe and start trawling through tops.

'It's today, isn't it? Shit, Susan, I totally forgot — '

'It's fine. Everything's fine.' I try for a smile but it's more of a grimace.

14

I remember Steve and I ogling our first test stick, like kids in a sweetshop. Those were the early days, when that wand was the key to Wonderland; when everything lay ahead of us. Or so we thought.

Don't cry.

'It'll happen, Susan. We just need to be patient.'

My fingers clench. I am so sick of these phrases:

Give it time.

Just keep trying.

Relax, it'll happen.

He pads up behind me. 'Really. It's going to be OK.'

Nearly four years. Forty-seven cycles of Big Fat Negatives. In what messed-up world is that 'OK'?

He pulls me to him, giving my back little pats. His gestures are well intended, but they've gone stale through sheer frequency.

'I know it's hard,' he whispers. 'But we're doing all the right things.'

Genetically personalised supplements. Fish oil and folic acid. No pesticides, caffeine or booze.

'Maybe you ought to . . . you know, give those apps a miss for a while. Stay off the forums.'

My lips tighten. My Trying to Conceive (TTC) forum is the only thing keeping me sane.

He swallows. 'The doctor said it's probably not a good idea to keep test —'

'Can we not . . . ? Can we just . . . not . . . ?' My voice cracks and I pull away.

'Listen to me, Susan. You heard what she said. There's nothing wrong with either of us.'

'Well, I bloody well wish there was. Then at least we could fix it.'

They call it unexplained infertility. It's like having some undiagnosed terminal disease. I have copious high quality eggs, my tubes are open and no growths in sight; Steve's sperm are plentiful and positively flying.

He squeezes my shoulder. 'We've got to try and stay positive.'

My breath snorts through my nose. 'You know how long it took Christine? Three months. And she can barely look after herself, let alone a child.'

His hand recoils. I know how I sound; how bitter this green-eyed monster has become. It's getting to the point he can hardly look at me, let alone make love.

'Everyone's different, Susan. Some get lucky.'

'It's the twenty-first century, Steve,' I snap. 'Luck has precious little to do with it.'

We must be the only couple I know who are still trying solo, without help, the old-fashioned way: just sex.

He sinks onto the bed and sighs. 'We can't keep doing this, Susan. It's like history's repeating itself.'

He means Katya: his ex. The ultimate insult. It's not my fault, what happened. I'm the one being punished, and I wasn't even there.

'As if work isn't stressful enough . . . I don't want to live like this.'

'And you think I do?' I cuff away a tear. 'All those pitying looks from mothers in the playground. The endless bulge of bellies in the staff room — '

'You think you're the only one?' Steve cuts in. 'Week in, week out, I have to listen to the same office banter about how *lucky* I am, how much *fun* I must be having: all those lie-ins and rampant sex . . . ' He turns to me and his face stills my heart. 'Every day. Every single day I wake up seeing how unhappy you

16

are. Because I haven't given you the thing you want most . . .'

I smooth my palm over his cheek. 'It's not your fault, Steve. You're right, though: this can't carry on. We *have* to try something else.' I swallow. 'Look at Carmel. It worked out fine for them, in the end, didn't it?'

He yanks away from me as if I've just bitten him. 'Christ. Don't you ever stop?'

I slam the mattress. 'It's my choice, too! How can IVF be any worse than this?'

He stands up and squints at me, as if from a great distance. 'Oh, it gets much, much worse, believe me.' There's a gravelled edge to his words that makes me shiver. 'We've barely even got started.'

He stomps to the bathroom and locks the door. Water smashes into the tiles.

I grab my phone and slide down the wall to the floor. I scroll through my history: relentless pink circles encasing straight blue lines, the word, 'NO', shouting in white capitals.

I hear my father's voice:

You can't do anything right . . .

These lines have become the story of my life.

Flat. Blue. And always negative.

3

I pull my collar up around my ears and pace the playground, trying to avoid the parents' eyes. I have no bandwidth this morning for the posse of petty plaintiffs: Greta's mum whining about school lunches and how *utterly exhausting* the new baby is, or Harry's dad laying in about phonics again.

A straggle of year twos darts past like startled fish, first one way, then the other. Did I ever run like that? It's hard to imagine. My body is calcifying; with every failed conception it grows more inert. Sometimes, it feels as if I've been dropped down a very deep well, and I'm lying there, watching the clouds roll past, listening to the far-off lives of others.

I risk a glance at the idling pushchairs, the red-faced toddlers straining against their straps. Two girls fly up to a pram and wave at a swaddle of pink inside. My chest tightens. Other mums crowd round, poking their fingers under the hood. The mother bestows on them a sleepy, beatific smile, her hand cushioning her belly as if she's already lining up number three.

I look away and spot Marty, his long legs striding across the playing field. I lift my arm and wave.

He nods at the babble of children, frolicking like puppies. 'It's as if they store it up over the weekend, ready for Mondays.'

I smile. 'Good weekend?'

'Loud.' He takes a swig from his travel mug. 'Grandparents are over, on Mamma's side.' Marty's mother is Sicilian. He makes a yapping motion with his fingers. 'Non-stop, I tell you. I had to send them into Oxford on one of those open-top-bus sightseeing tours. I've been craving silence for forty-eight hours.'

I remember Marty on his first day in the staff room: fancy shirt, olive skin and huge brown eyes. He looked like some tropical species that had inadvertently flown off course. After ten years in corporate law he joined an accelerated teacher-training scheme: I didn't think he'd last the year. Then I watched him at break, coaxing shy Holly Chipson off the Friendship Bench. I couldn't have been more wrong. The next thing, Holly was up playing football with Marty, and three other kids joined in.

'Take it steady, Danny.' Marty sidesteps two boys crashing past after a ball. The red-haired one whoops as he crosses in front, but then he teeters to a stop, as if his batteries have died.

He sways slightly. Marty rushes over. 'Danny?'

Marty gets there just as the boy crumples, catching him under the shoulders. Marty lays him gently on the ground. Danny's body is completely rigid, his eyes rolled back. Marty takes off the boy's glasses and checks his watch.

I kneel next to him. 'Shall I fetch another first aider?'

Marty wrestles out of his jumper and lays it under the boy's head. 'It's alright: I'm trained.'

Danny's back arches and his arms jerk out; his feet start pushing against the tarmac.

'It's OK, Danny,' says Marty softly. 'You're OK.'

Tremors ripple up Danny's body; his legs rhythmically thump the ground.

I glance at Marty. 'Tell me what I can do.'

Marty shields the boy's head with his hands, keeping the jumper close. 'Get hold of his mother. Let her know what's happened.'

'What's wrong?' asks a small voice. Danny's friend is staring at him, the ball clutched tight to his chest. 'Is Danny OK?'

'Yes, Ben: he's having a seizure,' says Marty. Danny's back stiffens and he hisses through clenched teeth. 'They usually pass pretty quickly.'

I give Ben a bright smile. 'Actually, Ben, would you do me a favour and run over to reception? Let Miss Jenner know what's happened and ask her to contact Danny's mum. She may still be by the gates.'

Ben nods and sprints off.

Saliva bubbles out of Danny's mouth as the spasms intensify. I notice a dribble of blood and someone squeals. Behind us, a circle of children has gathered. They're gawping at the boy, eyes wide.

I stand up and clap my hands. 'OK, everyone line up now, please: the bell's about to go. Let's give Danny some space. Nothing to worry about: he's going to be fine.'

I usher them away and flag down Aaliyah, one of my teaching assistants. I ask her to cover for me and organise something for Marty's class.

When I get back, Marty checks his watch again and scowls. 'You may need to call an ambulance. We're almost at four minutes. Five isn't good.'

I swallow. 'OK.'

Sweat is running down the boy's freckled face; his fists are tightly clenched. I count the seconds, phone at the ready, but the spasms begin to slow. Eventually, his body slumps. Marty rolls him onto his side as Danny splutters and gasps for air.

'That's it, Danny. Cough it up.' Marty wipes the boy's mouth and smooths back his hair. 'You're OK:

you've had a seizure. You're at school and you're safe. Just try to relax: your mum's on her way.'

Danny's eyes close. Gradually, his breathing calms.

I exhale. 'Should we call his doctor?'

'We'll let his mum do that. He's exhausted. He probably just needs to go home and sleep.'

'Well, thank goodness you were here. I mean, I know the basics, but when you see it for real . . . You were so calm.'

He doesn't take his eyes off Danny. 'My sister had epilepsy. I've been doing this since I was six.'

We stay with Danny until he's able to sit up. Marty virtually carries him to his mother's car. I wait in reception while Marty speaks to her outside. She's a small woman: pale face, dark rings under her eyes. At one point, Marty puts his hand on her shoulder. I think she's crying.

'Is she OK?' I ask as Marty trudges back in. 'Has this happened before?'

'Once.' He sighs. 'There's going to be an update at the staff meeting.'

'Epilepsy?'

He shakes his head. 'I wish . . . ' His jaw stiffens. 'Danny has Batten disease. We were only told on Friday.'

'What? I've never heard of it.'

'Neither had I. It's a genetic disorder: very rare. The family got the diagnosis last week.'

'Is it serious?'

He holds my gaze. 'It's devastating.'

Danny's in Marty's class: he's only eight.

'Sight goes first. Then the muscles. Dementia sets in.' Marty's fingers curl into a fist. 'By the end, he won't be able to see, or walk . . . Or even swallow.'

21

I think of what I said in the playground.

Nothing to worry about, Danny's going to be fine . . .

I inhale. 'But surely they must be able to treat him?'

'It's terminal: there is no cure.'

'God . . . His poor mother . . .'

'His parents were in pieces when they told us: they'd no idea. Danny had only been referred because his eyes had deteriorated so quickly.' Marty stares out the window. 'The consultant said he may not make it past his teens.'

My eyes veer to a wall display: lopsided paintings of cats and dogs, a little boy chasing a purple balloon.

'There's one hope. Some new gene therapy in the States. The hospital is trying to find out more, see if they can get Danny onto the trial.' He sighs. 'He's been prescribed drugs, to help with the seizures. But that's about it. All we can do is try to keep Danny safe and record any other symptoms.'

I shake my head. 'I'm so sorry, Marty.'

'Yeah. You know the worst thing? His parents blame themselves.' His forehead furrows. 'They found out they're both carriers for the disease.'

'It's hardly their fault, what's in their DNA.'

'Right. It was a one-in-four chance. And Danny was the one. They weren't tested, so how were they to know?'

I think of Danny's mother. How cruel. To finally get pregnant, only to have your child stolen from you by some time bomb lurking in their genes. No wonder everyone's getting themselves and their embryos tested.

'Anyway . . . ' Marty exhales. 'I'd better rescue whoever's covering my class.'

I catch his arm. 'You were brilliant with him, you

22

know, Marty. Really brilliant.' I meet his gaze. 'Whatever happens, at least Danny's got you looking out for him.'

Marty's mouth twitches. 'Thanks, Susan.'

As he walks off, my eyes return to the painting of the boy running after his balloon.

I know what legacy my genes have in store: I've been tested.

But Steve hasn't.

4

'Here, babe. Get this down you.'

Carmel hands me a decaf latte and sinks into her myco-leather sofa, curling her feet underneath her like a pedigree cat. If you'd told me five years ago that Carmel would buy furniture made from the roots of fungi, I'd have laughed.

'Thanks.' I grip the handle, trying not to scald my fingers.

She nods at me. 'This will blow your taste buds. New variety, only just designed. Vanilla and cocoa notes, all dialled up.'

She eyes me over the rim of the glass. 'Look, this hang-up of Steve's about IVF . . . I know only too well it's no tea party, but, Jesus, practically everyone's doing it: for the disease screening if nothing else. You shouldn't let him bully you out of it.'

I think of Danny, and my gut churns.

'Honestly, some men would rather die than ask for help.' She deposits her glass and inspects her nails. 'Steve should know better, particularly second time around.'

I recall Steve's face and feel a stab of guilt. I'm not sure I subscribe to such a black-and-white view.

'Of course, this not-having-a-reason only makes things worse. If you know who the enemy is, you can crack on with it, get things sorted. Like Barry and I did. But if you don't, well . . . ' She plucks some fluff from a cushion. 'I've seen it with couples before.' She pulls a face. 'Turns ugly.'

The coffee burns down my throat. I'm still waiting for the part where Carmel gives me hope.

'Come to think of it, I don't know any couples who are even *trying* to conceive naturally.' She nods at me. 'I'm telling you, Susan, conception through intercourse is becoming positively Neanderthal. What's the saying? 'Sex is for recreation and IVF is for procreation.''

I shift in my seat. It was different for Carmel: there was never any question about intervention. Barry's bank provides fertility insurance so they both got tested and discovered Barry carries a mutation in the Huntington's gene. Fortunately, his faulty gene is in what they call 'the grey area', which means he's highly unlikely to develop symptoms himself, but there was a one-in-two chance of him passing it on. So that was that. Barry and Carmel qualified for PGD — pre-implantation genetic diagnosis — to test their IVF embryos for disease, and got it all done through the company scheme.

Whereas the only intervention I've had is a few fertility pills that gave me hot flushes and bloating.

'Has Steve actually considered the risks he's taking, leaving it all to chance? He's had his own profile done, right?'

I hesitate. 'No.'

Carmel's face drops. 'But he works in biotech, for goodness' sake! You're telling me he's prepared to ravage the genomes of mosquitoes and mice, but not even get his sequenced?'

'He works in corporate affairs, Carmel, not the labs.'

It's a sore point but I still feel the need to defend him. Steve's dad died in his fifties. After a heart attack.

'And?'

I pick at my skirt as the argument floods back.

'He reckons it's like unwrapping some kind of 'disease fortune cookie'. He says, 'What difference does it make? So you find out you're going to get dementia or heart disease. It just gives you one more thing to worry about.''

Secretly, I used to agree. For all the support programmes and genetic counselling they offer, it doesn't necessarily change the end game. Like Dad's Alzheimer's or Mum's cancer: it was a curse they couldn't lift. Only the other day, I read about some guy who'd waded out into Farmoor Reservoir with a rucksack of bricks. His wife had bought him a DNA test kit for Christmas. Turned out he carried the mutation for Creutzfeldt-Jakob disease: a fatal brain disorder that has no cure.

Carmel puffs out a breath. 'I'm sorry, but that's just . . . irresponsible. I mean, how can you prepare yourselves properly for a baby if you don't get tested? It's Russian roulette.'

I dig my nails into the chair. 'I guess we'll just have to cross that bridge when we come to it. *If* we ever come to it.'

She sucks in her lips. 'You know what I think, Susie?' I look up. 'I reckon you should just go ahead and book it in yourself.'

I frown at her. 'It takes two, remember?'

'Tell him you'll bloody well use a donor if he doesn't say yes.'

I expel something between a sigh and a laugh. 'You know I could never do that. I can't really blame him. With everything that happened, you know, with Katya, his ex.'

26

Carmel slams her saucer on the table. 'Honey, that was nearly a decade ago. IVF has moved on. Back then only one in five made it: now it's one in three. And you're not Katya, you're you. You need to get on with it before your egg quality falls off a cliff.'

I gaze at one of the photos of Leo, just after he was born. Carmel's efforts sure paid off. Underneath the ludicrously large cotton cap is that cute little face, all crumpled and pink, as if he'd stayed in the bath too long.

'It's no use . . . He won't discuss it.' I sigh. 'Even now, I don't think I know the whole story . . . ' I clasp both hands around the glass. 'But what I do know is that IVF broke his marriage and nearly bankrupted Steve in the process.'

I choose to omit the other detail: that it nearly broke Steve, too. Five rounds, they went through: a relentless boot camp of injections, tests and scans. And waiting. Always the waiting. He did tell me about that. How he began to dread her ringtone, hearing her voice: so brittle with hope, followed by the suck of breath that made him want to take a hammer to that phone. He said that's what started him drinking: listening to her fall apart.

My head slumps into my hands. 'It's killing us, Carmel. Our lives are controlled by apps: what we eat or don't eat, how much we exercise, when we have sex, if you can call it that. More like some kind of insemination Olympics. What if he leaves me, like he left her?'

Carmel plonks herself down next to me. 'Steve's not going to leave you, Susie. Not in a million years. He loves you: that much is obvious. Even if he is a little . . . ' she meets my eyes '. . . controlling.'

Through the blur of tears I notice a small fist curled

round the edge of the door. Two round brown eyes peep at me.

I wipe my face. 'Ah, hello, young man.'

Carmel glances round. 'Leo! You little monster. You're *supposed* to be having your nap!'

He barrels into the room, all feet and arms, and buries his head in Carmel's bosom.

She ruffles his hair and tuts, unable to suppress a smile.

Leo peers out at me from under her arm. His brows knit together. 'Why crying?'

'Why *are* you crying?' Carmel bites her lip and glances at me. 'Sorry. Force of habit.'

'It's nothing, Leo.' I sniff. 'Grown-ups worry about things they shouldn't. Sometimes, they forget to be happy.'

Carmel clamps a hand on each of his cheeks and kisses his nose. 'Run and play with your Go-Go Track for just a few more minutes, and Mummy will find you a biscuit. Then you can show Susan your cars.'

He scrambles off her lap, eyes glittering. She waits until he's gone and taps my knee. 'Right, how long till you ovulate?'

'A week or so.' Carmel arches her eyebrows. 'Six days.'

She inhales through her nose. 'You need to plan something special. Remind yourselves that you're lovers, not just breeders.' She gives me the once-over. 'You're lucky, you've still got a *fabulous* figure. Buy something that makes you feel good. Black lace, thigh boots, whatever does it for you. Hell, I've got a bone-fide police uniform you can borrow —'

I groan. 'We've been there, OK? Frankly, I'm beyond it.'

28

She scowls at me. 'Look: I know how hard it is when you're low. Leo didn't appear overnight, you know. But unless you're part of the Second Coming you're not going to pull off an immaculate conception.'

I glower at the cushions.

'And it's no good going through the motions, Susie. You need to get those juices flowing.' She throws her arms in the air. 'Vodka. Wine. Jane Austen porn flicks. Whatever it takes.' She grasps my hands. 'Just. Do it.'

'OK, Carmel, here's the thing. You know what it is, next weekend? Mother's Day. I'm going to be about as juicy as a post-menopausal nun.'

In houses all over the country, children will bounce into their parents' bedrooms, clutching glittery cards with wonky hearts and pop-out flowers. I should know: I help make thirty of them every year.

Carmel grates a tooth over her lip, and I think she's done. But a slow smile breaks out. She claps her hands. 'Perfect. Just perfect!'

My frown deepens.

'Don't you see? Steve won't deny you anything.' She presses her mouth to my ear: 'Forget all that bollocks about not drinking. You've total licence to get absolutely, filthy hammered. And then fuck like rabbits. Like you used to.'

She slaps me on the shoulder, delighted with her cunning.

'And before you poo-poo it: by the time you pop out that egg, the booze will be well out of your system.'

I'm not convinced: Steve still has to be careful. But before I can muster a response, Leo pokes his head into the room. 'Biscuit now?'

A blue hydrocar spins across the tiles and ricochets

off my foot.

Carmel winks at me as my stomach sinks beneath her honed slate floor.

It's never too early to give your child the best start in life.

Bringing a child into this world is an exhilarating time for new parents, but it can also be an anxious one. Naturally, you want it to go smoothly, knowing you have done everything possible to give your baby the best start.

Optime™ pre-implantation genetic diagnosis brings you peace of mind by enabling you to eliminate the risk of genetic conditions that may lead to miscarriage or disease. Our genetic screening tests offer a glimpse into your unborn baby's future, so you can gift your child the chance of staying healthy, whether you require fertility treatment or not.

Gone are the days of having to cross your fingers and wait for post-transfer screening results, or agonise over three-month scans. Our internationally acclaimed specialists screen for thousands of diseases, providing you with benchmarked risk profiles for each embryo. Helping you make informed decisions just as your pregnancy starts.

No need for a fairy godmother.

Give your child the gift of good health with Optime™ baby screening.

Why leave such life-changing decisions to chance?

5

I wander through the Peace Garden, stopping to admire a clump of tulips: Mum's favourite. Sumptuous pink petals cup a ring of scarlet stamens; at their centre glistens the seductive yellow stigma.

My phone pings.

Reminder: Your fertile window starts in four days.

I sit on the bench and sigh.

The spring equinox is upon us. Buds are sprouting, birds are nesting and pigeons are climbing on top of each other with a relentless flapping of wings. It's reaching the point where I'm even resentful of wildlife, as if it's these creatures' choice to flaunt their breeding habits. Perhaps it's because my own reproductive instincts are just as urgent but don't get results.

Marty pokes his head round the pergola. 'Staff room not good enough?'

'Something like that . . . ' I make room for him. 'How's Danny?'

'OK, for now.' Marty shakes his head. 'It kills me. We can wipe out malaria and get cars to drive themselves, but we can't save an eight-year-old boy.'

We actually can't wipe out malaria, but that's not public knowledge yet. It's one of the reasons why Steve's so stressed. His firm engineered a gene drive that modified the disease-carrying female mosquitoes and effectively sterilised them. Just a few generations after they were introduced, wild populations crashed: it was hailed as a biotech triumph. But apparently mosquitoes can resist gene drives as well as insecticides,

32

and now a new malaria strain is running rampant in Nigeria.

Marty takes a breath. 'Anyway . . . Did you see Neesha brought her baby in?'

I yank a thread on my skirt. 'Yup.'

Every goddamned year someone at this school gets pregnant. I opened the staffroom door, took one look at the coddling crowd and stepped straight out. These days I can't even be subtle.

'It was pretty cute. As babies go.'

'Don't tell me you're getting broody, Marty?'

He puffs out his lips. 'I'm sticking to the practice side of things.'

I chuckle and think, not for the first time, what incredible lashes Marty has. They encircle his eyes like the kohl of an Egyptian pharaoh.

'So, who's the current flavour of the month?'

He raises an eyebrow. 'You make it sound like I've an army of them on the go.'

Every now and then Marty lets a name slip. Always a different one.

'I can't imagine what it must be like, going on a date,' I say. 'It's been so long. I'd be terrified.'

'It *is* terrifying. There's this new dating app: Genedr. Have you heard of it?' I shake my head. 'Like a genetic Tinder. People post their DNA profiles. DNA-Ps are the new dick-pics.'

My sandwich drops in my lap. '*Please* tell me you're kidding . . .'

'It's all about carrier status and compatibility. They call it 'genetically optimised dating'.'

'Oh my God. May I never be single again.' I give him a sideways glance. 'So, Marty, have you — ?'

'Hell, no!' he says, horrified. 'But when you tell

33

people you're not on it, some of them look at you as if you must have something to hide.'

I'm appalled but part of me can't help wondering how he might score. I stiffen. Or Steve.

'It gets worse. There's this tool on it. Find someone you like then mash up their data with yours. Spits out your 'maybe baby's' profile. Which way their earlobes hang, what colour eyes. Whether you're breeding the next marathon winner or some bloke who'll pop his clogs before he hits forty.'

I gawp at him. 'I'm sorry, that's just wrong.' But then I think of all the IVF couples doing exactly that.

Marty takes a swig of water. 'Anyway . . . what plans for the weekend?'

Fertilisation against all odds . . .

'Nothing special. What about you?'

'There's a music festival in Oxford. Mostly local bands, but a few names. You'll never guess who they've dragged out of rehab to headline Saturday.'

'Go on.'

'The Nostalgists.'

I spin round. 'I *loved* that band! I used to lie on my bedroom floor and imagine Curt was there, singing next to me.'

Marty nudges me. 'Look at you. You've gone all misty-eyed.' His face lights up. 'Hey, why don't you come?' My smile fades. 'It'll be fun. And you can protect me from all those genetic predators out there . . . '

'I'm not sure The Nostalgists are really Steve's thing.' I bite my lip. 'Plus, I have to be on form for Sunday. We always take flowers to Mum's grave. For Mother's Day.'

'I'm sorry. That must be rough for you.'

'It's not the best.' The last time I saw Mum, her

body was so emaciated it didn't look like her, at all. 'But it's been fifteen years now. It gets easier. With time.'

'Well,' he says, 'if, by some remote chance, you change your mind, just message me. I'll be there, propping up the stage.'

I picture Curt Brown and feel a distant stir. A flash of a different Susan, storming the dance floor, no inkling of what was about to hit.

I force a smile. 'Unlikely, but thanks, all the same.'

I contemplate my weekend plans with mounting dread. And then I remember Neesha's baby.

I make a mental note to order some gin on the way home.

6

I slide the silver hook through my ear and check the mirror. The pale-green stones have a leafy shimmer, like forest pools.

Steve sits back and nods. 'They suit you. Bring out your eyes.'

I smile.

'They're real jade. Not some resin print job.' He pauses. 'Meant to be good luck.'

This is Steve's way of trying to make up for Mother's Day, tomorrow. He used to buy me little gifts all the time, when we first met. I couldn't believe my luck: I'd been such a mess, for so long. I was paranoid something would happen to him, the way it did to everyone I cared about. My fretting didn't seem to bother him, back then.

I loop my arms round his waist. 'Thank you. I love them.'

He nuzzles my hair. 'Thought we might watch a movie later.'

'Sure.' I swallow. 'But first, I've knocked up a little treat of my own.'

I steal out of the room, heart thumping, as if I'm about to commit a robbery. Hidden behind two packs of chicken thighs, at the back of the fridge, are a six-pack of tonic waters and a bottle of D-Zine gin: personalised to my requirements. I slice the rind off a lemon, dunk a fistful of ice in two tumblers and slug it in.

The smell of juniper ambushes me: wicker chairs in

the garden; sun on skin. I add some tonic, and take a swig for courage. And another. I totter back to the living room and casually hand Steve his drink. He takes one sniff and stares at me. Before he can say anything I raise my glass: 'Cheers!'

The gin races to the back of my throat, making me cough.

He frowns. 'Steady on.'

For a moment, I think he isn't going to play along, but a smile creeps into his face.

'What's this, then? Some radical new fertility theory?'

I laugh, emboldened by the alcohol. 'Thought it was time to let our hair down. Stop taking things so seriously, like you said. Particularly given tomorrow's . . . Well, you know what tomorrow is.'

It's taken me all week to drum up this lie. It doesn't feel so dishonest now.

He takes a sip and rolls it round his mouth. 'Damn, that tastes good.'

I drain my glass. 'Fancy another?'

I see a flash of hesitation. He looks at his drink then at me. 'Sure.' He downs it. 'Why not?'

I head back to the fridge, wondering why we didn't do this before. Dull, depressed Susan is diluting with every sip: the old me is emerging like some glorious butterfly from its gin-soaked chrysalis. Even Steve seems more playful.

This may just work.

We finish the second. And the third. After the tonics have gone, I sway back to the kitchen and ferret out the contingency bottle of wine.

Steve lurches through the door. 'Now what are you up to?'

'Cab Sauv, darling?' I say in my theatre voice, slopping it over the side of my glass. 'Whoops.' I grab a cloth. 'Mustn't waste it.'

He eyes the bottle. 'Are you sure that's a good idea? I mean . . . we haven't sunk this much in ages.'

'We're enjoying ourselves, aren't we?'

His face darkens, like a cloud moving over the sun. But it passes.

'Yeah . . . About bloody time we did.'

We steer our limbs back to the living room. I scroll to my favourite slowies list and activate the speakers.

Steve pulls my face towards his and kisses me: a proper kiss, long and slow.

'Come on.' I give his hand a tug and slide off the sofa. 'We haven't visited this rug for a while.'

★ ★ ★

It was all going so well.

For the first time since I can remember, I actually wanted to make love. Not functional coupling; but slow, lustful sex. It made me realise how . . . mechanical things had become. Instead, we were exploring each other. Taking our time, like we used to.

I'd gone on top. Riding rodeo, as the girls used to say. Before we started failing at trying, this was my favourite position: satisfaction guaranteed. But then I'd read another of those damned articles which said that gravity could work against you. Better to go missionary, flat on your back: help guide those boys home.

Whereas tonight, it was my body that was instructing me, not faceless fertility gurus. So I was happily cantering away when I noticed a change down below. Let's just say my horse was going lame. I sped up to a

38

gallop, thinking this would resolve matters. It didn't. If anything, it made things worse.

'Is everything OK?' I panted, wiping my forehead. Boy, I was out of practice.

Steve was panting, too. 'Yes, it's just . . . ' His hands slid off my buttocks. 'All this rocking . . . ' He swallowed. 'It's making me feel a little . . . '

His eyes bulged. He shoved me off and scrabbled across the hall to the loo. A few seconds later I heard the unmistakeable sounds. Like a dog with a stuck bone.

Steve was mortified, saying he must have had some kind of reaction. I told him it didn't matter, and let him slope off to bed with a bowl. Inside, though, I was howling. This would be our forty-eighth fail. Four barren years of flat blue lines.

I slump against the cushions and stare at my empty glass. Is this it, my destiny? Should I just grieve for the child I'll never have and move on?

My phone beeps. One new message.

Nostalgists on at 11!

It's the strike of a match in the dark.

I turn to the smart speaker: 'Taxi to Oxford, in ten minutes.' A sudden rush of adrenaline makes me giddy.

'Paying by cash.'

7

The bass pumps through the walls. There's a loud sniff in one of the cubicles, followed by a flush. All of a sudden I feel very, very sober. If it wasn't for the fact Marty knows I'm here, I'd be heading straight back home. I appraise my face in the mirror. The lights are unforgiving, but, with a little help, my eyes still pop. My mouth, on the other hand, feels like something that's been left out in the sun too long. I touch up my lips, run my tongue over my teeth and take a deep breath, as if I'm about to launch into battle.

A cubicle door opens. My stomach drops. Aaliyah, my teaching assistant, stumbles out.

'Aaliyah . . . Hi!'

She looks up and her eyes go very wide. 'Oh, wow, Susan . . . ' She swipes at her hair. 'I didn't know you were here.'

'Just came for the final act.' I attempt a smile. 'Bit of a fan.'

'Right . . . ' She nods vigorously then brushes past me and thrusts her hands in the sink. 'Hey, guess what? Marty's here, too.'

'Yes.' I swallow. 'I . . . saw him.'

There's enough speculation about Marty's love interests in the staff room. I do not intend to join that queue.

'Anyway . . . ' I exhale, one hand on the door. 'Better get going. See you Monday. Enjoy the rest of your night.'

I push through the crowd, pulse racing. Great; I'm

not even meant to be here. What if Aaliyah says something at school? What if it gets back to Steve?

As I scan the room, a girl in impossibly high heels stares through me, making me feel even more of an imposter. How long is it since I went to a gig? Must be five years, at least.

It doesn't take long to spot him. Marty's sitting with his back to the bar, in a pale-blue T-shirt and jeans. His hair is slicked back, either gel or sweat, his skin a rich mahogany under the fluorescent lights.

I raise my hand. He breaks into a smile and strides towards me, cradling the drinks.

'Hey. You made it.' He leans over and kisses my cheek. I glance round, praying Aaliyah hasn't followed me.

'Better late than never!' I have to shout to make myself heard.

'Here you are: got you a large one. Nostalgists are up next. We should probably take our positions.' He grins. 'Assuming you want to get nice and close to the stage.'

We claw our way through the hordes as rotating coloured spots sweep the walls. The music is so loud I can actually feel it, resonating in my chest. I scour the crowd, but I can't see any sign of Aaliyah. She did look pretty out of it; maybe she's already left.

When we're about five rows from the front, Marty stops. The hard-core fans are welded together, impenetrable as a phalanx.

'This OK?'

I nod. I'm sweating already: all these bodies and lights. A rake-thin guy with a shaved head is bawling into the mic; a laser illuminates his elaborate dragon tattoo. A girl with wavy black hair gyrates next to me,

41

her hips bumping mine.

'Not long now,' Marty shouts, as the band finishes its encore. The crew starts changing over kit. 'Excited?'

I smile at him and nod, a loud buzzing in my ears. I think of Steve and feel a stab of guilt. I gulp some gin. As soon as it's over, I'll leave.

'Well, you're in for a treat. Apparently, your man Curt has been 'enhanced'.'

My eyes widen.

'Not like that . . . Although, he's probably had that done, too. Voice-box implants. I spoke to a guy who saw them play a festival last year. He said old Curt's pumping out those tunes better than ever.'

'Really?' I eye the stage. The roadies look as if they're almost done. 'So. What was the best gig you ever saw?'

He rubs his thumb along his jaw. 'I think it would have to be their *Golden* Tour. Must be fourteen . . . no, fifteen years ago. I'd just started law school. The Apollo, Leicester Square.'

'You're kidding me: *the Apollo*? I was there.'

'No way . . .'

'They did three encores.' I grin. 'Best set ever.'

I was twenty-one: sassy and single. No worries, beyond the next set of exams. Five months later, Mum died. I dropped out of veterinary school and fell apart.

There's a sudden hush as they kill the lights, followed by a few whistles and shouts. A drum thuds out the opening beats to 'Radiance', one of my absolute favourites. I grab Marty's arm, as if I'm twenty-one again and back in that arena. The keyboards swoop in, then the guitars. Lasers arc round Curt as he runs on stage, and the crowd erupts.

42

Curt looks good. Better than good. He grabs the mic and his voice booms out, fierce and throaty, sparking a surge of energy, all of us grappling for that same high. And as the pace picks up, there it is: that incredible rush I always used to get whenever I heard this song. As if the world was opening up to me, like a promise.

Minutes pass. Maybe hours. I marvel at the ease with which my body moves: light, almost weightless. Marty dances effortlessly, his long limbs surprisingly graceful, just the hint of a smile on his lips. A strobe passes over his face, illuminating his thick black lashes. I feel a pulse of desire, like a forgotten friend.

Then the music slows, and the mood shifts with it. A guy with dark-blue eyes pulls the girl next to me into a tight embrace. Marty sees me looking and smiles. Danger flutters in my belly.

I edge closer. We're centimetres apart.

Marty slips his arm around my waist. I sense his fingers through my dress and remember other moments. Other boys. Curt's voice echoes between us, his sad, sad words spinning round.

The song builds to its final chorus. Marty presses me tighter.

I don't want this to end.

My hand glides up to Marty's cheek. He stares at me, eyes shining. 'Are you sur — ?'

I stop his words with my finger and bring my mouth to his.

Somewhere deep inside, a knell rings. But I ignore it.

I am a woman, not just a womb.

And that is the best feeling of all.

8

I sense light: a brazen yellow. My head responds
with a dull throb. Consciousness sidles in: covert yet
purposeful, like a thief. My eyes stretch wide. The
curtains, the bed: they're not right. My brain skitters
for an explanation.

Oh, God.

I slide my knees up to my chest and tug the duvet
over my face.

I'm in the guest room.

And I know why.

* * *

I prise my head off the pillow and swallow. The room
is freezing and stinks of second-hand gin. I spot my
dress, bunched on the floor: accessory to the crime. I
jump out of bed and stuff it underneath, out of sight.
Bad idea, bending over. I collapse back on the mattress, skull buzzing.

I remember reading that, for the majority of animals,
promiscuity is the rule. It increases the chances of
conception, and improves genetic diversity. Probably
top of the philandering chart are Bonobo chimpanzees: both sexes mate with multiple partners.

But I am not a Bonobo chimpanzee, I am a woman.

And when humans commit to a partner, we make
a contract to remain faithful. We subjugate our urges.
At least, we're supposed to.

I picture Steve's face and a bitter taste fills my

mouth. Did he hear me come back?

Does he know?

Images of dark hair and olive skin flicker past. A dingy room off-stage, the band still playing. A soft blue couch that creaked.

Shame courses through me. Lord, what was I thinking?

What if Aaliyah saw us?

What if someone came in?

I think of the staff room on Monday and shudder: blushes and stilted hellos. I want to throw myself in the shower and scrub until I'm raw. But it's not the kind of dirt that washes off.

There's a muffled knock at the door. 'Susan?'

I freeze.

'Susan, are you awake?'

I screw my eyes shut. My heart sprints, sharp little bursts in my chest.

The door opens.

I'm not ready. I can't do this.

Steve places a mug on the bedside table and sits on the bed.

'Well, hello stranger. You had me worried. I woke up and you weren't there.'

My mind scrambles for words. Something. Anything.

'I thought you'd fallen asleep downstairs. But then I heard you in here.'

I swallow. 'Sorry, I . . . I didn't want to wake you.'

I carve my nails into the duvet. Embroidered white flowers feign order and innocence.

He inhales. 'Look, I'm sorry about last night . . . '

You're sorry?

'Steve, you really don't need to apologise — '

45

'You see, there's something I haven't told you.'

I glance up at his pinched face and my guilt spirals.

He runs his tongue over his lip. 'After the split with Katya, I had gene therapy. For the drinking.' His eyes dart to the floor. 'And, well . . . It gives you a bad reaction.' He sighs. 'I should have said something, but I know you were trying to make things . . . nice.' He shakes his head. 'Not *nice* . . . I mean, it *was* nice — '

I grab his hand. 'Steve, I'm so sorry, I should never have got us sloshed. It was a stupid idea . . .'

'No, the truth is, I was ready for a blow-out. This Nigeria thing's been so full on . . .'

'I know, but still . . .' Tears prick my eyes.

How could I? After everything Steve's done?

I have to tell him. But I daren't.

He takes a deep breath. 'Anyway, let's forget about all that.' He manages a tight smile. 'Here: I got you these.'

He hands me a dark-blue box wrapped in red ribbon.

'They're from that firm you like. No caffeine, nothing 'off-list' . . .'

I stare at the chocolates and swallow, hard.

Just as I thought things couldn't get any worse.

It's Mother's Day.

46

Give your child the head start they deserve with ProdiGyne

At ProdiGyne, we believe every child has exceptional talents waiting to be discovered.

Just imagine the possibilities if you knew what they would excel at before they even started school. That's why we've taken the guesswork out of parenting. To help you identify the skills your child is destined to have.

ProdiGyne's unique DNA profiling tool pinpoints your child's true gifts and natural character traits, so you can nurture them. Whether they have the makings of the next biotech whizz kid, tennis star or fashion guru, our detailed analysis of more than one hundred genetic indicators will reveal your child's innate strengths and personality.

No more money wasted on ballet lessons or language tuition when their real talents lie elsewhere. Whether it be an aptitude for sport or art, a strongly analytical mind or a creative one, all these traits can work to your child's advantage if you know about them early on. Book an appointment today and make the most of your child's potential.

***Help them realise their dreams and
unlock the prodigy within.***

9

I clap the soil off my hands, kick off my clogs and slump into a chair. The late-afternoon sky is a wash of cobalt blue. Goldfinches raid the feeder like flamboyant burglars, red-and-black masks strapped to their eyes. In the bed underneath, indigo and gold hyacinths bow their feather-duster heads.

'Kettle on.'

A pain sharpens behind my eyes. My head's been pulsing like a persistent wasp; I hope I'm not coming down with something. Steve's booked some new Italian place for dinner that's supposed to be amazing. I feel the familiar sting in my chest. The longer you keep a secret, the harder it is to tell. I haven't stopped fretting.

But guilt can be productive.

I dedicated my Easter holiday to my marriage. It paid off: the Cotswold minibreak I organised was a success, helped by ignoring my pregnancy apps and avoiding the forums. No calendars. No pressure. We even had sex whether I was ovulating or not. It was like the holidays Steve and I used to have, before we started trying. My notifications have held us hostage for too long.

I scroll through messages while my tea brews. Three from the head about Monday. My heart sinks. A whole day's training, trapped in the same room with Marty.

I think of that excruciating exchange at the end of term. He gamely apologised, claiming it was all his fault, while my eyes stayed pinned to the ground, like

48

some inept teenager's. When I finally found my voice, all the clichés tumbled out: 'carried away', 'too much to drink', followed by 'best to forget about it', and 'not breathe a word to anyone'. The look on his face. I didn't think it was possible to hate myself more. At least Aaliyah didn't mention anything. As far as I know, the staff gossip drums haven't been beating.

My finger hovers over a message from @goingbananas. Her real name is Terri, and she's one of the Bumpy Roadsters, my Trying To Conceive forum. Last thing I heard, Terri managed a single embryo transfer just before Easter.

Hi babes
Know you've been staying off the bulletin boards so wanted to give you my news.
2WW [2-week-wait] *over. Yesterday was OTD* [official test day] *and I finally got my BFP* [big fat positive]*!!!*
Hang in there. It's taken me five years. Miracles do happen and I know it will for you, too. xxx

The stab isn't as sharp as usual. That was her fifth round: she's been through hell, too. Another month gone, another cycle begins. Maybe this time.

And that's when I clock the pink alert on my calendar. I hesitate.

There are four pink menstruation squares. The fourth is today.

My brain fires into neuron overload. There's been nothing. Not even a cramp.

Tiredness, headache . . .

Shit: I can't be.

Can I?

49

* * *

I eye the test stick, as clammy paws scamper down my back.

Sixty seconds.

A tropical beach shimmers on my screen: froths of white cresting turquoise.

'Let your lungs expand . . .' croons the calming app, as palm fronds rattle in an azure sky. 'Imagine your body is a balloon and is slowly filling with air . . .'

Mine's more like an airlock: nothing's getting in or out.

I cling to the basin; try to steady my hands.

My phone chirps.

I suck in one breath, two. And two more, for luck.

CONGRATULATIONS!

The screen turns a luminous pink. White caps:

YES

You're pregnant!

A noise erupts that's half gasp, half shriek. I have to jump, jig, punch the air.

My phone pings, offering to calculate my due date. A little calendar page pops up:

14th December

A Christmas baby: the three of us together, Santa Claus and stockings by the tree . . .

I stare at my face in the mirror, as if I'm seeing myself for the first time.

Finally. We did it.

My palm glides to my belly. 'Hello there, little baby. This is your mother.'

I watch my mouth as it tests the words, roll the consonants on my tongue. Every fibre in me dances.

The app offers me tips for the first trimester, and

50

my heart soars.

I have to call Steve, right away.

And that's when I notice the other square on the calendar, that's highlighted with a star.

Date of conception

There's a faint ringing in my head, as a soft blue couch rises up, like a ghost.

No, no, no . . .

My fingers fly across the screen.

How early can you do a paternity test?

10

The alarm clock finally goes off.

There's a suck of air, then a sigh, like a dying breath. Steve curls his arm around my waist. 'Morning.'

'Morning.'

I've spent the past two hours staring at the wall. One minute, I'm high on the tiny life inside me, daring to believe in our happy-ever-after. The next, I'm in tears, convinced my nemesis is nigh. In certain cultures, infertility is regarded as a curse on a marriage, so some wives, who have no access to support, sleep with other men in a desperate attempt to conceive. They are unfaithful to save their marriage, not to destroy it. Although that strategy didn't play so well for Anne Boleyn.

As I lift myself off the pillow, it rushes up out of nowhere and hits the back of my throat. I clamp my hand to my mouth.

Steve pokes his head up. 'You alright?'

I tear off the covers and race to the bathroom. I run the taps full blast, praying they mask the gags.

There's a knock at the door. 'Susan? Are you OK?'

Shit!

I splash water on my face. I've spent years longing for these symptoms.

'Sorry, it's just — ' I clench my jaw. 'Salmon must have been off.' I just manage to get the words out before another retch comes.

'Really? Mine tasted fine.'

I gulp some air as water drips off my chin.

'Sure you haven't picked up another bug? That classroom is a veritable breeding ground.'

'Maybe.' I try deep breathing. 'You might want to use the other bathroom. Think I'll be here for a while.'

I grip the porcelain as another wave rolls in. His feet shuffle by the door. 'I just need my stuff.'

I thrust his deodorant, shaver and toothbrush into a washbag and hand it to him. My stomach loops. That's not morning sickness, though.

Yesterday, when Steve went for a run, I emptied his shavings into one of the tubes the clinic sent me for the DNA test. I felt like some kind of organ trafficker. I had to pay to upgrade to a forensic one, because I can hardly ask Steve for a cheek swab. Head hair proved more challenging: it must be attached to a follicle. I combed through his wardrobe, and then the sheets and retrieved two possible candidates. Just to be safe, I snagged a contingency sample: the head from his electric toothbrush.

This is how far I've fallen. It's not just the deception: I'm breaking the law. The Human Tissue Act prohibits non-consensual DNA analysis. Technically, it's theft.

I slump onto the toilet, poised to spring back round, just as Steve sticks his head around the door.

'How are you feeling?'

I look at him and want to cry. 'Not so bad.' I swallow. 'It comes in waves.'

I used to fantasise about the way I'd tell him. Leaving the test stick by his coffee mug. Drawing a cartoon sperm head-butting an egg, with *GOAL!* underneath.

But I can't say a word. All I can do is lie.

He frowns. 'You still look a bit pale.'

I flap my hand. 'Don't worry, you carry on. I'll be

fine.'

He gives me a stern look. 'You're not thinking of going in, are you?'

'I don't know . . . It seems to be passing.'

He wags his finger. 'If it's food poisoning, the voms will be back, you can count on it. You don't want to get sued for spraying a child.'

I manage a limp smile.

'I'll call later, see how you are.' He stops at the door. 'Oh, by the way, did you change the head on my toothbrush?'

'Yes, it was looking a little . . . flat.'

He blows me a kiss. 'You're a good one. Thanks.' He shuts the door.

My head sinks into my sweating palms.

I am the worst wife alive.

11

Rain hurls against the windows as the bus trundles through Oxford's morning traffic. I watch the drops fatten and slide down the glass.

One more stop.

My fingers curl round the samples, nestled in my bag like incendiary devices. Stickered with barcodes: no names. They call it non-invasive prenatal paternity testing, a 'peace of mind' test: the results aren't legally binding. But it doesn't feel very peaceful or non-invasive right now. One vial of my blood and a bit of Steve's hair will determine if my child is legitimate. Oh, and one thousand pounds, for the express service: results in three working days. Thank God I kept my old savings account going. Steve notices if fifty quid has gone out of our account, let alone a grand. Plus 'The Sunflower Clinic' on our statement might be a bit of a giveaway.

The bus slows to a stop on a sodden Beaumont Street. The iconic stone terraces look less sand-coloured, more cement. Water spools off their black, cast-iron balconies. I hold my umbrella low, shielding me from people as much as rain. Just my luck to see one of my class parents, wondering why I'm not at school. I step off the kerb, and notice something lying in the road: looks like a squirrel. It's only when I get closer, I see it's a toy bear. Its amber eyes gaze at me forlornly. I pick it up and stuff it in my bag.

I spot the gilt nameplate straight away. I peek through the Georgian windows, but the blinds are drawn. I walk up the stone steps to the intercom, but I can't bring myself to press it. It's as if I'm four again, gripping my mother's hand at the school gates:

Don't worry, Susie darling. It's going to be fine.

A face appears on the screen. As the door buzzes open, I'm hit by a wall of hot, fragrant air, a bit like the butterfly house at Blenheim Palace. My eyes dart to the waiting area. No shortage of customers. Thankfully, none I recognise.

The receptionist smiles at me: 'If you could just register here.'

Six sunflower heads loom behind her, dark circles of seeds gaping like mouths.

I press my thumb on the screen and my details light up.

'Do you have the consent forms with you?'

I hand them over, pulse racing. I could get three years for forging Steve's signature.

'The nurse will be with you shortly. Please, take a seat.'

I perch on a synthetic leather couch. The couple opposite studiously avoid eye contact; the man's knees jiggle as if they can't wait to get away.

My gaze sidles to the pictures on the walls. They haven't gone all out with the babies — careful to manage expectations even with the décor. My eyes linger on the wrinkled soles of two impossibly small feet; their pale pink toes are like seashells, pointing to the sky. I think of the tiny life inside me whose limb buds are beginning to sprout, whose heart is starting to form.

In the old days, when DNA testing had just become affordable, millions of people spat into tubes for fun. The focus was ancestry, not health; attempts to trace themselves back to Henry the Eighth or Attila the Hun. But what happened next wasn't so funny for some. As companies' databases grew, connecting far-flung profiles, secrets were dug up and detonated, ripping families apart. Long-buried adoptions. Closet sperm donation. Infidelities. Paternity fraud rampaged through the news like wildfire as alleged adulteries came to light. And now everyone could check.

A door springs open and a woman in a matching blue tunic and trousers sails towards me.

'Mrs Rawlins?' she mouths discreetly. I nod. 'I'm Jenny. Would you like to come through?'

I follow her down a corridor. The treatment room is an immaculate white. I note the crisp cotton sheets on the bed: no disposable towels here.

She cocks her head. 'So, how are you feeling, Mrs Rawlins?'

I swallow. 'A little nauseous. The odd twinge and ache.'

She nods. 'And the test? How are you feeling about that?'

I look down. She's the only other person apart from the lab technician who knows there's a question over this pregnancy. Hell, she's the only other person who knows there *is* a pregnancy.

'Nervous . . .'

'That's understandable. But I assure you, you're in good hands.' Her lips pull back in a smile. 'Whatever the outcome, we're here to support you. We want this process to be as stress-free as possible.'

To my horror, my eyes suddenly well up. Despite furious blinking, one tear escapes.

She rests her hand on my shoulder. 'It's alright.' Despite her youth, there's something maternal about her. 'This can all feel rather overwhelming.'

I scrabble in my bag for a tissue; my fingers close round the soggy bear. One sob huffs out, and then another.

'I . . . I'm so sorry. Must be the hormones.' I attempt a laugh.

She offers me a box of tissues. 'Dealing with uncertainty is hard at the best of times, let alone when you're swimming with oestrogen. There's no rush. You take your time.'

I blow my nose, while she tactfully busies herself with the packets on the trolley.

'Better?' I nod. 'So, you understand how the test works?'

'Broadly speaking. You analyse the baby's DNA in my blood and compare it to the samples.'

'That's right. We analyse the DNA sequences in twenty different locations. We compare those locations in each sample to determine the number of matches.' She pauses, checking I've understood. 'That number will identify whether the alleged father is the biological father of your baby.'

Alleged father . . .

My gut tightens.

'Each test is processed twice by separate teams of human and AI technicians. If the results say the alleged father is *not* excluded, the statistical probability that he is the biological father will be almost 100%.'

'Wow. Not much room for error, then.'

She holds my gaze. 'No. No room at all.'

This should reassure me, but for some reason it doesn't. I think of that old aphorism: 'Maternity is a matter of fact, whereas paternity is a matter of opinion.'

Not anymore.

She pulls on her gloves. 'If you could just roll up your sleeve, please.'

She applies the tourniquet, and I try not to tense. As she picks up the needle, I stare at the row of canvases on the wall. Each picture has intersecting circles, a bit like the patterns you see through a kaleidoscope. They're spotted with white flecks, like seeds in a fruit. And I realise what I'm looking at. Human egg cells, photographed through a microscope.

I watch my blood filling the collection tube. And, with a jolt, I remember. This test won't just confirm whether Steve is the father. It will reveal my baby's gender, too.

'There. All done.' She removes the tourniquet, slides the needle out and presses a ball of cotton wool against my skin. 'Did you post the father's sample?'

'No, no. I've got it here.' I rummage in my bag. 'I brought a selection.' Lord, I've made it sound like a box of chocolates.

She gives a perfunctory nod, as if this is quite routine. 'We'll send you a link in three days. You can access the report using your security PIN. If you have any questions, please feel free to give us a call.'

Three days.

Seventy-two hours.

Roughly four thousand minutes.

I head back through reception and stumble out into what seems like a normal day. The rain has subdued to a light drizzle. Cars queue at the lights as students drift past in untidy gaggles.

As I shake out my brolly, a woman approaches me: 'Hello.'

Her dark hair is slicked to her head; her coat is sopping.

Two pale-blue eyes appraise me. 'You look a little lost. This might help.'

She thrusts a leaflet into my hand.

DON'T SCREEN US OUT!

There's a photo of a child with Down's syndrome holding a sign:

I AM NOT A RISK!

Underneath is a quote:

'Behold, children are a heritage from the Lord, the fruit of the womb a reward.' Psalm 127:3

The woman steps closer. 'God's children are a blessing.' She smiles. 'Each and every one.'

Irritation spikes; as if the day isn't tough enough without some pro-life preacher on my tail. I try to hand the leaflet back, but it drops in a puddle.

Her smile withers. 'Do you know how many embryos die as a result of genetic screening and IVF?'

'I'm sorry but I need to catch a bus.'

She moves in front of me. 'Thousands. Every year. Innocent lives, discarded like rubbish. Even worse, experimented on.'

I try to push past her, but she blocks me. I sigh. 'Look: you shouldn't accost people like this. It's not fair.'

'Do you think murdering babies is fair?'

I scan the road, desperate to cross.

'Every life deserves a chance . . .' She lifts her arm and something flashes.

I gasp. She's taken a photo. My photo.

Right outside the clinic.

'What the hell — ?' I lunge for the phone; it flies out of her hand into the road, just as a bus sprays past.

She jumps off the kerb and brandishes the flat-tened metal. 'Look what you've done. It's completely

60

smashed.'

I stare at her, cold waves of panic rising. 'I'm sorry; I didn't mean to do that. But you can't just take photos without asking.'

'I'm going to report you. For assault.'

'What? Don't be ridiculous.'

She veers round. 'Help!' A man eyes her warily as she strides towards him. She jabs her finger at me. 'This woman just assaulted me. She tried to steal my phone.'

What? 'That's a total lie. I was only trying to delete a picture. It was an accident. She should never have taken it in the first place.'

The man hurries past, but she's still shouting and pointing. A car slows by the kerb. The woman in the passenger seat throws us a worried glance.

I can't afford a scene. Not now, not here.

'Look . . .' I hold up my hands. 'Let's just calm down, OK? We can sort this out. You must have insurance?'

She screws up her face as if I'm the crazy one.

'Alright.' I swallow. 'I'll give you the money for another phone. We'll go to a cashpoint: there's one round the corner.'

Something crosses her face. 'OK.' Her tongue slides over her lips. 'But it wasn't cheap.'

My chest tightens. I try to inject some confidence into my voice. 'In which case, three hundred pounds should cover it.'

Her eyes meet mine. 'Four.'

'What?' I splutter. From what I glimpsed, it didn't look like a four-hundred-pound phone. 'Come on . . .'

Her gaze doesn't waver. 'Four. Or I go to the police.'

This is a total rip-off, but I'm in no position to

negotiate. And she knows it.

She collects her bag of leaflets from the railing and we head off in an uneasy silence.

I hunch over the touchpad, my mind racing. How on earth am I going to explain the cash to Steve? I'm meant to be in bed with food poisoning. I'll just have to say I lost my card and hope he swallows it.

I fold the notes into my palm and shuffle into a shop doorway. 'There.' I slip her the wad, like some dealer. She pockets the cash without a word.

As I turn to go, she reaches into her bag. 'You really should consider what I said.' She tries to hand me another leaflet, as if nothing's happened. 'Children are a gift from God.'

'I'm not even having bloody IVF,' I snap, and stomp towards the bus stop. But, when I get there, some instinct makes me turn.

She's still standing by the shop, watching me. The leaflet crumpled in her fist.

12

I settle on the bench and contemplate my salad. My appetite has perished, but I must eat, constantly, to keep the nausea at bay. My body is suffused with hormones: one set clamouring for nourishment, the other stuck in fight or flight. What with agonising about the test results, trying to stave off morning sickness and still hold down a job, it's no wonder the cortisol has free rein.

Clouds clump across the sky, blanketing in the heat, as gingham dresses whizz past in full sail. My gaze veers to a troupe of year fives swinging a skipping rope; I can just make out the familiar chant.

Suddenly there's a cry, which escalates to a wail. I spin round. Olivia, from my class, is face down on the tarmac. I dash over and gently lift her up.

'Oh, Olivia. Did you trip? Let's take a look at you.'

I scan her hands and knees: just a graze. She collapses into me, as I whisper reassurances, tears bubbling from her china-blue eyes.

'Feeling better?' She nods. Her hair has that sweet, buttery smell that melts me every time. 'OK, then. Off you go.'

'Another casualty restored for battle?'

The air squeezes out of my chest, as if someone just dropped a stone on it. That was a punishment, in mediaeval times, for refusing to plead to a crime.

Guilty . . .

'Marty, hi . . .'

He must know I've been avoiding him. Fear slices

through me: that he can read my thoughts, that, just by looking at me, he will know.

I retrieve my lunchbox and feign fascination with the skipping girls. Their chanting gets louder:

'Ice-cream Sunday, cherry on the top.

'Who's your boyfriend: I forgot?

'A, B, C, D . . .'

Marty swallows. 'Well, you missed another canteen triumph: toad in the hole. Just the thing for a hot day. Maybe it's time I brought in my own lunch, too.'

I risk a glance at his mocha eyes, that jet-black hair. Marty looks nothing like me or Steve. It won't take a fancy DNA profile for that to show.

'J, K, L . . .'

The heat is stifling. I fan my face, but the air doesn't budge. Pressure builds in my head. Marty's still complaining about the food, when all of a sudden the ground swoops in front of my eyes.

Someone grips my shoulders. 'Susan? Are you OK?'

Marty's staring at me, eyes wide. There's a dull ache in the base of my skull, like a hangover.

'Lean forward and put your head between your knees.' He folds me over.

'What's going on?' My voice is muffled by my skirt.

'I think you just fainted. Take deep breaths.'

Sweat beads on my face. I curse myself for being such an idiot.

'It's awfully hot down here, Marty. Can I sit up?'

'OK, but take it slow.'

My head feels too heavy for my neck. 'Sorry . . . Must be the heat . . .'

The girls have stopped skipping and are staring at us, giggling behind their hands. Marty looks up. They turn and flee.

He frowns at me. 'Has this happened before?'

'No, I just overheated.'

I see the worry in his face and guilt weighs back in. What would Marty say if he knew I might be carrying his child? Probably run a mile. I bite my cheek. No. That's not fair.

'I should let the office know. They can sort out cover for you.'

I grab his arm. 'Please, Marty, I don't want to make a fuss.'

My phone pings. I resist the urge to check it. The clinic said not to expect anything before five, but maybe the report's in early.

I muster a smile. 'Well, I'd better get myself out of this sun. Thanks for saving me from a concrete nose dive.'

'Shouldn't you at least get yourself checked?'

I shake my head. 'No, honestly. It's much cooler in the classroom. I'll be fine, don't worry.' I grip the bench and push myself up. 'Thanks again.'

I pick my way carefully across the playground. As soon as I'm inside, I fish out my phone.

Number not recognised.

I frown.

No message, just a photo.

It's me, outside the Sunflower Clinic. In the middle of Oxford.

Name plate in full view.

★　★　★

It's almost five.

I pace round the garden, clutching my phone. I've spent the past four hours stressing about that photo.

65

So stupid: of course she'd still have it; everything instantly uploads. But how did she trace my number? And what does she want: more money? Or is it penance she's after, for whatever sins she thinks I've committed?

Something cackles by the maple tree. There's a flash of blue and a lone magpie sails onto a branch.

I check my inbox, as the nursery rhyme flits through my head:

One for sorrow, two for joy.

Three for a girl, four for a boy . . .

A sunflower emblem appears and my mouth goes dry.

My fingers tremble as I enter the PIN.

Five for silver, six for gold . . .

Three columns of numbers spill into view:

'Child', 'Mother', 'Alleged father'.

And seven for a secret never to be told . . .

My eyes race down to the score at the bottom.

I sink my knuckle between my teeth as the magpie sniggers and takes off.

Probability of paternity: 0%

The alleged father is excluded as the biological father of the tested child.

13

I read the report for the hundredth time. Numbers and letters twirl past my eyes, genetic markers sashaying with chromosomes. My brain is scrabbling like a trapped animal, desperate for a way out.

The alleged father lacks the genetic markers that must be contributed to the child by the biological father...

I check my messages, praying there's an explanation. These aren't my results: they're someone else's. Those technicians confused their matches and an apology is on its way right now. Someone else's DNA got caught up in my samples...

No new messages.

My finger hovers over the call button. I think of Jenny's face:

Not much room for error then.

No. No room at all...

What am I going to do?

What can I do?

And then I notice it, hidden away at the bottom, last row on the left: number 21. The amelogenin locus.

The amelogenin gene encodes the protein that forms tooth enamel. It's also the genetic marker used to determine sex.

In the column next to it is a single X.

For a moment, the chaos clears.

My baby is a girl.

Catholic Church condemns burgeoning fertility industry and urges world leaders to 'get tough' on governance

OneWorld News Agency
By Sharmila Gupta

As the fertility industry enjoys another record year, the president of the National Catholic Bioethics Center, Charles Minten, has condemned what he calls 'immoral and discriminatory practices' ahead of the G20 summit in Moscow. He insisted governments must stand firm against the unborn being 'sacrificed on the altar of scientific research'.

Minten said:

'The Catholic Church has repeatedly condemned the enormous number of abortions involved in IVF through the destruction of so-called 'unfit' embryos during selective screening. It has also warned that treating the human embryo as mere 'laboratory material' through experimentation would erode human dignity. Sadly, these practices have become routine. It's time for regulators to step up and address their failures. And to respect our future children's inviolable right to life.'

14

I step along the travertine stone path, rehearsing my words. Box hedging flanks the porch, trimmed in perfect straight lines; tubbed lavender trees guard the step. Before my hand even touches the fox knocker, the door swings open. The security cameras are concealed; Carmel relishes taking people by surprise.

'Well, hello, stranger.' She leans in for a kiss. My lips brush an earlobe. 'Naughty girl. You've been avoiding me.'

'Hardly . . .' My heart thuds a little faster. Carmel can sniff out a lie a mile away, and I've a few too many on my lips right now. 'Just a shame our dates clashed over Easter.'

I kick off my shoes and pad along the cream-carpeted hallway, Carmel's skirt billowing out in front. My eye, as ever, is drawn to the baby photos on the wall. I did another pregnancy test this morning, just in case. Still positive. My euphoria was slightly dampened this time round.

I hoist myself onto a stool. 'No Leo today? Or is he hiding?'

'We're trying out a nursery.' Carmel stretches up for the cups. 'Thought it might do him good to socialise. And me to get my mind back.' She nods at the coffee machine. 'The usual?'

I hesitate. Coffee hasn't been agreeing with me. But if I say anything, she might guess. Then again, if I don't . . . 'Actually, have you got a decaf tea?'

She raises an eyebrow. 'New regime?'

I shrug. 'Just fancied a change.'

I feel like Judas, keeping this from her and Steve. I want to scream it from the rooftops: *Carmel, guess what? I'm pregnant!*

Hot water fizzes from the spout. 'So, come on, then. What have you been up to?' She purses her lips. 'Any news?'

I bury my nose in my cup. 'Nothing exciting.'

'Really?' She cocks her head and gives me the once over, like a cat sizing up its prey. 'If you don't mind me saying, you're looking a bit peaky.'

'Yes, well, that's what you get teaching a class of snotty five-year-olds: it's a constant assault on your immune system.'

She slides her latte over and hops up next to me. 'Well, you'd better fill me in anyway.'

I'm suddenly ambushed by coffee and musk.

I swallow. Hard.

Carmel eyes me, as if from a great distance. A slow smile spreads across her face.

'How many?'

'Sorry . . . ?'

'How many weeks are you?'

I blink at her. If it was that easy, then who else might have guessed?

She slaps my thigh and laughs. 'Oh, come on, Susan. You didn't think you'd get away with it, did you? The moment you walked through that door, I knew. Tiredness rings; the tea; a bit blue around the gills.' She ticks off the clues on her fingers. 'And as skittish as a fish in a new tank.'

'Jesus, Carmel. You're like frigging Sherlock.'

'Honey, you don't go through four rounds of IVF without learning a thing or two about pregnancy.'

Four rounds? I thought it was three.

She claps her hands. 'Oh, this is wonderful.'

I smile, despite myself, to see her joy: to celebrate this news, even for a second.

Her voice lowers. 'Don't worry, I totally understand why you're keeping it quiet. We did the same at this stage: very wise.'

My smile evaporates.

'Hey, what is it?'

I don't answer.

She grips my arm. 'Is it the tests? Have they found something?'

'I . . . ' My shoulders heave. 'I've really screwed up, Carmel. You have to promise, no matter what. This stays between us. Always.'

Carmel's eyes widen. I can't tell if it's excitement or alarm.

She gives me a solemn nod. 'I swear. Nothing will pass these lips.'

My insides roil. I think of the report. Of Marty's face, creased in concern.

'I . . . ' I exhale. 'The baby . . . ' I force myself to look at her. 'It isn't Steve's.'

To her credit, Carmel's face holds. No immediate signs of horror or dismay.

She sucks in her lips and swallows. 'Holy fucking shit.'

71

15

Carmel points a banana at me like a gun. 'Get this down. You need to watch your potassium levels. Good for fluid retention and staving off the old leg cramps.'

I twist the top off the banana and mechanically start to peel.

'I understand you're worried about Steve. But, whatever happens, you *cannot* get rid of it, Susan. You'll always regret it.'

'I know, I know . . .'

She grips my knee. 'After the torment you've been through, you're going to have a baby. And a daughter, no less.'

The banana splits in half and topples to the floor. 'Sorry.' Carmel waves my apology away. 'This baby . . . she's part of me.' I'm whispering, as if she can hear us. 'I hate even *mentioning* that.'

I remember seeing a history programme about infanticide. In the 1800s, court records showed that half of England's murder victims were babies. Mothers driven to kill by desperation or shame.

'God: how could I be such a fool? It's a miracle Steve hasn't cottoned on already. Let's face it: you did.'

'Yes, but I know what I'm looking for.'

'Well, I'm just about managing the sickness, but only because he leaves early for work. Weekends are a different story.'

She sighs. 'This wouldn't have been a problem in our mothers' day. Thousands of women passed off other men's babies as their husbands'. Even when blood types were blatantly incompatible.' She frowns. 'That's the downside to all this genetic testing. Back then, people didn't check. No one had even heard of NPEs.'

NPE: 'not parent expected'; the acronym born in the wake of cheap ancestry tests.

Because DNA doesn't lie. Just people.

I press my fingers into my eyes. Speckled circles drift across a pink moonscape. I think of those egg pictures at the clinic.

'All this sneaking around, the stress of getting caught . . . I'm worried what it's doing to her. I'm seven weeks: I should have contacted my doctor by now. Booked in with a midwife for tests.'

Carmel leans forward. 'So *tell him*.' Her eyes burn. 'Yes, he'll be furious, initially; yes, he'll be hurt. But it was a drunken moment of aberration. A total one-off. He'll come round.'

I think of those stories Steve told me about Katya. The anger he still carries.

I shake my head. 'He won't tolerate betrayal. You don't know him.'

Carmel's mouth tightens. 'Maybe not. But, from what you've told me, he wants a child as much as you do.'

'*His* child, Carmel. The product of *his* seed, not someone else's.' I claw my fingers through my hair. 'Even if Steve agreed to go along with it — and that's a big if — it would always be there, like a wedge between us. Every time he looked at her, he'd be reminded.' I swallow. 'And so would I.'

'And what if you don't get pregnant again?' she retorts. 'How will that make you feel? I wouldn't fancy

73

that hanging over your marriage . . . '

She has a point.

I hesitate. 'There's something else.'

Carmel inhales through her nose. 'Really? Isn't one shitstorm enough for you?'

I show her the photo. Carmel winces at least three times when I tell her what happened.

'I've literally no idea how that woman got my number. What if she sends it to Steve? I've already lied to him about the cash; I told him my card must have been stolen.'

Carmel whistles out a breath. 'OK, first things first. You haven't replied, have you?'

'Of course not.'

'Good. Forward me any messages you get, straight away. You need to get off social media. School sites, too. Ask them to remove all photos: say you're getting trolled.'

I swallow. 'That all sounds very . . . serious.'

Her face hardens. 'Look, I don't want to freak you out, but some of these people are fanatics: they don't give up.'

I feel a sudden wave of nausea. As if things aren't dire enough.

'D'you remember which group she was peddling?'

I try to visualise the leaflet. 'It mentioned something about God and wombs . . . Hang on . . . ' I do a quick search. 'Yup, got it: Fruit of the Womb.'

Carmel scrolls through their details. 'So: is it money she's after, or 'harassment for the cause'?' Carmel clocks my expression and squeezes my arm. 'Leave this with me, Susan: OK? I'm good at this stuff. This isn't your priority, right now.'

'Thanks, Carmel.' I sigh. 'Sorry to dump all this on

you.'

'Hey, it makes a pleasant change from Go-Go Tracks and pirates.' She smiles. 'But I think I need some sustenance of the grape variety.'

I glance at the wall clock: almost six. I should get back. Steve will be home soon.

Halfway to the fridge, Carmel takes a sharp breath. 'There may just be a way . . .'

She abandons the fridge and perches back next to me.

'When you told me about the baby, you asked if you could trust me.'

'Yes . . . ?'

'Well, now I need to ask the same of you. Can I trust you, Susan?' Her tone is deadly serious.

'Of course. But what's this got to do with — ?'

'I have a secret, too. One I've never told anyone.'

Images of Carmel *in flagrante delicto* flit through my mind. 'You don't mean . . . Is Leo not Barry's — ?'

She barks a laugh. 'No: not that. Bit hard to cheat with IVF, unless you're wielding the pipette. No, something else entirely . . .'

She grates her teeth over her lip. 'As you know, things weren't exactly straightforward with Leo. The first round, we managed to conceive. But we only produced one viable embryo. The biopsy showed it carried the Huntington's gene. So we started a second round.' Carmel sighs. 'My egg quality wasn't great. Like most things, it starts going downhill once you pass thirty. The second round didn't produce any embryos at all.'

It's a sobering tale, but I've heard it before and am wondering how it's relevant. 'Third time lucky, I guess.'

75

Carmel slowly shakes her head. 'I did get pregnant. But we lost the baby at seven weeks. We didn't tell anyone.'

I stare at her. The same age my baby is now.

'Oh, Carmel. I'm so sorry.'

She smooths her palms over her knees. 'The IVF rollercoaster is rough, Susan. Rougher than I've let on, particularly when you have a one-in-two chance of passing on a terminal disease. We were desperate for a result, and I wasn't getting any younger.' She swallows. 'We spent a lot of time researching different options, looking for somewhere that could . . . optimise our chances. A clinic in the Czech Republic came highly recommended.'

I lean forward. 'Hang on, you went abroad? How did I not know about this?'

Carmel smiles. 'I can be discreet when required, Susan.'

'Oh my God, I remember now . . . Barry was off working with some client in Prague. You used to visit him weekends. At least, that's what you told me.'

'You become rather good at deception when needs must.' She gives me a knowing smile. 'Anyway, we got two embryos. One was a carrier for Huntington's, one wasn't. The non-carrier didn't make it to transfer.' She fixes me with her gaze. 'And this is where we reach the material part.'

I brace myself. This secret she's about to reveal. I'm not so sure I want to hear it.

'They carried out a procedure. On the one that was left. PGO.'

'PG what?' So many acronyms. It's like studying a foreign language, trying to keep up.

'Pre-implantation genetic optimisation. They

76

zapped the Huntington's gene, corrected the mutation. Then implanted the embryo. Which grew into Leo.'

I stare at her, mouth agape. 'They *edited* Leo's genes?'

She nods.

'I didn't think that was allowed. I mean, only in very limited situations.'

'Huntington's is on the approved list. We could have applied here, as a special case, and we'd probably have met the criteria. But we didn't want to risk months clearing all the administrative hurdles.'

'Wow . . .' I shake my head, still trying to process it. 'I thought they were really strict about those edits, because the changes are permanent. Don't they pass on to future generations?'

'Exactly, which is what we wanted. To rid our family of that curse. Obviously, we had to be careful, and keep it under wraps. Not everyone is as . . . open-minded. Particularly Barry's parents . . .' She rolls her eyes.

'But . . .' I hesitate. 'Weren't you worried? How could you be certain it's safe?'

Her face pinches. 'Do you honestly think I'd have risked our only child? PGO is practically routine in places like Russia and India. Barry says all the funds are investing in it. We're just a lot more risk averse in this country, because of the damned HFEA.'

I don't say anything. From what I've seen on the forums, the Human Fertilisation and Embryology Authority does a pretty decent job. It regulates the clinics, ensures standards are maintained. Balances medical ambitions with protecting people.

She gazes at Leo's photo. 'He's all we ever wanted.

77

Fit and healthy, no threat of that awful disease. And he'll never have to go through what we went through when he has children. I tell you, Susan: it was a blessing.'

I am suddenly reminded of what Carmel used to do for a living, before Leo. She was a corporate fixer, and a very good one, by all accounts. The firm she worked for specialised in corporate bungles. Carmel routinely smashed through barriers to get a result.

'So, you're not concerned about any — what do they call them? These unknowns they always talk about?'

''Off-target effects'?' Carmel flaps her hand. 'There'll always be scaremongering when something's new, Susan. Look how people reacted to IVF. They called them 'Franken-babies', for goodness' sake. I saw a documentary on it: the poor parents got hate mail. Did you know the Pope even weighed in, saying it was a 'moral abomination'? Imagine if they'd strangled that idea at birth.'

It's a cute point. But the Pope was no scientist. When it comes to gene editing in humans, even the science world is divided.

'Anyway, we digress . . . The whole reason I brought this up is *you*.'

My stomach thuds. In the wake of Carmel's revelations, I'd momentarily forgotten my own.

She shifts on her stool. 'It's just an idea, OK? And it might sound a little crazy, so bear with me.'

I swallow. If Carmel's offering a disclaimer, it must be bad.

'So, I was thinking . . . If they can cut out bad genes that cause disease and paste in good ones . . . If they can switch certain traits on and off . . . ' She eyes me

78

carefully. 'Then maybe they can swap other types of genes, too.'

I frown.

'Each baby inherits twenty-three pairs of chromosomes: one pair from Mum, one from Dad. What if they could . . . separate them, somehow? Take out the father's. And insert someone else's?'

'Are you . . . ?' I stop and try again. 'Are you suggesting that . . . ? That Marty's DNA is, somehow, swapped for Steve's?'

'Exactly.' She beams at me: top of the class. 'Radical, huh?'

There's a whining in my ears, like a low-flying plane, about to crash.

'Have you *any* idea what you're suggesting? How big a deal that is? This is a human body we're talking about, not a Word document: you can't just do a quick cut and paste.'

She holds up her hands. 'Alright, no need to bite my head off.' She throws me an injured look. 'I warned you it was a bit 'out there'. I'm only trying to help.'

I clamp my palm to my belly like a shield. 'Carmel, it's straight out of a Mary Shelley novel.'

'But technology moves so fast. And this industry is booming. Things we never could have imagined even five years ago are happening for real.'

I shake my head at her.

'OK, Susan, imagine you were living in the 1950s, and I told you that in twenty years' time doctors would be growing babies in petri dishes and planting them in women's wombs.' She raises her eyebrows. 'You'd probably have had me sectioned.'

I take a deep breath. All this talk of genetic slicing is making me queasy.

79

'OK, let's say, for the sake of argument, that something like that *were* possible, not to mention safe . . . It's about as far from legal as you can get. No clinic in their right mind would touch it.'

Her mouth puckers. 'In my experience, you never know what's possible until you ask.'

'Well, I appreciate you trying to help, Carmel. Really, I do. But I just can't cope with — ' My phone beeps. I jump up. 'Shit, Steve's home.'

Carmel clasps my hand. 'Before you go, are you at least going to consider what I've said?'

Typical Carmel, pushing for the close.

I shoulder my bag. 'There's nothing to consider, Carmel. It's a pipedream.'

Her jaw stiffens. 'So, what are you going to do, then?'

'I have absolutely no idea.'

16

I stand in the hallway and listen to the thump of cupboards, the rattle of plates. I'm aware of my heart, beating too fast. I think of that tiny second heart, growing inside me. Not as fast as hers.

'Susan? Is that you?'

I stare at the photo framed on the wall. The two of us, on a whale-watching trip in Canada, Steve's arms wrapped tight around my waist.

I head through to the kitchen. I sense the mood before Steve even opens his mouth.

'Where have you been?' He slings some cutlery into a drawer.

'I stopped off at Carmel's. Sorry, lost track of the time.'

He snorts. 'Maybe you should have married Carmel. The amount of time you two spend together.'

I keep my tone light. 'Tough day?'

'Yeah, you could say that.' He folds his arms and leans back against the sink. 'We need to talk.'

All the secrets in my head collide.

'On my way in this morning, I thought I'd chase up the bank card.' He locks eyes with me. 'While I was on, I told them I wasn't happy about them refusing to refund our money. They had no idea what I was talking about. They said you never mentioned any cash being stolen when you cancelled the card.'

The blood drains from my face.

'So I told them. About the four hundred pounds. And, after a bit of pushing, they said they'd look

81

into it.'

I swallow.

'ATMs have built-in cameras. You obviously didn't realise.' He steps closer. 'They thought we were trying to scam them, Susan: they could have pressed charges. It was you who took the money out, not some thieving skimmer. Why did you lie? What the hell's going on?'

I sink into the chair and grab on to the truth. Or, at least a version of it.

'I did something really stupid.' I clasp my hands. 'That morning, when I was sick, I decided to go into work after all . . .' His face darkens. 'I know, I know . . . And I ended up in an altercation, with this woman. On the bus.' I run my tongue over my lips. 'It was silly, really. I shouldn't have let myself get drawn in. She was one of those pro-life religious types.'

Steve's frown deepens.

'Anyway, I ended up missing my stop. And when I got off in the middle of town, she followed me. Before I knew what was happening, she'd taken my picture. Well, I couldn't have her posting my photo on one of those sites. So I tried to snatch her phone, but accidentally knocked it under a bus.'

I pause. Steve is staring at me, aghast.

'She completely lost it, started accusing me of all kinds of things. So I . . . I panicked. Said I'd give her the cash for a new phone . . .'

Steve slaps his forehead and groans.

'I wasn't thinking. I just wanted to make her go away.'

'Why didn't you tell me this before?'

My eyes dart to the floor. 'I knew I'd been conned. It's a lot of money . . .' I bite my lip. 'I didn't want you to get mad.'

He sighs. 'Oh, Susan, what are you like . . . ?' He walks up and rests his hands on my shoulders. 'You know there's one thing I cannot abide, and that's lies . . .'

'I know: I'm sorry . . . I should have told you.'

'Well, what's done is done. The cash will be long gone, by now. As for that woman . . .' He shakes his head. 'She better not cross my path, or she'll be needing more than God on her side.'

I risk a tentative smile; at least one storm is passing. What's this day going to throw at me next?

I squeeze Steve's hand. 'I'll just grab a quick shower, then I'll make us some tea. I picked up some of that fresh pasta you like.'

I slope upstairs and rip off my clothes. It feels as if I've been drugged. I bend my head under the jet and furiously soap my skin. The scrubs are a little gentler over my belly. Nothing showing yet, thank goodness.

I dry myself off, sit at the dressing table and drag the brush through my hair. The tear of bristles at the roots feels good.

Steve appears in the doorway. He studies my reflection. 'You look done in. I think that school is working you too hard.'

I brush a little harder. 'You know what it's like, this stage of term.'

'It's barely worth it, for what they pay you.'

I stiffen. 'I enjoy it, Steve. It's my job.'

His eyes meet mine in the mirror. 'You haven't mentioned any tests lately. Is everything OK?'

My phone beeps. I ignore it.

He sniffs. 'We could, you know . . . Give those apps another whirl.'

Maybe Carmel was right: I should just tell him. Let

my mouth crack open, and the secrets spill out, like babies from a spider's egg sac.

I clear my throat, ready. But the words won't come.

Steve's phone chirps. 'Ah, that's probably Eghardt, about tomorrow: better take it. See you downstairs.'

I stare at the mirror. I look like the same wife on the outside.

My phone beeps again. I frown. Carmel's message flashes:

Maybe pipedreams CAN come true . . .

What the . . . ?

I check her first message.

Call me. Don't say anything to Steve.

17

Two grey squirrels spring across the grass and stop, casing the park with their funny head jerks. One flicks its tail and scampers up a horse chestnut. Another eyes me with unblinking black spheres. It's a strange feeling, being observed by a squirrel: they're much smarter than you think. Like Carmel and I, these animals are capable of deception. They pretend to stash food in elaborate digging displays, to divert thieves from their real hoards elsewhere. There was talk of using another gene drive to curb their population, give our native reds a chance. The anti-intervention lobby kicked off big time. It appears these nimble Americans not only invaded our country, they invaded our hearts. The government caved, and the greys' fertility and future were saved.

'Sorry.' Carmel huffs round the corner, Leo in tow. 'My neighbour wouldn't stop talking. She minds Leo for me sometimes, so I couldn't cut and run.'

Carmel applies the same strategic approach to motherhood that she used with her job. It's remarkably effective.

'Hi, Leo,' I wave. He peeps his head out from behind his mum and smiles.

Carmel produces a fleet of trucks from her bag. 'Here you go, darling. See which ones go fastest along the path.'

Leo dutifully squats and lines them up.

'So, then.' She drops onto the bench beside me, eyes glittering. 'Ready to eat your words?'

85

'Not unless they've got ginger in them.'

She grins. 'You came, didn't you?'

'Carmel, I'm here because you're like a nuclear reactor in meltdown: I need to contain you.' I lower my voice. 'When exactly did I ask you to start ringing up clinics? Swear to me you never mentioned my name.'

She waves her hand. 'I was the epitome of discretion; these people are professionals, you know.' Carmel leans in. 'But before we get on to that, I've been checking out your 'womb stalker'.'

I wince. I hope that phrase isn't going to stick.

'The good news is, you don't feature on any of their message boards or other media. So she hasn't 'outed' you yet.'

'Thank God for that.'

'She's not stupid, though; she's using a burner phone. I take it you've not had any more messages?' I shake my head. 'Shame. I haven't managed to locate anyone fitting her description. We could do with a name.'

I grip the bench. 'I just wish she'd come out with it, whatever it is she wants.'

'Don't worry: I reckon she'll be in touch soon enough.'

A mother strides past with a pushchair; her young boy jogs beside her, trying to keep up. Instead of the usual lurch of envy, I feel a flutter of anticipation.

She suddenly yanks him to one side: too late. The boy flattens a dog poo. 'For God's sake, Richie. Look at your shoe.'

'Ow . . . ' he bleats. 'You're hurting.' Tears melt from his eyes; his sister wails and strains against her straps.

'I'll report it,' I say, launching myself off the bench. I hand the woman a tissue. She gives an uncertain smile. 'If it's any consolation, once they ID it, the owner will get a hefty fine.'

Carmel grimaces as the woman wipes her son's shoe. 'Boy, I don't envy those lab guys.'

'No,' I say, snapping a photo and trying not to gag. 'Me neither.'

I post it on the warden's page, with the location, and sit back down.

'Come on then, Carmel: what's this 'mega-news'? I have to get to work.'

'So, I managed to get hold of my consultant — '

'In the Czech Republic, yes.' That much I gleaned from last night's brief hushed exchange.

'I explained the situation to him . . . ' My eyes widen. She silences me with her hand. 'Don't panic, I emphasised how delicate it all was.' She giggles. 'God, you know, I really did have to insist it wasn't me.'

I pinch the bridge of my nose.

'He said the case was 'intriguing' . . . So I asked him, straight out, whether there was anything he could do.' She pauses. 'He went a bit technical at that point, and started rabbiting on about single nuclear polymorphs . . . ' She frowns. 'Or something like that . . . Anyway, he said he'd speak to a couple of people and come back to me.'

I stare at her. 'And?'

'Well, to be honest, I didn't expect to hear anything for at least a day or two. So when he rang back first thing . . . That's why we had to meet.'

Carmel is positively fizzing.

'Turns out he's spoken to a colleague of his.' She arches her eyebrows. 'An *extremely* clever doctor in

87

Ukraine.'

'Ukraine?'

'Yes, Susan. It's one of the top European destinations for assisted reproduction. And it just so happens this doctor's a real pro in genetics. He's pioneered all kinds of breakthrough treatments. No kidding, these were my consultant's words: 'this is your guy'.' She gives an emphatic nod. 'So, they exchanged messages, and — this is the really exciting bit — he's over here for a conference next week.'

'Next week?'

'I know: it's like it was destined to be. The best day for him to meet is Saturday, in London, before he flies back.'

'Carmel, I've barely got my head around this, let alone — '

'It's just an exploratory meeting: I'll come with you. This man is a legend in the fertility world. Don't you want to hear what he has to say?'

I steady myself against the seat. 'I can't just . . . bugger off to London, at a moment's notice. What am I going to tell Steve?'

'Make out it's a shopping trip . . . That I begged you. It's only a day, for goodness' sake.' I shake my head. 'Look, I know you've got doubts, but this could be your one chance.' She glances at my belly. 'What other options do you have?'

A wave of nausea sweeps through me. I grab a ginger biscuit from my bag and cram it in my mouth. The crumbs absorb the gathering saliva, cementing into a sickly paste.

Carmel frowns. 'Are you alright?'

I leap up just as the bile hits my throat. I dash behind a tree and throw up on the grass.

As I lean against the trunk, I think of the weeks stretching ahead of me, trying to hide this pregnancy and not trip over the lies I've told.

Out of the corner of my eye, I see a squirrel digging furiously in a border. On the branch above, another squirrel watches it intently.

Maybe this trip to London could be a good thing.

MyBodyMyHealth.net

Procreation vacations: are they safe?

Going abroad for fertility treatment has never been more popular, but new procedures may pose new risks.

Sabina Wise investigates.

Couples seeking fertility treatment have been venturing oversees for decades to escape long waiting lists and save money, but 'procreation vacations' are no longer just about the price tag.

Tougher regulation in Britain means some pioneering new treatments can now only be accessed abroad.

Almost all IVF patients opt for genetic tests before implantation, to assess their embryos' risk for certain diseases. But some overseas clinics have been screening for physical traits too, which is illegal in the UK, including gender, eye colour, height and even personality type. Other fertility centres have gone further, offering 'corrections' to IVF embryos if there are insufficient healthy ones in the pool. This is against WHO guidelines, which only permit genetic edits for a handful of terminal disorders. This is because such modifications, known as human germ line genome editing (HGGE), are passed down to future generations, and this technology is still relatively new.

Supporters claim the risks are negligible as

long as treatment is well managed, but regulators in the UK insist it would be 'highly irresponsible' to relax the rules, warning these procedures could have 'far-reaching, unknown impacts'.

The controversy surrounding these practices has not stemmed the flood of investors or customers. Thousands of aspiring parents appear happy to ignore the warnings and jet off abroad to follow the dream they've been sold: of conceiving a 'disease-free, healthy baby'.

18

Carmel puckers her lips, expertly navigating the twist of peel. Serene in coat dress and heels, she appears perfectly at home in this opulent lobby. If I'd known we were hitting up a five-star Kensington hotel for brunch, I'd have made more of an effort. Sometimes she can be very economic with the details.

'Ah,' she sighs, swirling her glass, 'you can't find a Negroni this good anywhere in Oxford. And, believe me, I've tried.'

You could purchase a two-course meal for less. I inhale a pulse of citrus: bitter and sharp. Part of me is tempted, just to dampen my nerves, but aside from the fact alcohol's a no-no, and I'm struggling to keep porridge down, let alone gin, I'm not sure cocktail consultations with fertility specialists are the done thing. I did hint as much, but Carmel's like a teenager who's bunked off school.

I tug my skirt down over my knees. 'What I still don't understand is how that woman got my number in the first place.'

I received another message from the 'womb stalker':
Does your husband know?

That so-called Christian is obviously out to black-mail me. As Carmel cheerfully pointed out, with the amount of cash I handed over, it's no surprise. She says we just need to sit tight and draw her out. The thought of Steve seeing that photo makes me want to howl.

Carmel puts down her glass. 'Facial recognition,

most likely. You've got to remember, organisations like hers are professional stalkers, and the software's cheap and easy to use. They record patients outside clinics then track them over the Internet for their vicious little harassment campaigns.'

My pulse throbs. 'How come you know so much about this?'

'A few years back, one of our VPs got targeted by the anti-abortion brigade. It got really bad. They published her picture and personal details all over their sites. Even sent campaigners round to her house.'

'Jesus. You don't think the same could happen to me, do you?'

'I mean, it's possible . . . ' Carmel curls her fingers, as if she's playing an invisible harp. 'But if she was going down that road, she'd have posted stuff by now. Plus, they usually hunt in packs. No: I think this one's out for herself.'

I bite my lip. 'Is that better or worse?'

'Oh, definitely better. Because, once that photo's out in the public domain, it's worthless to her.' Carmel wags her finger. 'Sooner or later, she's going to ask you for something. Probably money. And when she does, we set a trap.'

Carmel seems in her element.

'In the meantime, I've called in a favour. Just so happens that ATM is covered by the council's CCTV. Assuming the recording's good enough, we can play her at her own game.'

'And what game is that?'

Carmel rattles her ice and smiles. 'Facial recognition, baby. Facial recognition.'

My head is spinning. All this talk of spy software and blackmail is freaking me out even more.

I eye the foyer. 'This consultant did say eleven-thirty, right?'

'Yup.'

'Do you think we should message him?'

Carmel swallows a sigh. 'He's a keynote speaker, Susan. That fertility show is vast. He probably just got delayed.'

I scan the clocks above reception as the concierge bots glide back and forth: *New York, London, Moscow, Beijing, Tokyo*. Five gilt rings of artificial candles are suspended from the ceiling like fiery doughnuts.

Carmel pushes the menu over. 'Why don't you order something? You need to keep your energy up.' She winks. 'Especially now you're eating for two.'

'Shush.' I glance at the other seats in the lobby; thankfully, most are empty.

I slide my palm over my stomach. My daughter is the size of a blueberry. Her upper lip and nose have already formed. Small swellings are the start of ears. She has a face.

And then I see him. Or at least I think it's him; there was no picture on the website. A tall, grey-haired man in a dark navy suit is striding towards us, a swish leather briefcase clutched in one hand.

'Do you think that's him?' I whisper. He marches past and takes a seat in the far corner.

'Given he didn't so much as glance at us, I doubt it.' Carmel sucks the last beads of moisture from her glass. 'Lord, you're making me nervous. Just relax, will you?'

But then her gaze sharpens. A young man in faded black jeans, a loose grey jacket and cobalt shirt is walking purposefully towards us. That *cannot* be him . . .

Carmel pushes herself up: 'Dr Stakhovsky?'

94

My eyes drop to his lanyard: *Viktor Stakhovsky, Medical Director, Mokosh Fertility Clinic.*

He smiles. 'Mrs Hunter, I presume.' He holds out a hand.

'You presume correctly.' Carmel shakes it, with a coquettish bob.

He has bewitching grey eyes, tinged with green, ruffled black hair. The shadow of a beard that's too well shaped to be a casual missed shave.

'May I introduce my friend, *Susan*.' The emphasis is for my benefit: Carmel's under strict instructions not to mention my surname.

He turns his eyes on me, and I feel like Eve after the Fall.

'Pleased to meet you, Susan.' The stress on the soft 's' makes it exotic.

'Thank you for making time to see me.'

'My pleasure.' He surveys the seats. 'Are you happy to talk here, or would you prefer somewhere a little less . . . public?'

His English is immaculate, enhanced by the crisp Ukrainian accent. Only the hard 'v' instead of 'w' gives him away.

'My suite has a lounge. With rather splendid views of the gardens.'

I assume he means Kensington Gardens. These guys must be raking it in. Although the conference organisers are probably footing his bill.

Carmel rushes in: 'That sounds wonderful. Don't you agree, Susan? A little more privacy?'

I suppress a snort. Privacy has precious little to do with it; she just wants a nose around his suite.

I nod anyway. 'If it's not too much trouble.'

We follow him through the lobby to the lifts,

Carmel's heels clacking across the marble tiles. As the lift doors open, a tingle creeps up my spine.

What are you getting yourself into?

I take one step back, but Carmel presses in behind. Stakhovsky lifts his palm to the scanner. Ten flashes up in red digits, and the doors slide shut. I gulp the stale lift air as Carmel bludgeons him with questions. Eventually, we glide to a stop.

The doors open. Up-lights shimmer over copper-flowered walls. A vase sculpted like a claw perches on a credenza.

Stakhovsky walks up to a polished black door and raises his hand.

I hang back, in the corridor.

Carmel takes my arm. 'Come on,' she whispers. 'It'll be fine.'

19

Carmel gasps. The suite must spread over the entire floor.

A vast sofa faces the bank of windows, a balcony garden visible through sliding doors. A screen takes up most of the left wall, projecting silver swirls of light. On closer inspection, I realise they're cells and DNA: customised lighting, of course. No possessions clutter the surfaces, no dirty plates or cups. It looks as if he's barely been here.

I steady myself with the view: a sea of green punctuated with skyscrapers and farming towers. From this high up, the trees look like cake decorations. Limes and oaks flank the avenues; florets of horse- and sweet-chestnuts bunch in between.

'Please.' He sweeps his arm. 'Do sit.'

Carmel arranges herself on the animal-print cushions; I perch next to her, on the sofa's edge. There's a faint aroma of coffee and spice.

He claps his hands. 'So, what can I get you? Tea, espresso?' He glances at Carmel. 'Or something a little stronger?'

I run my tongue over my lips. 'Tea for me, please. Something herbal.' Carmel settles for a latte. He picks up the phone. Just water for him.

Stakhovsky shakes off his jacket. 'So, Susan.' He leans forward, one arm draped across his knee. 'Maybe you're wondering what you're doing here. And who, exactly, I am.'

I don't say anything. I don't think I'm expected to.

'I want to stress that you're under no obligation to take this conversation further. I'm simply here to offer suggestions.'

He has the same expression I remember from Mum's consultants: earnest and well meaning but powerless to change the outcome.

'Also, I want to reassure you that nothing discussed here will go beyond these walls. Do you understand?'

'Yes.' I nod. 'Thank you.'

'Why don't I start by introducing myself, explain a little about what I do? Please, stop me at any point to ask questions. And you must tell me off if I lapse into jargon: it's a bad habit of mine.'

'Oh, don't worry,' says Carmel. 'We will.'

He settles back in his chair. 'I'm what they call a reproductive scientist. I graduated from Luhansk State Medical University, specialising in reproductive technology and fertility treatment. I work with patients in the clinic, and I also do research.' He is watching me closely. 'That's just a complicated way of saying I help women have children. And, for me, that's the best job in the world.'

It's his usual patter, I'm sure, but it has the required effect: I unclench, just a little.

'I help men, too. As you're no doubt aware, when it comes to fertility issues, it's pretty much fifty-fifty.'

'Not that you'd know it,' mutters Carmel.

'Mokosh Fertility Clinic offers the full range of assisted reproduction services. We have an excellent track record: the highest IVF success rate in Europe, which is why we attract a large clientele from abroad. Our patients come from more than twenty-five countries, including the UK, Germany, the States . . .'

My eyes start to glaze over. It's a bit like some of

the conversations with the Bumpy Roadsters. I recognise the lingo, but it's not applicable to me.

'But so what, right?' He throws up his arms. 'You're already pregnant. Why should any of that matter to you?'

I bite my cheek: I feel like one of my class, caught drifting off.

He strolls to the window and slides his hands in his pockets, apparently consumed by the view. My eyes dart to Carmel's; she shrugs.

'Innovation. That's what sets us apart.' He turns to face us. 'I am fortunate enough to have a team of scientists who are at the forefront of reproductive research. Together, we develop novel fertility treatments using the latest technologies. Which means we can offer services to our clients that aren't yet available elsewhere.' He smiles. 'A decade ago, CRISPR revolutionised this industry: a pair of genetic scissors that could help rewrite our genetic code. Since then, the application of AI and quantum computing has pushed the boundaries of what's possible even further.'

There's a knock at the door, and I start.

A young woman in a fitted black dress entirely unsuitable for bending deposits a silver tray on the coffee table. She asks him a question in what sounds like Russian. He shakes his head and slips something into her hand.

'Please. Help yourself.' He hands me an engraved wooden box and waits for me to assemble my tea before he continues.

'Each of my team has a specialised interest. Mine is genetic optimisation *post*-implantation. Which involves administering gene therapies in the womb.

99

Typically, these babies have chromosomal abnormalities or other genetic disorders. Our ambition is to correct them.' He takes a sip of water. 'It's a relatively new field, but the technology's moving very fast. We've already corrected several disorders *in utero* by delivering editing agents into the embryo, through the placenta.' Carmel is sitting forward, hanging on his every word. 'These correct the mutations. And prevent these babies passing on the same disorders to their children.'

'That's ... extraordinary,' says Carmel. 'I assume this is still at an early stage?'

'We're in clinical trials. These women couldn't access IVF so hadn't benefited from genetic diagnostic tests. The first time they knew something was wrong was when they got their prenatal test results back. Which left them with two choices: have the baby anyway, or terminate the pregnancy.'

He looks me in the eye. 'We offered them a third choice. For free.'

I take a breath. 'So, these pregnancies ... They're progressing to term?'

'Most are, yes.'

My face drops. *Most* ... I think of those recent news articles.

He spreads his palms. 'There are risks, as there are with any pregnancy: natural or assisted. One in four pregnancies ends in a miscarriage. Genetic abnormalities account for over half of those. Without intervention, many of these mothers would most likely lose their babies. Even if they went to term, their babies would have serious health conditions. Thanks to our efforts, their odds have vastly improved.'

I try to picture these women: celebrating their BFP

after who knows how many tries, tentatively planning colours and names. The plummet of shock when those first test results arrived.

These mothers are my fellows in desperation. Pushed to extraordinary lengths, not by infidelity, but disease.

'But, even so, they're effectively guinea pigs?'

Carmel expels a breath. 'Dr Stakhovsky is here at our request, Susan.' Her tone sharpens. 'Remember, he's a busy man.'

Stakhovsky's smile does not waver. 'Would you describe Louise Joy Brown's mother as a guinea pig?'

'Absolutely. A lucky one: for her, it worked out. But if the pregnancy had terminated, we'd never have known. Hundreds of women took part in those early IVF experiments. No one talks about how many failed cycles and miscarriages they suffered.'

His eyes sparkle. 'In Russian, the phrase they use is 'white rats'. But that's not how these mothers see themselves. This trial gives them hope. We monitor them closely; give them the best possible care.' He scratches his stubble. 'Innovators have to break new, sometimes uncomfortable, ground. Look at Edwards and Steptoe. Less than a decade before they produced the first IVF baby, their pioneering work was dismissed by the great and the good of medicine as worthless. Four decades later, Edwards was awarded the Nobel Prize. Since Louise Joy Brown, millions more IVF babies have been born.'

Carmel coughs. 'Yes, indeed, and we are eternally grateful. Thank you so much, Dr Stakhovsky. It's clear you have a tremendous wealth of experience.' She lavishes him with a smile. 'However, as your time is no doubt limited, I wonder if perhaps we should

101

move on to discuss the issue at hand.'

He holds out his arms. 'Please.'

'Susan, would you care to elaborate?' She smiles at me sweetly. 'Then we can hear what Dr Stakhovsky recommends.'

My throat constricts. 'Before I start, I know you've already mentioned it, but this conversation . . . ' I carve my nail into the leather. 'It *has* to remain completely confidential.'

He regards me with his cool grey eyes. 'Of course. Patient confidentiality is a top priority.'

I look past him, to the park. Two cumulus clouds float languidly across the sky.

'My husband and I were diagnosed with unexplained infertility. We've been struggling to conceive without assistance for the past four years.' I swallow. 'But now I've discovered I'm eight weeks' pregnant.' My eyes flee to the floor. 'With another man's child.' I cringe as I think of Steve. 'But I can't just . . . Now that I finally have a baby, the thought of . . . ' My voice cracks. Carmel wraps her arm around my shoulders. 'I can't lose her now.'

Stakhovsky leans forward and rests his chin on his fingers.

'I understand how distressing this must be, Susan. Life is precious.' His gaze drops to my belly. 'We must strive to hold on to it.'

I'm suddenly ashamed of how I behaved earlier. This man performs miracles. I'm in no position to throw stones.

He swallows. 'In my view, the shame that still accompanies illegitimacy in many cultures, and the devastation it wreaks, is archaic and unfair. A healthy baby is a blessing; it doesn't matter how it was conceived. Why should the mother or child be tarnished with some label because of an outdated moral ideal? Even worse, got rid of. Surely, we are better than that.'

I think of those small, stiff bundles abandoned in Victorian streets or buried under floorboards. It still happens.

'So here is my proposal. My team is part of a research consortium. We collaborate with scientists in medical establishments across Russia, Georgia and the Czech Republic.' He gives Carmel a fleeting nod. 'It is our belief that, just as every woman should have the right to conceive, every man should have the right to father his own child. But male infertility is a growing problem. Sperm count and concentration have continued to deteriorate, despite improvements in diet and lifestyle. There still aren't many solutions out there, certainly not compared to what's available for women.'

I'm wondering where this is going. Steve's never been told his sperm are sub-standard. And Marty's sperm had no issues, that's for sure.

'Are you familiar with a fertility procedure commonly known as three-parent babies?' Carmel nods. 'A donor egg's nucleus, which contains that donor's genetic material, is replaced by the intended mother's nuclear DNA. Which enables her to carry her own biological child. It's quite straightforward. So, what if we could do something similar with men?'

Carmel slaps my arm. 'See? Not so crazy, after all!'

He ignores her. 'If we were able to replace a male donor's genetic material with the intended father's, it would remove any legal obligations from the donor and give the father true biological status. We already

103

know how to identify the paternal genes; we just have to find a way to disable them and insert the new ones.' His eyes flash. 'It's not dissimilar to correcting a complex polygenic disorder: same base editing principles, same AI. Just a few more algorithms.'

I stare at him. God, is that what it comes down to, in the end? A few more algorithms?

He leans closer. 'There is great appetite to pursue male fertility solutions, Susan. Funding, too. If we get this right, we could rescue relationships, as well as babies.'

I feel a tingling, all the way up my spine. Stakhovsky gets it. He's on my side.

I see, now, why some women worship these doctors like fertility gods.

'I know it's a lot to take in, Susan. I've rather bombarded you. Why don't I send you some information, which you can absorb at your leisure. Then, when you're ready, I suggest we have another conversation.'

Carmel nods. 'Very sensible.' She flashes me an excited smile.

'You said you were eight weeks, yes?' I nod. 'In which case, I'm afraid, you don't have that long to decide. Things become a lot more complex beyond ten weeks, which is when the immune system starts to develop. And, I imagine, time is a consideration for you, too.'

My heart thumps. He's right. It won't be long before I'm starting to show.

'If you did decide to proceed, I should warn you there's a fair bit of administration. Consent forms, medical details, that kind of thing. Probably the most urgent requirement is the DNA samples. But we can discuss all that later.'

He stands up. Carmel takes his cue and jumps up, too.

'Thank you so much, Dr Stakhovsky. It's been a privilege. Your work is truly groundbreaking.' She pumps his hand.

I lever myself up. 'Thank you. I appreciate your time. You certainly have given me lots to think about.'

'My pleasure,' he says, with a little bow, and presents his card. I didn't think anyone used business cards anymore; perhaps it's cultural. My eye is drawn to the picture above his name: a statuesque woman with long, golden tresses cradles a cornucopia overflowing with seeds. Her naked torso is encircled by tendrils.

'Mokosh: the goddess of earth and water,' he says. 'Protector of women and bringer of fertility.'

Two rings glow above her head, like haloes; a sheaf of wheat rests at her feet.

'Ukrainian women still perform dances in her honour, with the return of spring.' He smiles. 'Some believe she's also the goddess of destiny.'

The sockets of her eyes are white. She's either blind or has no eyes.

Stakhovsky holds out his hand. 'Goodbye, Susan.' His grey eyes weigh me up like a prize filly: is she going to saddle up or bolt?

I grasp his palm. 'Goodbye.'

Such power in those fingers.

'Wasn't he amazing?' gushes Carmel as we wait outside for the lift. 'I swear, someone up there is smiling on you.'

I think of the sightless goddess in my bag as the lift doors open.

I steady myself against the wall and offer up a silent prayer.

20

I turn my face into the late-afternoon sun and inhale the scent of peonies and freesias. A desperate rush of love squeezes the air from my throat and flutters loose, like a sail catching the breeze. Nine weeks, now; my daughter is the length of a penny. Her muscles are starting to grow. She has elbows and toes.

For the past three days, the arguments have raged in my head. I can barely sleep, and even when I do drift off, Stakhovsky's stubbled face awaits me, his complex rhetoric tangling my dreams. My mind keeps summoning grotesque images: ghostly foetuses in glass jars, rows of pregnant women on operating tables, eyes closed. In one nightmare, Carmel appeared, in a tight nurse's uniform, clattering instruments on a tray. I woke up in a sweat. That dream has haunted me ever since.

My phone buzzes, but I ignore it. Amongst the warbles and trills, two clear notes ring out. I open my eyes and see a starling on the branch above me. Its glossy black feathers flash iridescent pinks and greens.

My phone buzzes again. I sigh. There's no escape.

'Finally,' Carmel huffs. 'Where are you?'

'In the garden. *Trying* to rest.'

'Well, I need you to look at something. It's important. Should be in your inbox.'

I'm about to ask what it is when I spot the video file. I swallow.

'Got it?'

'Yeah.'

106

I clamber off the lounger and move into the shade as the CCTV file loads.

It's a shock when my image appears. It doesn't look like me, at all.

I watch this other self hurry down Magdalen Street to the ATM. I note my tight face, my frantic rummaging. The constant checking behind . . .

And there she is: limp hair, navy rain jacket. She lifts her face, just for a second.

'That's her. Two paces behind me.'

'Blue jacket and a shitty cloth bag?'

'Yeah.'

'Great. I'll get the guys on to it.'

I delete the file. 'Carmel?'

'Yes?'

'What you're doing: it's legal, right?'

She makes a puffing noise. 'Bit of a grey area.'

My eyes narrow. 'Which means what, exactly?'

She exhales. 'Which means that all's fair in love and war, and you should be focusing on more important things.'

I brace myself for the inevitable question.

'Have you spoken to him yet?'

Carmel's acquired the fervour of someone who's just found God; she believes Stakhovsky's the answer to my prayers.

'I've arranged a call with him tomorrow.'

'Good. Because that clock is ticking. Apart from anything else, we need to think about flights.'

'Jesus, are you on commission or something?'

'Susan!' She actually sounds quite offended. 'I just don't want you to miss this opportunity. That's all.'

'I know, sorry. I'm just tired. I'll update you after the call.'

I think of Steve and my stomach roils. He worked late again last night. Just as well he's consumed by another crisis; I can barely look him in the eye.

To distract myself, after flicking aimlessly through channels, I ended up watching a nature documentary about a floating barnacle which uses crabs as hosts, to reproduce. The female barnacle sheds her own shell and most of her body, and burrows into the unfortunate crab, latching on underneath its belly. After she lays her eggs, the female crab lovingly tenders them as if they were her own. If the barnacle happens to land on a male crab by mistake, she triggers hormonal changes that effectively switch its sex and render him infertile, so he behaves like a female and protects her eggs.

There's a lesson there.

Nature has no moral code. No ethical qualms about collateral damage.

It's about survival: of yourself and your progeny.

That's it.

21

I scurry along the footpath, keeping an eye out for other walkers. Sunlight dapples the beeches, flickering across their leaves. The wood is ablaze with bluebells, their delicate fragrance battling the more pungent aroma of wild garlic.

'As you're no doubt aware, a child receives a maternal and paternal copy of every gene,' says Stakhovsky, through my ear buds. 'It's not easy to tell them apart. But there is a technique we can use.'

His face is cupped in my hand. In this light, his eyes are the colour of an angry sea.

'Once we identify which copies are inherited from the biological father, we can train a deep-learning algorithm to target them. We synthesise design guides and set about replacing those genes with your husband's.'

I check the path ahead. 'You're confident that you can do this?'

He smiles. 'What we're proposing here, Susan, even a couple of years ago wouldn't have been possible. But there have been huge advances . . . Not just in gene editing, but also in the accuracy and scale of computational models. We will, however, need special permissions. That will require some . . . manoeuvring.'

A flag goes up. 'What do you mean?'

'Getting approval for new trials can take time. But my connections with the relevant authorities are good. I know the bioethics committee well. And the Ministry of Health is keen to accelerate any research that aids male fertility. So, if we position this correctly, I think we'll get the necessary traction.'

It's clear Stakhovsky's willing to jump through all manner of hoops to pursue this, but I'm not naive enough to believe that's solely for my benefit. When he looks at me, he sees published papers and scientific accolades. Dollar signs and glory.

'But the risks . . . ' I bring the mic closer to my mouth. 'The documents you sent mentioned birth defects. Even miscarriage — '

'*Potential* risks, Susan. All procedures have them, including routine diagnostic tests that millions of mothers undergo every day. Many experts predicted an IVF baby would never survive. They were wrong.'

I'm beginning to think Carmel has primed him.

'Just because something is unproven doesn't mean it cannot work.'

It doesn't mean it *can* work, either.

I skirt a small holly that's sprouted in the middle of the path and feel a familiar pang. How many times have I pictured the three of us, under a Christmas tree?

'Obviously changes of this magnitude do have *some* risks attached. Have you heard of off-target events?'

I think of Carmel and swallow. 'Yes . . . '

'Our edits are targeted to specific regions, but they might inadvertently cause changes in different locations, that occur at the same time, or later.' He pauses. 'However, we know a lot more about them than we used to. Our monitoring systems have vastly improved, and, if we detect them early, we can correct them.'

'But if you didn't . . . what would that mean?'

A tiny goldcrest flashes across the path, like a gilded

110

bullet.

He tilts his head. 'Potential developmental complications.' He hesitates. 'It's *extremely* unlikely, but, worst case: spontaneous abortion.'

My hand rushes to my belly. I can't risk that. I can't risk her.

'Susan, these are worst-case scenarios.' His urgency steps up. 'I understand you have concerns, but we'll be actively managing these risks, not leaving things to chance. Apart from the odd urine test or scan, most pregnant mothers are largely left to fend for themselves. My team will be monitoring you all the way. So, if anything doesn't look right, we will spot it and address it.'

It's easy for Stakhovsky, reeling off his reassurances. All scientists like him have got to lose is someone else's money, their own egos and time. It's the white rats who risk their lives.

There's a beeping noise. Stakhovsky rattles off something in Ukrainian. 'I'm afraid I'll have to go shortly, Susan; I have another meeting. Is there anything else you need from me at this point, to help you reach your decision?' His chair swivels slightly.

I name the elephant in the room. 'You haven't discussed payment, Dr Stakhovsky. This all sounds very complicated. How much is it going to cost?'

His lips pucker. 'Well, on that I can definitely reassure you. This is a trial, and you are 'first woman in', which means we would absorb the costs. All you need to cover are your flights. We'll take care of the rest, including accommodation. There are, however, two conditions.'

'Which are . . . ?'

'We'll need to monitor your daughter regularly. Not

111

only during pregnancy, but after the birth, during childhood. To check things are progressing normally. Which means we need your consent for follow-up tests, including interviews with you.'

I slow to a stop. 'I . . . I don't know about tha — '

'It's for her own wellbeing. The tests won't be onerous. After the first year, probably once a quarter, at most. Any research we publish will be anonymised. No one will know your identity or hers.'

I grind my palm into ridges of bark. 'I'll have to think about it.'

'Of course . . . The second condition is confidentiality. You'll need to sign some papers. You can't talk to anyone about the procedure or the research.'

'Well, that suits me.' I spot a dog walker and veer off, down a different path.

'Excellent. Well, before you go, just a quick word about the DNA samples.' His eyes flash. 'If you *do* decide to proceed, we'll need access to records or new samples sequenced ASAP.'

I think of the next robberies I must commit. Steve's I know I can get, but Marty's . . . ?

'I appreciate this may not be easy, but could you obtain samples from your parents and your husband's parents? It gives us a baseline to compare. Helps us assess which DNA changes are hereditary and which are random.'

My chest tightens. 'I could send you my father's. He was diagnosed with early onset Alzheimer's in his fifties. But my mum . . . she never had any genetic tests.'

I've been thinking about Mum a lot lately. It suddenly dawned on me, I'll be the same age as her when she had me. And I remember the circular blue box, faded now: the wisp of hair curled inside.

'I *do* have a lock of her hair . . . ' As soon as I say the words, I regret them. That hair is the only piece of her I have left. 'But it's from when she was a baby. I doubt it will be any use.'

'No matter,' he says, casually. 'Our forensic team are excellent — send it.' I bite my lip. 'What about your husband's parents?'

'That won't be possible, I'm afraid. His father died some years back, and I have no idea if he was tested. And there's no way I can ask his mother.' I pause. 'Is that a problem?'

He sucks air through his teeth. 'Not necessarily. We could comb the biobanks and public databases, do a few long-range searches. If they don't crop up we'd likely locate near-relatives.'

Stakhovsky hasn't touched on the issue of consent. Is it legal in Ukraine to take people's DNA without asking them? Either way, it's illegal here.

'I have a colleague at a laboratory not that far from you who could take your blood sample and process the others. Arrange secure delivery to me.'

He makes it sound like a pair of trainers.

'In the meantime, I suggest you have a good think about everything, Susan. I'm happy to talk again. But, given your stage of pregnancy and the preparations that need to be made, I think it would be best to confirm one way or another by end of play tomorrow.'

'Tomorrow?'

'Yes. I don't mean to rush you, but as you know, time is precious. And I have other potential candidates waiting, should the need arise.'

Is that a threat?

A warm wind rustles through the canopy. I think of her, as she might be. Soft, olive skin in a babygro with pink bunnies. Dark-brown eyes.

If my baby had a life-threatening disease like Leo's, I wouldn't hesitate.

But not doing this *does* threaten our life together, as a family. And Stakhovsky promised we'd get the very best care. What if she develops some condition that, without his vigilance, might grow undetected?

I think of the barnacles jettisoning their body parts, burrowing into the bellies of crabs.

There's another, more practical problem. One that Stakhovsky can't solve.

How am I going to negotiate a weekend away abroad, without Steve?

114

22

I lift my palm to the scanner and march through the school gates. Amidst the flurry of masks, hats and wings, I recognise the usual characters: the hastily assembled Matildas, the BFGs. Fur-clad Gruffalos, face-paint slopping down their chins. I totally forgot about Book Week: I had to panic-print a Victorian nanny costume. Not only is the hat too small and the dress too tight, but I can't stop sweating. I certainly attracted some looks on the bus.

Goldilocks pants past, her satin dress caught in her knickers, pursued by a scowling Snow White. My eyes veer to the playing field. Towering above a mob of zombies, a gangly scarecrow races for the ball, wisps of straw drifting in his wake. He passes the ball to Hermione Granger, who slams it into the net.

I take a breath. OK. This is it.

I wave. Marty looks up, surprised. I've been making myself scarce. He waves back.

As he ambles over, I think again about the child we might have made. His eyes, or mine? Tall, or short, like me? It's like that app we joked about, where you mash up your profiles. Not remotely funny now.

Marty pushes back his hat and wipes some straw that's stuck to his forehead. He's painted on huge, arched eyebrows, just like the original scarecrow's in *The Wizard of Oz*, but they've run a little.

I nod at him: 'Nice work.' No matter how hideous the costume, he always carries it off.

'Thanks . . .' He scratches his nose and eyes my

costume.

'You have no idea, have you?' I brandish my umbrella. We both stare at the handle: more like a dinosaur's head than a parrot's. I sigh. "Everything is possible. Even the impossible . . ."

Mary Poppins had no children of her own but wielded an indomitable optimism. I'm hoping some of that might rub off on me.

'Ah, I see it, now: Mary Poppins!' He slaps his forehead. 'Sorry: must be my lack of brains . . . ' He scratches his neck. '*Man*, this straw is itchy.'

I tuck my dino-parrot under my arm. 'Hang on. You've got a bit tangled in your . . . ' I give his fringe a yank.

'Ouch!' He flinches. I snatch my hand away. 'I think that was the real thing.'

My gloved fingers curl into a fist. 'Sorry.' I slide my hand into my pocket, pulse racing.

'So, where are you flying off to today, Miss Poppins?'

Shame burns through me. 'Nowhere, sadly.'

I should have come as Cruella de Vil.

I try to lighten my voice. 'How about you? Off to see the Wizard?'

He sucks in a breath. 'More like the Wicked Witch. I've been summoned to the office. Think I'm in for a roasting.'

Mrs Purcell, the office manager, has a formidable reputation. I shake my head. 'What have you done this time?'

'My assessments. Apparently, they're late.'

'Oooh. Bad scarecrow.'

'I know.' He sighs. 'It's the torch for me.'

The bell rings. I tip my umbrella. 'Well . . . have fun

116

with the witch.'

He touches a finger to his hat and lopes off towards reception. I walk a few steps and stop.

I imagine a room: white walls alive with tropical birds, a unicorn mobile twirling above a cot. Marty, leaning over the rail, such love in those mocha eyes . . .

I swallow.

In some alternate world, we are there: the three of us.

A world where I met Marty first. And we raise this child, just the way she is.

23

'I do have one last question.'

My heart hasn't stopped hammering since I told Stakhovsky I'd do it.

'Of course; go ahead.' He smiles, patient as ever. But there's fire in his eyes.

'What happens, if . . . if not *all* the DNA changes? If some of the original father's remains?'

A little boy barrels past the car, his mother in hot pursuit.

'You're talking about mosaicism, Susan?'

I nod.

'You've certainly been scrutinising those documents.'

Stakhovsky arches his fingers and presses the tips together, one by one. 'Given the scale of the edits, that is a *small* risk. It may initially seem that the editing is quite accurate, but later, you discover locations which haven't been changed . . . ' He clears his throat. 'But, as you know, we're going to monitor your daughter regularly, to ensure that doesn't happen.'

'Right . . . '

'And even if it did, it's highly improbable a standard paternity test would pick it up. Plus, there's a plausible explanation.' His eyes flicker. 'Do you know about chimeras?'

I immediately think of a fire-breathing lion with a serpent's tail. 'Not the mythical creatures, in Greek legend?' I frown. 'Whose bodies are made up of different animals?'

He smiles. 'Not that kind. Are you aware that there are human chimeras?'

I shudder. 'You're not talking about some kind of . . . hybrid, are you? Like a humanzee?'

I remember those awful experiments they did, trying to cross a human and a chimpanzee.

He throws back his head and laughs. 'No, no, Susan. Nothing like that, I assure you. A human chimera has *two* sets of DNA.' I stare at him blankly. 'Maybe you've heard of vanishing twin syndrome?'

The penny drops. 'Hang on, yes . . . Where one twin dies early in the pregnancy?'

'That's right. If one twin doesn't survive, its DNA is effectively absorbed by the other. It's actually much more common than people realise. It occurs in around a third of multiple pregnancies.'

'Really?'

He nods. 'It also happens with some organ and bone-marrow transplants. The body continues making blood cells that have the original donor's DNA, inside the recipient's body.'

Wow. That's macabre.

A little girl skips along the pavement, singing, her socks half-way down her calves.

'It caused havoc with paternity tests early on, before the syndrome was more widely recognised. In one landmark case, a DNA test concluded the actual father was the child's uncle, not his biological parent. Turned out he had different DNA in his saliva and his sperm. In another case, a woman didn't test positive as the mother of her own child because she had different DNA in her blood and her ovaries.'

My mind spins. 'So you're saying — '

'In the unlikely event we don't change *all* the

genes . . . If challenged, you could attribute it to chi-merism.'

I relax, just a little. Although I can't stop thinking about the humanzee.

I lower my voice. 'This is all . . . within the regulations, isn't it?'

He frowns. 'Susan, what we're doing here may be groundbreaking, but I assure you, it complies with the regulatory framework here in Ukraine.'

I think I may have offended him. 'Good. Right.'

'Now, please remember what we discussed, about communication and privacy. It's vital for your protection and for ours. Only use the designated data room. You can complete all forms securely, with full encryption. Nothing gets in or out, without our say-so.'

'Understood.'

'And, Susan?'

'Yes?'

'Let me congratulate you, once again, on your decision. Such a choice takes bravery. Determination.' My stomach tightens. 'I promise I will do everything in my power to make it a success.'

I think of the nerves branching out in my daughter's brain. The buds in her gums that will soon be teeth.

I look straight into his cool grey eyes. 'Please make sure that you do.'

Activists clash with police in worldwide protests against 'commodification of babies'

Helena Sanchez, Science Correspondent for Guardian Online

A global 'week of anger' against the genetic selection and manipulation of embryos began today in more than one hundred cities across the US, Europe and South America. Thousands of campaigners staged die-ins outside fertility clinics, demanding an end to what they call 'the commodification of babies'.

In Washington DC, police clashed with hundreds of protestors, while in Paris, activists picketed fertility clinics, brandishing embryo dolls printed with the slogan: GM baby for sale.

The unprecedented, week-long campaign follows months of growing controversy over the surge in genetic procedures taking place during IVF. Opponents accuse fertility clinics of cashing in on costly and unethical services in pursuit of 'the perfect child'.

The protests have been coordinated by the group Genome Defence Alliance (GDA) based in Richmond, Virginia, who have joined forces with disability-rights activists and religious groups.

Marlese Stant, campaign coordinator said: 'Prospective parents are sleepwalking into medically endorsed discrimination and murder. What started in the name of disease prevention is sliding down the slippery slope of eugenics. We need to stand up for the rights of the unborn child.'

Dr Alana Pritchard, Founder of the New Beginnings fertility clinic in Washington said the protests had gone too far. 'Our patients aren't breaking any laws. It's a basic human right to conceive a child. The last thing these families need is strangers threatening them with hell for eternity.'

But with a booming global fertility market valued in excess of $50 billion and joined-up governance looking unlikely, the fight between anti-interventionists and pro-choicers shows little sign of abating.

24

I bite into my wrap, scowling at the paint trapped under my nails. We're celebrating One World Week, so my class threw their hands and most of their bodies into 'rock art' this morning, and I've lined up a holographic djembe drummer after lunch who's going to teach them some moves. Normally, I relish these breaks from the standard curriculum, but there is no normal, anymore. These past few days, I've barely slept. The thought of thirty pairs of hands hammering away all afternoon makes me want to weep.

A message arrived last night — the one Carmel had been waiting for. The timing couldn't have been worse:

My silence has a price.

The way things are going, that awful woman will find out about Stakhovsky and derail the whole thing.

My phone beeps:

BIG NEWS! Call me ASAP.

Carmel picks up on the first ring. 'We've found her.'

A courgette lodges in my throat. I force a swallow. 'That was quick.'

'These guys don't hang around, Susan.'

She launches straight in.

'Helen Tomlins: thirty-five-years old, married, but we think separated, no kids. Get this: used to work as a teaching assistant but was made redundant two years ago, hasn't held down a job since. Which confirms our suspicions.' She snatches a breath. 'She's in it for the cash. Probably held out till now, thinking the media furore about those protests would up the stakes.'

It has.

The Sunflower Clinic was targeted yesterday. It was all over the Oxfordshire news. Protestors wearing baby masks lay on the pavement outside, holding posters with the caption: 'Mummy, don't kill me because I'm not perfect.'

'This is it, Susan.' Carmel's eyes shine. 'We know who she is, where she lives . . . So now we can turn the tables. Start rattling her cage.'

My throat tightens. Rattling cages isn't something I do. I'm usually the one being rattled.

'But we haven't got anything that connects her to these messages, have we? You said the phones are burners.'

'That's why you're going to arrange to meet her.'

I nearly choke: 'What?'

'We need her on record.'

I grip the phone. 'I'm a primary-school teacher, Carmel. I can't get embroiled in something like this. Have you seen what's happening on the news? These people are practically terrorists.'

Even on screen, Carmel's stare is withering. 'Susan, Kyiv is barely a week away.' Her mouth looms closer; it must be practically kissing the phone. 'This woman could ruin everything. Do you want to be rid of her or not?'

I look into Carmel's dark, oval eyes. I wish I had her strength. Maybe Dad would have liked me better.

I graze a tooth over my lip and nod.

She exhales. 'Right. In which case, it's time to text her real phone. She'll either disappear for good, or take the bait. Let's keep it simple. How about: 'We

124

need to meet'?'

She sends me Helen Tomlins' number and I dutifully assemble the words.

I hesitate and hit send. 'Done.'

'Excellent. We'll sort out the details later. Next up: Kyiv. What's the situation there?'

I twist my hem. God, Carmel must have been a nightmare to work for.

Her face falls. 'You haven't told him, have you?'

'I just don't think Steve will buy it, Carmel, not at such short notice. He's crazy stressed about work.'

Carmel's grand plan is to make out that she's the one with the appointment, and needs me there because Barry can't make it.

'Hang on. It's a weekend, isn't it?'

'Steve doesn't really have weekends . . .' I sigh. 'You know what he's like — he gets a bit funny when I'm away . . . He already thinks we spend too much time together.'

Carmel mutters an expletive. 'I see his firm's still copping grief about that mozzie gene drive.'

'Yeah, he's under a lot of pressure. And there's another major launch supposed to be happening tomorrow that he's been working on. A new gene therapy for prostate cancer.'

She purses her lips. 'What if I was able to help him out . . . ?'

'What do you mean?'

'An old contact of mine — what you might call a 'covert influencer'. He's got an uncanny knack for narratives. Trained by the very best on cyber disinformation storms.'

I blink at her. 'I have absolutely no idea what you're talking about, Carmel.'

125

She rolls her eyes. 'He cleans up PR disasters. Basically muddies the waters and deflects the shit elsewhere.'

My head begins to throb. 'How's that going to get us to Kyiv?'

'Steve could use a man like him on this malaria debacle. And I'm a great believer in that old adage, 'One good turn deserves another'.'

Despite everything, I have to laugh. 'I hate to break it to you, Carmel, but I'm not sure Steve would accept a beer from you right now, let alone some massive work favour.'

'Oh, I don't know about that.' Carmel smiles at me, as ever, undeterred. 'I'm betting Steve's career-protection instinct is pretty strong.'

25

'Shit. Shit, shit, shit!'

I stir. My eyes are like bricks. Steve throws off the duvet and leaps out of bed.

'You OK?'

'Slept through the alarm. Today of all days.'

I glance at the clock. That's a miracle. I must have slept through it, too.

He barrels to the bathroom door. 'It's the prostate press launch. Can't be late.'

I knead my temples. I don't know if it's the stress or the hormones, but I seem to have a continual headache.

I hurry downstairs, pop my folic acid and force down a bowl of cereal to ward off the morning retch. I make Steve a tea and head back up to the bathroom. As I open the door, a blanket of minty steam wafts out.

'There you go.' I pass him the mug.

'Ta.' Steve's standing in front of the mirror, a towel wrapped round his waist. 'Eghardt would bloody love it if I mess this up.' Steve braces one hand against the basin and flips on the shaver. 'He's been on my case ever since Nigeria went south.'

The shaver buzzes over his face like an angry mosquito.

'Eghardt's an idiot. Everyone knows that. He's only lasted this long because he's got you.'

Steve angles it round his jaw. 'Doesn't make things any less painful.' The shaver makes a whining sound.

'Damn . . .'

A dark red spot pools on his cheek. He snatches some tissue to blot the cut. It blooms a deep crimson.

I stick my head in the cabinet and fish out a plaster. 'Here.' I swap it for the plug of tissue. 'Don't want you bleeding all over your shirt.'

'Thanks.'

I close my hand around the bloody wad, horrified by this thief that I've become. The DNA samples are due at the lab tomorrow. Now I'm a serial offender.

Steve glances at me. 'By the way, Carmel left some cryptic message about work. Asked me to give her a call. You haven't been blabbing to her about Nigeria, have you?'

'No, of course not. She's probably seen it on the news.' I take a breath. 'Actually, while we're on that subject, she asked if I could help her out next weekend. She's got an appointment. In Kyiv.' I swallow. 'Women's stuff.'

Steve frowns.

'Barry was supposed to go with her, but something's come up at work. They were going to make a weekend of it.'

The heat in here is smothering me, and the pounding in my head steps up. 'I think she's pretty desperate.'

Steve snorts. 'Well, we can't let our precious Carmel get stressed now, can we? Not with that full-time job of hers, lounging around the house.' He splashes water over his face. 'I could do with a break myself. These next few weeks are going to be hell. I see little enough of you as it is without you swanning off with her again.'

I feel myself sliding into surrender, the way I always do, the way I did with Dad; anything to avoid that flare

128

of anger. But then I remember Stakhovsky's words:

Such a choice takes bravery. Determination . . .

I tap the tiles. 'I know you're busy. But let's face it, you'll probably be working all weekend anyway.'

Steve turns. Water drips off his chin onto the floor.

'I've never been to Kyiv, before.' I swallow and meet his gaze. 'Carmel said she'd foot the hotel bill. It's only two days.'

Steve swerves back to the mirror and smooths some gel through his hair.

I wet my lips. 'I'll tell her it's a yes, then, shall I?'

I don't wait for an answer.

I just walk out the door.

26

I survey the park, trying not to stare too hard at people's faces. Particularly Carmel's, who's ensconced on the bench opposite. Behind her, copper beeches are in full leaf, like russet peacocks on display. A terrier races past; it leaps in the air and snaps a ball in its jaws.

My eyes are drawn to the graceful arcs of a Tai Chi group practising under a Turkey oak. I wish I could absorb some of their fluid calm.

Carmel briefed me to arrive early, so I could get in position and secure the seat. I'd usually make a beeline for the rose garden; there's supposed to be some new strain that glitters all the colours of a rainbow. But flowers are not my focus today.

My phone buzzes. Twice. My stomach drops: that's the sign.

Helen Tomlins is here.

Carmel has planned this sting operation with the punctilious rigour of a military campaign. She's researched everything, down to which seats to sit on and what microphone to use. We even did a dummy run with the hidden mic. I just want to get it over with.

I don't recognise her straight away. She looks younger. Her hair is scraped back in a ponytail, and she's wearing a loose T-shirt and jeans. She wanders over the grass, as if she's just out for a stroll. A sudden rush of anger takes me by surprise.

I lift my hand in a discreet wave. She scans right

and left, and takes a seat at the far end of the bench. She doesn't look at me. Neither of us speaks.

I try to remember how I'm supposed to start. Carmel warned me not to talk too much, just let my stalker speak, so she can, in Carmel's inimitable words, 'hang herself'.

I inhale. 'Before I hand over any more money . . . I need to know what proof you can give me that my photo will be destroyed.'

Her gaze remains fixed straight ahead. 'The proof is my word.'

I cough. 'Right. Maybe you can understand why I might have some concerns about that.'

She shrugs. I grip the wooden slats.

'Seeing as I gave you four hundred pounds for a one-hundred pound phone, and you've been blackmailing me ever since . . .'

Whoops — definitely off-script. Not supposed to antagonise.

'That's an interesting accusation.' She inspects her nails. 'What we have here is a simple transaction. I took a picture of you in a public space; there's no crime against that. For reasons of your own, you want to buy it off me.'

Her cool confidence rocks me. Would any of my objections actually hold up, in a court of law?

I try a different tack. 'Why are you doing this? You seem like a reasonable person. I'm just an ordinary woman, trying to get on with life.'

Her lip curls. 'Oh, so life's *difficult* for you, is it?'

Her sarcasm makes me reckless. 'Maybe not as difficult as it's been for you, *Helen*.'

Her eyes dart to mine. She jumps up, but I grab her arm.

'I'm not here to make trouble. Whatever you think about me, you're wrong.'

She shakes me off. 'You've made it abundantly clear you don't care what I think. And you were at that clinic for a reason.'

'Yes. I was.' I swallow. 'But before I ever set foot in that place, I had four years of heartbreak. Before finally getting pregnant, the old-fashioned way.'

Her brow pinches. 'You're pregnant?'

I nod.

'Without intervention?'

I nod again. It's true, so far. My palm gravitates to my stomach. 'Nine weeks. And I want this baby, more than anything in the world.'

A shadow sweeps over her face, but she shutters it up behind her eyes.

And I recognise what's at the heart of this. It has nothing to do with money.

She turns, as if to go, and I press on.

'My husband and I had unexplained infertility. It's a very lonely place. I honestly thought I'd never get pregnant.' I glance at her. 'I used to mask my pain, too.'

Her lips tighten. I think she's going to leave, but she sinks slowly onto the bench.

We sit, watching families amble round the park. Her gaze rests on a young couple pushing a pram.

She takes a breath. 'Before we started trying, my husband suggested we get ourselves screened. I was oblivious to the issues. So I agreed.' Her voice is monotone. 'Turned out I'm a carrier for DMD: Duchenne Muscular Dystrophy. I had no idea. And there's a one-in-two chance of passing it on.'

'I'm sorry.'

One of the boys in my class had DMD, when I first started teaching. Like Danny's disease, it's a cruel condition that targets the young. Progressive muscle wastage, severe respiratory and cardiac complications. Most sufferers don't make it to their mid-twenties.

'My doctor said I qualified for three rounds of IVF, including something called PGD. I'd never heard of it, but he said it was 'the responsible thing to do'.'

Her eyes drop to her hands. Her nails are bitten and raw.

'The first round, I only had one embryo: a little girl. But I lost her; she didn't implant.' She swallows. 'The next cycle they harvested three eggs. One of the embryos didn't survive to transfer. The second wasn't what they called 'viable'. The third was a boy who carried the DMD mutation.' She pauses and her lip quivers. 'We were advised to try again.'

I think of Carmel and the Bumpy Roadsters. All these couples, going through hell.

'After a break, we started our final round.' She takes a deep breath. 'The first embryo failed to implant. I lost the second after a week.'

I reach for her arm but think better of it. 'I am genuinely so sorry, Helen . . .'

'We couldn't afford to go private. I wanted to keep trying, the natural way, but Tommy — my husband — said he didn't want to risk bringing a child into the world with DMD.'

She shakes her head. 'We could have had our little boy. He was ready for life — perhaps not a long one, but still a life. And we threw him away, like rubbish.' Her eyes burn. 'I realised then that we deserved to be childless: it was God's punishment. But Tommy didn't see it that way. We couldn't salvage our marriage after that.'

I clench my fingers and try to think of something, anything, to say.

'Tommy left. Then I lost my job. It got to the stage where I could barely leave the house. But then, one day, Fruit of the Womb posted a leaflet through my door.' She turns to me. 'And I thought, if I can stop just one person making the mistakes I made, save one tiny soul, maybe God will forgive me. Maybe He'll give me another chance.'

'You shouldn't blame yourself, Helen. You were just following the advice you were given. It wasn't your fault, what happened —'

'But I had a choice, didn't I? I should have been grateful for the child I was gifted.' Her jaw stiffens. 'And now they're saying there's some new therapy that might cure DMD. So you see, he could have lived, if I'd just had faith.'

I am besieged by conflicting emotions: sympathy, remorse, fear. But I cannot accept her vengeful God.

Two boys fly past on moto-scooters, gravel spitting up behind.

She pulls out her phone.

'This is your photo, in the cloud.' She taps the phone and my face vanishes. 'I haven't stored it anywhere else.'

'Thank you, Hel —'

'I shouldn't have asked you for money. But sometimes, when people won't listen, when they fob you off . . . ' Her eyes darken. 'The anger and the pain just . . . eat you up.'

I remember how I felt before I got pregnant. That scalding resentment inside.

'There are groups, Helen. For women who've gone

through similar things to you. Those forums can help you get past this. They helped me.'

She shakes her head. 'I've found my support group, and they've been good to me. But I haven't forgiven myself.'

She pushes herself up and eyes my belly. 'Take care of that baby, won't you? It's the most precious gift.'

'I know.' My gut churns as I think about next weekend. 'Goodbye, Helen. And . . . good luck.'

I watch her hurry along the path, her back slightly bowed, arms swinging stiffly by her sides. A dull ache throbs in my chest.

After a few minutes, Carmel hurries over.

'Crikey, that was a result. Even though you did go *completely* off-script.' She grins. 'I think I need a stiff drink.'

I hold out my hand. 'Phone, please.'

One eyebrow lifts. 'Why?'

'You know why.'

Carmel scowls. 'Are you sure about this? She's a bit of a nutcase, she might — '

'Absolutely positive.'

She sighs and taps her screen with a scarlet nail. 'Very well.'

I highlight the recording and press delete.

My eyes narrow. 'You haven't sequestered it anywhere else, have you?'

'No!' Carmel pockets her phone and glowers at me. 'You know, for a self-proclaimed pushover, you really can be quite pig-headed.'

27

'Good evening, Susan.'

Stakhovsky graces me with a dazzling smile. The screen's reflection imbues his face with a blue glow, like one of those creatures from that old classic *Avatar*.

I press my palm to my stomach. 'Good evening.'

It's only been three days but they've run the tests already. If there are any genetic abnormalities, he'll know.

'So, the samples were all good, then?'

'Absolutely. And we traced some relatives of your husband, so we have the required baselines.' He pauses. 'I assume you're alone?'

'Yes. I'm parked up at my local supermarket.'

'Good.'

I examine his face, try to gauge what's coming, but those eyes are inscrutable. Years of practice delivering life-changing news.

He clears his throat. 'Now there's nothing major to concern you, but, as you know from your own test, sequencing can throw up a few things.'

My pulse quickens. I think of Helen.

'It's Alzheimer's, isn't it? I heard it can skip a generation. Has it passed to her?'

'No, no, your daughter has no indicators for Alzheimer's.' I breathe out. 'In fact, there are no signs of any chromosomal abnormalities or serious genetic disorders. Your daughter appears to be in fine shape.'

'Oh, thank God.' I slump back in my seat.

'Yes, it's great news.' There's a slight hesitation. 'But, there are a couple of risk areas we should discuss. From your husband's results.'

I stiffen. I'd forgotten about Steve's profile, with all the other worries flying around my head.

'Has your husband ever experienced any palpitations or black-outs?'

I swallow. 'No . . . Well, not to my knowledge. Why?'

'Your husband carries a mutation in the gene associated with LQTS. That stands for Long QT syndrome. It's an inherited condition that can cause irregular heart rhythms, triggered by abnormal electrical activity in the heart.'

I inhale.

'Now, I don't want to alarm you, Susan. The rhythms *may* return to normal by themselves. However, in a small number of cases . . . it can lead to sudden cardiac death.'

My hands fly up to my face. 'His dad died of a heart attack in his fifties — '

Stakhovsky leans forward. 'This doesn't mean your husband will necessarily develop these symptoms; some people carry the same mutation without ever experiencing problems. The condition is determined by a number of factors, including environmental ones.'

I try to focus on what he's saying, but all I hear is 'sudden cardiac death'. I want to hang up and call Steve, get him checked right away. But what could I tell him?

'Susan, listen to me. Treated early, this condition is completely manageable. Your husband just needs to make an appointment with his doctor.'

I *have* to get Steve tested. Maybe, if this works, he'll

do it. For the baby.

'However, as this is a heritable disorder, we wouldn't want to pass it on.'

My thoughts instantly stop spinning. 'To the baby, you mean?'

'Exactly. We've good experience of editing the affected genes. We can incorporate those changes and eliminate the risk of your daughter inheriting this condition and passing it on to her own children.'

I take a long, slow breath. Thank God he spotted it. This is precisely the kind of issue an untested pregnancy would have missed.

'Are you happy for me to continue, Susan?'

I look up. God, there's more. I claw my fingers through my hair and nod.

'As you know, we don't just search for physical conditions. We screen for mental and psychological conditions, too. There is one other potential concern in your husband's profile.' He coughs. 'We identified thirteen genetic variants that are implicated as risk factors for alcohol use disorder.'

My eyes close. I think of that fateful night, with the gin. The reason I'm here.

Stakhovsky presses on. 'Now, as I explained before, just because he has a genetic predisposition, it doesn't necessarily mean the disorder will manifest. Environmental and social factors are just as important.' He swallows. 'However, we found other mutations that indicate he may have had therapy to treat it.'

I sigh. 'He had an alcohol problem. During his first marriage. He was under huge stress and, well, he was in a bad place for a couple of years. He underwent gene therapy. He doesn't drink very often, but if he does . . . ' I cringe at the memory. 'It makes him sick.'

Stakhovsky nods. 'I'm sorry, Susan. This is a complex area, with multiple genes involved, but we know how to target the defective ones. We can make those changes. You just need to decide what you would like us to do.'

My eyes well up as I think of Steve struggling in those dark years. 'And you're sure this is safe? It's been done before?'

'There've been many successful trials. As you can imagine, this research is in high demand. However, I would strongly recommend you talk all this through with one of our genetic counsellors. You don't need to respond now.'

A woman walks across the road in front of me, a little blonde-haired girl in tow. I'll bet she didn't have to go through any trials. I'll bet she was one of those that just 'fell pregnant'. Christ, I hate that expression. As if pregnancy were as easy as tripping up the kerb.

'As I said before, please try not to worry. It's good we found out about these conditions now.'

I think of the goddess on Stakhovsky's card, white eyes upturned. How fitting that she holds sway over both fertility and destiny. The very essence of Stakhovsky's trade.

'Before you go, Susan, there is one last thing . . . '

My face drops. *Now what?*

He holds up his hand. 'No genetic disorders, nothing like that.' He hesitates. 'In fact, we don't even need to discuss it now; you've more than enough to think about.'

I exhale. 'Might as well get it over with. I'll only fret.'

He purses his lips. 'Very well. I debated whether I should tell you. But, I think you have a right to know.'

Dread curls across my tongue. It tastes bitter, like the worst kind of medicine.

'Your father's DNA . . .' Stakhovsky's eyes flick away and back again. 'There's no easy way to say this. It isn't a genetic match.'

'I beg your pardon?'

'I'm sorry, Susan. There's a zero percent chance of him being your biological father.'

Dad's face rears up, clouded with anger; Mum in the background, trying to placate him.

My head suddenly feels too heavy; I brace my hands against the wheel.

'I appreciate this must be terribly difficult, Susan. I have one of my counsellors on standby.'

I shake my head. 'I don't . . .'

My mind fills with pictures of Mum, scurrying round the kitchen. On her knees, trowelling the soil.

I try again. 'It's not possible . . . My mother would *never* have been unfaithful.'

Stakhovsky's mouth flattens. I know what he's thinking.

Like mother, like daughter . . .

'She loved my father . . . They were devoted. Even if he was . . . difficult, sometimes.'

Difficult doesn't get close . . .

I try to picture it. A shared joke with a colleague. A lunch break together, drinks after work. And then . . .

No. *No!* I cannot accept it. I won't.

Stakhovsky takes a breath. 'There is another possible explanation . . . Do you know if your parents had trouble conceiving?'

I stare at him.

'I apologise, I know this is delicate. But if there *had* been difficulties . . . they may have used a donor.'

140

My eyes widen. 'A sperm donor, you mean?'

He holds up his palms, as if in surrender. 'It's just a theory. But there tended to be a lot of secrecy about such things, with that generation. It wouldn't be unusual not to disclose it. There wasn't the transparency we have today.'

My brows knit together. Mum had me when she was thirty-six. How long had they been trying?

'Mum never said anything . . . ' She would have told me, I'm certain of it. Unless . . . Did he forbid it? Hold her hostage? Her silence for a baby?

My brain speeds back over memories; replays them through this new lens. And it's as if a trap door opens up beneath me. And I plummet down, into a whole new world.

It would explain so much. The resentment I always felt radiating from him. His disappointment. I'd try and tell myself it was because of the bond Mum had with me. Perhaps it was a different kind of envy; the kind that would eat a man like him up.

'Susan, if you like, the counsellor can speak with you now.'

All these years, I'd thought it was my fault, something that was wrong with me.

Perhaps that's why Mum forgave him his moods, because he had granted her this wish. Because she knew he was ravaged by some primordial jealousy he couldn't control.

It fits. It all fits.

'Would you like me to transfer you, Susan?'

I stare at my hand, on the wheel. My mother's genes run through it, but who else's?

'Susan? Are you OK?' Stakhovsky's brows are knotted in concern.

'Not really, no.' A wave of exhaustion billows through me. 'But I haven't been for a long time now. I think I'm getting used to it.'

Xtra-GeneY: the smart, affordable way to health!

Do you expect every shirt you pick off the rail to fit you and feel good?
Of course not. Nor do we. So why settle for a one-size-fits-all diet or gym routine?

We all know that what we put into our bodies and how we exercise has a major impact on our health. But every one of us is different. Generic dietary products and fitness regimes don't work, and could actually be doing you more harm than good.

That's why we designed the Xtra-GeneY app. It analyses your unique DNA profile to personalise diet, nutrition and exercise plans, enhancing your body's natural resilience to help ward off hereditary risks.

Xtra-GeneY studies your genes to find out how your body metabolises fat and carbs, what nutrients you need boosting, and what food intolerances or sensitivities you may have. Using the latest technology, our meal planner customises diet plans just for you, taking the guesswork out of nutrition, with recipes that are both nutritious and delicious.

Xtra-GeneY's personal work-out planner designs genetically optimised training routines to build the right intensity, plan perfect recovery times and avoid any sporting injuries that your body could be predisposed to. Whether your goal is to burn fat, build muscle or increase endurance, Xtra-GeneY will devise a precision work-out just for you.

Don't settle for less. Order your kit today and get fit and healthy the Xtra-GeneY way.

28

'Well, it could have been worse.'

So speaks the oracle.

'How, exactly, Carmel?'

I've spent the past twenty-four hours in a frenzy, researching everything that exists on Long QT syndrome. I'm convinced Steve's going to keel over any second.

'Steve could have Tay-Sachs or . . . lung disease.' Carmel flaps her hand. 'Something much more difficult to treat.'

I suppose it's true; if drugs don't work, Steve can always resort to one of those lab-grown hearts. But still . . . I haven't even told Carmel about my father yet. Or rather, the man who claimed to be my father. It would feel like a betrayal: not just of him, but Mum, too.

Sun streams through the skylight, catching gold flecks in the granite. A memory surfaces with the familiar sting: murky rock pools, a pink bucket and lime-green net. A stone glitters under a mop of kelp. Treasure! I fish it out and race back to Mum. As she turns it over in her slender fingers, its gold veins sparkle. She beams at me: yes, what a find.

My father eyes us over the edge of his paper. 'Treasure, you say . . . ?' She hands it to him. A smile quivers on his lips. 'I don't think so.' He looks at me and tosses it on the sand. 'Fool's gold.'

Carmel offers me a plate of ginger biscuits. 'Thank goodness you decided to go ahead. I mean, imagine if you hadn't found out?'

'I still can't tell Steve, though, can I?'

Carmel cocks her head. 'What about the twelve-week scan? They'll bring up genetic testing, for sure.'

It's not a bad idea. If a midwife tells Steve it's for the baby's sake, he's much more likely to say yes.

I stare at the photos of Leo. Try to picture Steve and I, with our daughter: big smiles and hugs, a family at last.

'There are so many changes, though, Carmel. The chances of this actually working, of me not losing her . . . I keep thinking about what happened to Helen Tomlins. She ended up with nothing.'

Carmel perches next to me. 'Honey, this is completely different. You already have your baby. You don't want her inheriting a heart condition, do you? Or snorting vodka for breakfast?'

I wince. 'It's easy for you to say; you only had one edit. And yours was tried and tested.'

She opens her mouth and closes it. Her tongue pushes into her cheek. 'Actually, that's not *strictly* true . . .'

'What?' Here we go again. I'm beginning to wonder if I know Carmel at all.

'Similar story, really. The test flagged up a couple more risk factors.'

And when exactly were you planning on telling me?

'So they made a few tweaks.'

'Jesus, Carmel. You make it sound like a haircut.'

Her eyes dart to mine. 'Look, Susan, it boils down to this: you can go old-school, cross your fingers and hope your baby turns out OK.' She pauses. 'Or you can find out the truth. And do something about it.'

I sigh. 'Come on, then. What did you have done?'

She picks at a thread on the cushion. 'Don't judge me, OK? One of them wasn't exactly terminal.' She hesitates. 'Male-pattern baldness.'

I swallow a laugh.

'I know. Poor Barry. We didn't really need a test to tell us *that* runs in the family.' She shakes her head. 'The other condition wasn't as straightforward. They found mutations in a group of genes they said were linked to certain mental-health disorders. Like schizophrenia. And depression.' She meets my gaze. 'Those came from me.'

'You're serious?'

She nods. 'I mean, obviously I knew it was a risk from my own profile.'

Carmel? Depression?

'I'm so sorry, Carmel. I never knew — '

'Oh, I've never suffered myself. Well, not that I'm aware of. But I certainly didn't want to take any risks with Leo.'

I hesitate. 'But isn't the jury still out on all that? I didn't think those conditions had been approved by the regulators. That's what's worrying me about this alcohol disorder.'

'Well, they've certainly been approved in the Czech Republic. As, I imagine, they have in Ukraine.'

I think of what Stakhovsky said about the addiction genes. I didn't challenge him enough at the time. How can we really know what is possible? What is safe?

'Dr Stakhovsky knows what he's doing, Susan. You've got a real heavyweight looking after you: state of the art systems and tech. Most mums would jump at the chance. We had to pay an arm and a leg for our extra treatments, and you're getting all yours for free.'

'I know, but he's said it all along: this is new

146

territory. There are risks . . . ' I squeeze my fingers. 'Right now, she's perfectly healthy. If I do miscarry, it won't be some random biological act. It'll be *my* fault.'

Carmel rests her elbows on her knees. 'If this is how you really feel, you need to speak to Steve.'

I groan. 'I've tried, so many times . . . But each time, he says something that stops me. That reinforces it, this certainty: he'd never forgive me; he'd leave me, too.'

Carmel takes my hands. 'You're not Katya, Susan. Your marriage, this situation . . . It's entirely different — '

'She lied to him. When that last round of IVF failed, she secretly started hunting for egg donors. He said that was the final straw. The realisation he couldn't trust her anymore.'

I think of my father. That slow resentment, seeping out like poison. I couldn't do that to my daughter.

'I just *hate* all these lies. The longer it goes on, the more desperate I am to tell him. And the more afraid I am that it'll just blurt out.' I sigh. 'I need to get to the point where I can stop worrying and we can start *enjoying* this pregnancy. Together.'

'Come here.' Carmel pulls me into a hug. 'It's like labour: once your baby arrives, all the pain will be a distant memory. Your hearts won't have space for anything else but her.'

She bends her head and gently presses her palm to my belly. 'Hello in there, little lady. This is your Auntie Carmel. Now, listen up.' She's using that special voice she normally reserves for Leo. 'Hang in there, OK? Because we're *so* excited to meet you. And I have a little boy with lots of toys who's itching to play.'

147

I cuff away a tear.

Carmel looks up. 'Two days, Susan, and we'll be on that plane. Think of it as a new beginning, for you and for Steve. A new life, as a family.'

I look into her eyes and wish with all my being she's right.

But instead of her onyx eyes, it's the other eyes I see: white and empty.

And Destiny neither makes nor keeps her promises.

29

Mokosh Clinic is a stern construction of metal and glass. She's there to welcome us, engraved into the thick glass door: cornucopia in arm, sheaves of corn at her feet. Mokosh: protector of women, goddess of fertility and destiny.

'Nice boobs,' says Carmel.

I press the intercom and try to marshal my emotions. I'm already exhausted.

'Good evening, Mrs Rawlins,' says a voice that sounds more Dutch than Ukrainian. The lock clicks.

An immaculately made-up lady with spiky red hair walks out from reception to greet us. 'Hi, I'm Danaya.' She stretches out her hand. 'Pleased to meet you. How was your flight?'

'Wonderful.'

I cried for most of it. It was just over three hours. I think Carmel was sick of me by the time we landed in Kyiv.

The worst part was saying goodbye to Steve.

'And is your accommodation satisfactory?'

'More than satisfactory,' interjects Carmel. 'Top notch.'

When Carmel saw her room, she squealed. Our adjoining suites have views of the Dnieper River; you can watch the little tourist boats chugging up and down. The opulent decor could give Kensington Gardens a run for their money. If circumstances had been different and I wasn't so strung out, I'd have squealed, too.

Danaya smiles and gestures towards the seats. 'Dr Stakhovsky will be with you shortly.'

Carmel gazes round the room and whistles. 'This takes me back.'

We stare at the pictures. Some are subtle in their manipulation, some not. A pair of baby shoes, cupped in a palm. A pregnant woman in a meadow, holding pink balloons. An enraptured couple gazing at their scan. Behind reception is a wall of words in different languages, in white raised letters:

Motherhood. Family. Happiness.

It doesn't matter where we live: Germany, America, Russia. We all want the same things.

'Susan!'

Stakhovsky appears in a white coat and black trousers, very much the doctor now. He greets me with open arms, as if we are long lost friends.

'How wonderful to see you.'

I even warrant a kiss on the cheek. Except it's not just one, it's three: left, right, left, which is entirely unexpected.

'And, of course, you too, Carmel.' He clasps her palm in both hands. 'You had a good journey, I trust?'

'Oh, yes.'

'And is the hotel to your liking?'

'Very much so. It's very generous of y —'

'What a location: right in the historical centre.' Carmel looks as if she might burst. 'And the suites . . .' She rolls her eyes. 'Exquisite.'

'Good, good.' He nods vigorously. 'Now, I just need to run through a few more forms with you, Susan. Shall we get the boring stuff out of the way? And then we can proceed with the health checks, make sure everything's looking good for tomorrow. Including

150

the moment you've been waiting for.' He smiles as my eyes shine. 'Your ultrasound scan.'

Today, I will meet my daughter for the first time. See her heart, maybe even hear it. The hope this instils, the sheer longing, is just about holding the dread in check.

Carmel waits for me in reception while I scribble my name across more consent forms, data privacy sheets and liability waivers. I scrutinised them all at the beginning, but recently I've become more laissez-faire. They're all variations of the same thing: I understand the risks, so if anything goes wrong, I have no one but myself to blame. The confidentiality clause applies both ways: I'm not allowed to discuss any aspect of this procedure without prior permission. They've even made Carmel sign a form, too.

Eventually, we're done. Stakhovsky leads me through a set of double doors and stops outside a room. The sign above the door makes my heart skip:

Operating Theatre

Like the other signs, it's in English and Ukrainian. Machines, screens and monitors encircle an operating table, poised like predators on a kill. Looming over a black mattress are two white discs with multiple lenses that resemble some enormous insect's eyes.

'I wanted to show you where we'll be tomorrow,' says Stakhovsky. 'So you can familiarise yourself.'

I swallow. The empty mattress reminds me of Mum's hospital bed on my final visit. Its resident gone for good.

My gaze veers to a curved white hood that looks like one of those hairdryers that salons used to stick ladies under. Next to it, waiting patiently, is the metal tray where they put the instruments.

151

He glances at me. 'There's nothing to worry about, Susan. I assure you.' He gives me a friendly nod. 'The procedure itself is relatively simple; the complex part is already done. You're in good hands.'

I find myself staring at them. In some religions, people used to kiss the hands of holy men in reverence and devotion. These days, our miracle-makers work in laboratories and hospitals. I imagine sinking to my knees, bending my lips to Stakhovsky's gloved fingers, as he bestows on me a benevolent smile.

'Hello, Mrs Rawlins. I'm Veronika.' I turn. A woman with cropped brown hair in a white, short-sleeved tunic is standing at the door. 'I take you for check-up.'

She's wearing tortoiseshell glasses; must be a fashion thing. Hardly any adults need glasses these days.

'Veronika is one of our obstetrician-gynaecologists,' says Stakhovsky. 'She specialises in prenatal diagnosis. One of our leading lights.' A faint blush colours Veronika's temples. I notice she doesn't quite meet his eyes. 'Shall I ask Carmel to join you, Susan?'

'Please.'

He turns to Veronika. 'Give me a buzz when you're ready.'

She nods. 'Please. Follow me.'

She leads me down a different corridor and into a room that looks a lot less clinical: a normal bed with sheets and pillows lies next to what I assume is the ultrasound machine. The grey walls are decorated with forests of white trees.

There's a knock at the door, and Carmel appears. She takes one look at the monitor and claps her hands. 'Ooh, when does the film start?'

The machine's keyboard looks like a laptop crossed with a games console.

Veronika addresses me: 'If you could please give urine sample.' Her English, though excellent, isn't quite up to Stakhovsky's. There are no articles in Ukrainian or Russian.

I ferret in my bag for the container. 'There we go.'

Stakhovsky thoughtfully sent a collection pot to the hotel as I need a full bladder for the scan.

Carmel grins when she clocks my sample. 'Jeez, it's not a competition, you know. They only need a few drops.'

Mine is full to the top. I exhale. 'I think it's an acquired skill.'

Veronika dips the testing strip in the pot, waits a few seconds and holds it against some kind of scanner.

'Protein and sugars good . . . ' Her lips purse. 'No sign of infection.' She drops the strip in the bin. 'Excellent. We take blood pressure now and check heart. Then bloods to see hormone levels.'

I submit only too willingly: these are my first antenatal checks. If Carmel were Steve, I could almost kid myself this was a routine appointment.

My chest tightens. I wish he could be here for the scan.

Veronika fills four tubes with my blood and sticks a plaster on my arm. 'OK. Now, good part.'

My eyes light up. 'The scan?'

She nods. 'You know is trans-vaginal? Better picture than abdominal. At this stage.'

'Yes, Dr Stakhovsky told me.'

'Good. You undress bottom half and put this on.' She passes me a white gown with egg-like pink spheres. 'Then get under sheet.'

I see Carmel suppress a giggle at the pronunciation

of 'sheet'. I glare at her. Veronika busies herself typing notes in the adjoining room while I pull off my skirt and pants. Carmel looks on, oblivious to my modesty. As I scurry under the sheet she smirks.

'Better get used to it, babe. All the prodding and probing. Strangers gazing up your wazoo.' She grins. 'By the time I gave birth, I couldn't have cared less if the entire rugby team was watching.'

Veronika comes back in, freshly gloved. 'Ready?'

I nod.

'We use transducer for ultrasound.' She holds up a white plastic stick that looks like an electric tooth-brush, without the brush. Veronika pulls some kind of sheath over the end and applies two squirts of gel. 'This is probe; may feel cold. Try not to tense.'

Telling me not to tense only makes me tense, so I distract myself with the huge screen on the wall. It really is like a cinema.

Now showing: Up Susan Rawlins' wazoo!

'Please, bring knees towards chest. Now let knees flop out.'

I oblige.

'Lie back and think of England,' adds Carmel, unable to resist.

Veronika adjusts my feet and rests her arm on my leg. 'Putting probe in now.'

I forget the discomfort as a whole new world appears on screen. A twilight world of black, greys and whites, continually shifting.

'Scanning uterus now . . .'

As I search for my baby amidst grainy shadows and shapes, I'm suddenly possessed by a fear that she isn't there. The more seconds that pass, the more convinced I am that there is no body for the sound waves to bounce off, no echoes flying back to the probe.

'One baby: no twins,' Veronika says, matter-of-factly.

Relief floods through me, although I can't see one baby, let alone two. I think of Stakhovsky's vanishing twin: the human chimera.

Veronika angles the probe and holds it still. She presses a button and enlarges the image. 'You see now? Small black circle?' A white cursor moves over what looks like a black hole. 'Gestational sac. Black is fluid. And there, inside?' I spot another, smaller circle. 'Yolk sac.' It's like Russian dolls. The cursor shifts slightly. 'And there . . .'

I suck in a breath.

' . . . you see? Little bean?'

She's there. My daughter is a seed. The image enlarges. And I see a hand. An actual hand that moves.

Carmel squeals. 'Oh, Susan . . .'

Veronika gives her first proper smile. 'Baby is waving. Say hi!'

Tears spill into my eyes as her hand reaches up to her face. Five tiny fingers, growing their own arches, loops and whorls.

'You see flutter, here?' Veronika points the mouse at a slight flickering. 'Baby's heart.'

I gasp.

Veronika clicks the keys. There's a rush of static. And then, distant but undeniable: a muffled beat. She adjusts the probe slightly, and the beat swells to a pounding whoosh, fast and regular, like someone flapping a wobble board. A sudden warmth floods my chest. It's a sound that's felt, not just heard. The sound of life.

Veronika presses another button and a row of spikes

runs along the bottom of the screen.

'Heart trace. One hundred forty-nine beats per minute.' She nods. 'Is good.'

I stare at my daughter's constantly shifting shape, as her heart gallops through the room. It's magic, really. That I can see and hear her. That she's there at all.

'Her foot just moved,' blurts Carmel. 'Did you see it, Susan? There. She's going to be a kicker.'

My baby's legs push up as though she's riding a bike, her bones shining through translucent skin. Stakhovsky told me that up until the third trimester, when pigmentation develops, all babies' skin colour is the same, no matter what their ethnicity. Genes then dictate how light or dark the skin will be. I think of Marty's olive complexion, his deep-chestnut eyes. If Stakhovsky's elixir succeeds, those gifts will be taken from her. Switched off. Silenced. Replaced.

Veronika points out my baby's spine. Her neck. Her brain. The machine beeps, and a line appears across her body, then another, making a cross. 'Take measurements now. You say ten weeks, yes?'

'I think so.'

Veronika juts out her bottom lip and tilts her head. 'Ten weeks. Yes. Plus maybe one or two days.'

More kite shapes appear while Carmel and I just gawp. A knock at the door makes us both jump. Veronika discreetly adjusts my bed sheet. 'Yes?'

Stakhovsky opens the door. His gaze is immediately drawn to the monitor and his mouth stretches into a grin. 'Well, well, well . . . Look at your baby girl.' His eyes flick over the scan. 'Moving well. Good strong heart. No risk of ectopic.' He glances at Veronika. 'Other indications good?'

'Yes. Everything is normal.'

'Just sweep the uterus for me again.'

Stakhovsky moves closer. I detect a pulse of fragrance: earthy and sweet, like sandalwood. As he studies the screen, I study his face, just to be sure.

'Excellent. Nothing there that shouldn't be.' He claps his hands. 'Well, that's great news, don't you think, ladies?'

I beam at him: 'It's the best news I've had for a very long time.'

Carmel wipes the mascara smudges under her eyes. 'Goddammit, Susan.' She sniffs. 'You've made me want to go through the whole damned pantomime again.'

My daughter is healthy. I have seen her move. I have heard her heart beat.

But then comes that sharp prick in my chest.

This might be the last time that I do.

30

I hadn't really taken it in, that she would be there, in front of me, while he did it.

My daughter seems more coy today — not as many wriggles, as if she senses the changes to come. I make out the profile of her nose, just visible amidst the monochrome greys, before her head tosses, and I lose it again. Carmel gives me a thumbs-up and smiles. I don't smile back.

Stakhovsky's almost unrecognisable in his blue theatre scrubs, complete with surgical cap and mask; all I can see are his eyes. His jovial calm has been replaced by intense focus, Veronika scurrying at his side. I wonder: does he have children? Why is it I've never asked? Does he really comprehend, beyond professional experience, the agony of loss?

'Right then, Susan. I think we're ready.'

My eyes swerve back to the screen. I feel a swell of nausea. She begins to fidget: a series of spasmodic jerks.

Stakhovsky swabs my belly with antiseptic; Veronika tears a needle out of its packet and connects it to a syringe.

'First, the anaesthetic. To numb the area.'

His voice seems unnecessarily loud, as if he's presenting to a group of students. I grip the bed, dazzled by the lights' multi-lensed glare.

Stakhovsky draws the vial's contents into the syringe.

There's a faint pricking sensation, like a tiny bee

sting, as he inserts the needle into my stomach. I check the screen. No reaction from her.

'We'll just give that a couple of minutes.'

Stakhovsky glances at the monitor and adjusts the probe. He nods at Veronika.

She fetches a cool box and presents it to him, lid open, and I have a ridiculous image of him pulling out a beer. Instead, very slowly, he lifts out a different vial.

My heart stills. That tiny bit of glass holds all Stakhovsky's promises.

He spikes a needle through the rubber cap and pushes the plunger down. He rotates the vial and draws a milky potion into the syringe.

I stare at it, transfixed. Are those few drops all it takes, to reassemble the building blocks of life?

There's a ripping noise, and I flinch. Veronika extracts an obscenely large needle from its wrapper. The tips of my fingers tingle. Carmel shifts in her seat.

Stakhovsky twists the needle spear onto the tip of the syringe. If he's nervous, he doesn't show it. His gaze turns to me: the white rat, primed to test his algorithms.

My toes twitch. It's barrelling up inside: the urge to flee. I imagine throwing off the sheet, yanking out the probe and rushing to the door, gown gaping, as they stare at me, open-mouthed.

Would Stakhovsky stop me, if I ran?

Would Carmel?

Veronika's glasses sparkle under the surgical lights.

I look at my baby, silhouetted on the screen. It's now or never.

'This may feel a little uncomfortable.' Stakhovsky's masked face looms above me, his eyes glued to the monitor.

It's as if he's cast a spell on me: I cannot move.

'I'm going to push on your tummy now. Sharp push coming.'

The needle slides into my belly. Veronika takes my hand.

'Remember: try and keep very still.'

The point of the needle appears on screen, gliding towards my placenta. Towards her.

'OK, I'm going into the uterus now.'

I cry out: the pain is intense, as if he's just stabbed me. And I remember what he said: the anaesthetic doesn't work on the uterus. Veronika squeezes my hand and leans closer, her hand-holding a cover for restraint.

'You're doing brilliantly, Susan,' Stakhovsky murmurs, as he guides the needle in further, just centimetres from my daughter.

Tears prick my eyes. *Forgive me . . .*

'I'm penetrating the placenta now.'

Sweat beads on my forehead. I'm pinned, like a specimen on a board.

'OK, we're nicely in position. I'm going to inject the agents.'

A wave of giddiness rolls through me; it's as if I'm plummeting down a tunnel of grey.

Veronika brushes my arm. 'OK, Susan? Remember: breathe.'

Stakhovsky plunges the syringe. My baby's head flops back, and her arms shoot up to her face, like a startle reflex.

'Is she alright?' I blurt. 'Did it hurt her?'

'Keep still, Susan.' Stakhovsky's thumb presses down further, his eyes riveted on the screen. 'She cannot feel a thing, I assure you.'

'Breathe, Susan,' says Veronika, more stern.

My daughter's hands stretch out, as if in supplication.

'Nearly done,' says Stakhovsky, like it's some routine flu jab. 'There.'

He carefully extracts the needle and drops it on a tray. I hear Carmel exhale.

'Now, the magic begins.'

Tears spill down my face. I have to gulp back a sob.

'You did really well, Susan.' He takes off his mask and smiles. 'And so did she. Look.'

I see a flash of movement. Spikes race along the bottom of the screen.

'Perfect beat: not too fast. Or slow.'

The breath I've been holding for hours escapes. She twists away from me, and one foot kicks out. I think of that baby picture with the wrinkled soles, the tiny toes pointing skyward.

Carmel creeps forward. 'Can I . . . ?'

Stakhovsky sweeps his arm. 'Please, of course.'

Carmel strides up to me and clasps my hand. 'Well done, you,' she says, in a hushed whisper.

I don't deserve congratulations. This is my daughter's fight now.

'You may feel a little sore,' says Stakhovsky, snapping off his gloves. 'Possibly a few cramps.'

I try to focus on what he's saying. 'Like period cramps, you mean?'

'Similar. Veronika can give you some pain relief. The key thing is to rest.'

'Don't worry, I'll make sure of that,' says Carmel, squeezing my hand.

'If you have any sudden pain in your abdomen, call

161

me immediately.' He glances at Carmel. 'Or if you feel unwell, in any way.' Carmel nods solemnly. 'But don't worry if there's spotting; that's perfectly normal.'

How can bleeding during pregnancy be 'normal'?

'Anything heavier, though, or any discharge, I need to know. But, as I've said many times before, I'm not expecting that.'

I take a breath. 'But, if she . . . If things *did* start happening, then . . . How soon would that be?'

He appraises me with those cool grey eyes. Was that a flicker of impatience?

'If you *were* to have complications, it would usually happen within three days. Sometimes, a little later.'

'How much later?'

'Up to two weeks.'

I inhale through my nose. 'And you're *sure* it's safe to fly tomorrow?'

'Absolutely. You're on the evening flight, aren't you?' I nod. 'Usually, we advise a gap of twenty-four hours. So you're well beyond that.'

I wish I could stay here for three days. Under observation. Hell, I wish I could stay for the whole two weeks.

He lays his hand on my arm. 'Remember, Susan, you can call me, any time. And when you get home, you'll have access to local care, 24/7.'

He's back to the calm, agreeable Stakhovsky.

'But for now, rest is what you need. Danaya will bring you some tea. Veronika will do a few checks in a little while. Assuming everything's normal, you'll be free to return to your hotel tonight, and we'll see you back here, first thing tomorrow.'

I wince as the first cramp kicks in.

I think of that woman in the meadow, holding her

bright balloons.

And I pray that Mokosh magic is good magic. The benevolent kind, that lasts.

31

I'm almost home when Stakhovsky's number flashes up on the console. My heart races, as if I've knocked back a fistful of amphetamines. Just as well the car drives itself.

I've spent the past seven days obsessively monitoring my body, interrogating every twinge or tweak. Each toilet trip engenders a paralysing dread. It's like the monthly agony I endured when we were trying to conceive — constantly checking the calendar, hoping against hope that no pink stains would come. Stakhovsky's been calling me daily, showering me with reassurances. They haven't dispelled my unease.

I pull up to the kerb. The phone rings another three times before I summon the courage to answer.

He's sitting at his desk, in that high-backed chair, like a king on his throne.

'Susan! How are you?' His voice oozes through the speaker. 'Are you able to talk?'

'Fine, yes. Fine.' I carve my nails into my palm and study those eyes. Is he excited? He doesn't look excited.

'I have the results.'

I swallow. He means the results of the CVS: chorionic villus sampling, which will show if the procedure's worked. I'd thought the one in Kyiv was painful, but this was worse. The needle was the same size, but it wasn't just the injection, it was the stabbing the doctor did after, scraping off shreds of my placenta to send to Stakhovsky. I don't know if I actually screamed or whether the scream was silent. My hand clenched the nurse's so tight she yelped.

He takes a breath.

'We conducted the paternity test. In all analysed PCR systems, your daughter shows the required genetic markers to be your husband's biological child.'

I stare at him, speechless.

'The probability level is 99.9%. Which means we did it, Susan. We really did it.'

I force a breath. 'And she's *safe*? No . . . anomalies?'

He grins. 'None. She's perfectly healthy. No inherited disorders. And now she's biologically Steve's, as well as yours.'

I slump forward over the wheel.

'There are some new mutations, but they're within the expected range. All the intended edits are present in the required threshold of cells.'

He starts burbling about benchmarks, about mosaicism and monitoring, but I'm no longer listening.

She's safe.

It's over.

Now, finally, I can tell Steve.

165

32

I step away from the fridge and survey my handiwork. Adrenaline bursts through my veins.

It's almost time. Best nip upstairs.

I've given this a lot of thought; I've had to. Our daughter is eleven weeks old. It's all been for nothing if my dates don't add up. I can explain one missed period — it's not unusual for new mums to get their dates wrong. But two? Surely a woman desperate to conceive for four years would recognise the signs? Even if she turned off her apps?

I'll say I thought I was pregnant back in May, but the test was negative. It happens, although it's rare. It's called the hook effect. If you have very high levels of pregnancy hormones in your urine, the antibodies that pregnancy tests use are overwhelmed, so the result gives a false negative. I'm counting on the midwife to back this up when the true date comes out at the scan.

The door bangs. I hear his satchel thump in the hallway, two thuds as he kicks off his shoes.

'Susan?'

There's a strange effervescence in my stomach, as if someone's just popped a bottle of champagne.

'Down in a minute!' I gulp a breath. 'I've made risotto. Just needs heating up.'

He heads towards the kitchen. I wait a few seconds and creep down the stairs. My hands are trembling. I crouch on the bottom step.

He opens the fridge. There's a clink of glass as he

grabs a soda. The door thumps shut.

I wait for the pause. The suck of breath. There's a delightful torture in this moment. I wonder if she feels it, too.

He ferrets in a drawer for the opener and slumps into a chair.

How can he not have seen it?

That's the problem with perfect plans. They're not cut out for an imperfect world.

I tiptoe up a few steps, so I sound like I'm still upstairs. 'Could you grab me a drink, Steve? There's some cordial, in the fridge.'

I slink back down, clutching the bannister.

Steve reaches out one hand to the fridge, and stops.

He frowns. Just a slight frown, not the kind that storms over his face and has me rushing for compromise. He glances into the hall, and I dart back, smothering a laugh with my hand.

I feel like a child again, playing murder in the dark — that same heady mix of thrill and fear.

I peer back round. He takes the post-it note off the fridge and stares at it. I can't read it from here, but I know what it says:

OV (bun) EN

A pink-and-blue arrow points towards the cooker.

He looks at the oven, and, for a second, I think he's actually going to open it. Instead, he turns: 'Susan?'

Just the one word.

My eyes squeeze shut. There's a tenderness in his voice I haven't heard for years.

I tread lightly down the hall. His gaze meets mine. 'Are you . . . ?' He licks his lip. 'Is this . . . real . . . ?'

I smile. Let his question flutter in my heart, the way I always dreamed it would, before it became the

167

question that shall not be named.

A grin breaks out across his face. 'Seriously?'

I beam at him and nod.

'I can't believe . . . It's actually . . . *We're* actually . . .' He shakes his head. 'Come here!'

He lifts me up and spins me round, hooting.

'This is amazing. *You're* amazing. When did you find out?'

'This morning, for sure.' My cheeks burn. 'Although, I've kind of suspected for a while.'

He tilts his head.

'Long story. I think I got a false negative. But, well, I wanted to be certain . . .'

The lie grizzles. I ignore it. I take Steve's hand and press it to my belly. 'Come and say hi . . .'

He splays his fingers and glides them over my stomach. A jubilant laugh erupts. 'I *knew* it. I just knew, if we kept trying, eventually, we'd do it.'

I slide my hand over his. 'Yeah, it's really happening. We made a baby.'

'Clever, clever Mummy.' He pulls my face to his and kisses me.

And, for the first time since I can remember, perhaps since Mum was alive, I am suffused with unadulterated joy.

33

My baby is the size of a small orange. She can smile and scowl. She responds to noises and pokes.

She can stretch, somersault and forward roll.

And she is old enough for me to tell others she exists.

I prod the pasta with my fork and try to identify the vegetables as the rumpus throbs in my ears. After a couple of mouthfuls, I give up and check the line. A rabble of year threes are slapping each other with their trays by the hatch. Towering above them, like Gulliver, is Marty, in chinos and a crisp green shirt. My gut clenches. He must have just cracked a joke because the lunch ladies erupt in high-pitched cackles, like tickled geese.

I catch his eye. The look on his face is priceless, as if he's just spotted a giraffe in the canteen.

He slides his tray onto my table and folds his long legs underneath. 'So, what happened? Local food shortage?'

I fish a pallid pasta tube out of its tinned tomato sea. 'Thought I'd treat myself. Just this once.' I pop the tube into my mouth and start chewing.

'Well, I hope your day is going better than mine.' Marty stabs a slab of chicken. 'My entire class was derailed by a prepubescent boy with a penchant for farting.'

I force the pasta down. 'Well, at least you'll get a break from them tomorrow.'

He swallows. 'Ah, yes. Staff development day.

169

Apparently, we're going to implement an 'emotionally literate ethos'.'

'Lord. Kill me now.'

He arches his eyebrows. 'Thought you were in favour of all that . . . '

'I am, but . . . Sometimes, I think we overcomplicate things.'

I push the pasta round my plate. 'Actually, I wanted to catch you, Marty. I have some news.'

He frowns. 'You're not leaving, are you?'

'No, no, nothing like that.' My cheeks flush. 'Well, not permanently, anyway . . . ' I swallow. 'I . . . well, we — Steve and I — are going to have a baby.'

He puts his fork down. 'Really? Congratulations.'

'Thanks. I mean, it's still early days and everything, so we're not shouting it from the rooftops . . . But, well, I wanted to let you know . . . '

He meets my gaze. 'I'm happy for you, Susan. Really.'

My eyes seek refuge in my plate. 'Thank you.'

'You and Steve must be over the moon.'

I squeeze my knife. 'Yes. We are. We'd been trying for some time.'

Marty's far too discreet to say anything, although he must have guessed as much. I was hardly subtle.

'So: when's the due date?'

My pulse steps up. 'Just before Christmas. Unless she's late, of course. Like her mother.'

A smile creeps onto his face. 'So, it's a girl, then? Or is that wishful thinking?'

Shit.

'Oh: yes,' I stammer. 'Although I'm not really supposed to say . . . Not yet, anyway.'

'Don't worry, I won't let anything slip.' He smiles

again. But it's not the same, easy smile from before.

He checks his watch. 'Well, I've got an observation this afternoon. Better make sure the tech's working.' He slides back his chair.

Marty's barely touched his food.

'Oh, right. Sure. Good luck.'

'Thanks.' He grabs his tray. 'See you later.'

I watch him stride across the hall, and something sinks inside.

I'm losing him.

The father my daughter already lost.

34

As soon as I pull up outside Carmel's, a grin breaks out on my face. In stark contrast to the neighbours' ghoulish remnants of Halloween, her prim Victorian porch is emblazoned with pale-pink balloons that look like the eggs of some exotic amphibian. The lavender tubs are dusted with pink and white petals; even the brass fox has a strawberry ribbon through its nose.

I heave myself out of the car and waddle up the path. The front door flings open, and Carmel scuttles out with a squeal, sporting a silk rose dress that looks expensive, and a gold fascinator on her head. Six more friends and colleagues follow, modelling the same fascinators, which I realise are miniature crowns.

Carmel curtsies. 'Welcome, fecund fairy queen!' She pins a much larger crown on my head.

'I think you mean phenomenally fat friend . . . '

Carmel wags her finger and shivers. 'No self-deprecation. Not at your baby shower. Now let's get you inside before we all freeze.'

She takes my coat and leads me down the hall to the kitchen. My hands fly to my mouth.

An entire wall has been draped with rose tulle, cinched at the top with gold ribbon. Pink cupcakes with glitter icing rival a tower of white macarons; sandwiches have been cut into stars. I count six glass jars of sweets, tied with pink ribbon. Crowning it all is a white palace cake, complete with pink frosted turrets and iced roses. It's straight out of those storybooks I

172

used to drool over — the kind of cake Mum used to bake for me.

'It's . . . beautiful. Thank you *so* much.'

A gold pennant says: *Welcome, Baby Princess*. Nine months ago I would have scorned such indulgence.

I attempt a sideways hug, trying not to topple Carmel with my belly. 'Oh, Lord: I'm blubbing already . . .'

At thirty-four weeks, Baby is packing a good two kilos. The skin has stretched taut over my bump, popping my belly button out. Terri, my friend from the Bumpy Roadsters, is even bigger. Her baby is due within days of mine.

'We've got a few games lined up,' says Carmel, eyes twinkling. 'But first: drinks and eats. We will serve you, as befits a queen . . .'

She leads me to the patio window. The sofa has been moved back; in its place stands a chair draped with gold organza. Enticing packages are stacked on the counter under a handwritten sign: *Gifts for the Fairy Princess*. Two photo screens have been positioned either side. One is an album of Steve and I on our wedding day. The other is childhood photos: mostly me with Mum.

'Those were Steve's idea,' Carmel nods, twisting the wire cage off a bottle. 'Impending fatherhood does wonders for a man. How's he getting on with those beta blockers, by the way?'

I hoist myself onto my throne. 'Much better, thanks.'

Steve was officially diagnosed with Long QT syndrome, following the results of his test. With the right drugs, he should be fine. I have the midwife at our scan to thank for that.

Carmel pops the cork, sending my palm rushing to my belly. I wait for the startled prod. Nothing. Unlike

173

me, my daughter now spends most of her time sleeping.

Carmel distributes the frothing flutes. 'To Susan. May her labour be short, and her sleep be long.'

'Good luck with that,' says Nicola, another Bumpy Roadster. Her labour lasted fifteen hours. She takes a gulp and raises her glass. 'Here's to hanging in there. And small miracles. God bless 'em all.'

Everyone heads to the table and starts filling their plates. There's a comforting hum as the wine loosens tongues.

After a while, Carmel claps her hands. 'Right, ladies: time for our first game. The Due Date Sweepstake . . . Kessie will explain.'

The bubbly keeps flowing. As the games continue, the mood becomes more raucous. Nicola springs a leak and doesn't even notice. When Terri points out the two dark circles of milk on her top, Nicola squeals and dashes off to the bathroom to 'pump and dump', and everyone cheers.

'So, Susan, do you know the actual moment when you conceived?' slurs Aaliyah. 'Was it *terribly* romantic?'

My smile freezes. 'I . . . Not exactly . . . It wasn't — '

'Honey, things aren't how they're cracked up to be in the films,' says Carmel, swooping to my rescue. 'These days, it's romantic if we're even *present* at conception.'

Nicola and Terri roar with laughter. Both of the teaching assistants' young faces are blank.

Nicola leans over. 'She means if it happens *naturally*, like Susan's. After sex. As opposed to it all cracking off in a petri-dish . . . '

Aaliyah's eyes widen. 'Oh . . . right.'

174

As if in response, I feel a poke in my belly. My breasts respond with a sharp tingle. I rub my tummy in slow circles, until . . . There. Jutting against my palm. One tiny, upside-down heel.

'Is she kicking?' asks Carmel, leaping up.

'Sure is.' I grimace. 'Must be the sugar.'

They all flock to my belly and lay their hands on me, like tipsy apostles. I cannot help but smile.

'Right, before we get too sloshed, I've something you all need to do,' says Carmel, gripping the neck of another bottle. 'On that table is a book of wishes for Susan's baby girl.' She nods at a white, cloth-covered album. 'Think of something special and grab a pen.'

A book of wishes: what a fabulous idea. Although they didn't do Sleeping Beauty much good.

My thoughts slide to the bad fairy.

In the fifteenth year of her age the Princess shall prick herself with a spindle and shall . . .

What?

Discover that her father is not her real father?

That she was genetically altered, in the womb?

I clamp my palm to my belly.

This is my wish: that she never finds out what I did to her.

Like my mother before me, I intend to take that secret to my grave.

Part Two: The Consequence

'In nature there are neither rewards nor punishments; there are consequences.'

— Robert G. Ingersoll

I didn't ask for it. Any of it. None of us did.

Hair as fine as spun gold.

Deep ocean eyes.

Skin, white as snow.

I just wanted to be normal, whatever that means.

Like everybody else.

But they did what they thought was best, like parents do. To give us an edge over the others.

So they changed our bodies, and they adjusted our minds.

We never had a choice.

But they did.

'They hacked my fatherhood!' Sex Island star Kwento Jelani speaks to *OK Magazine* in celebrity exclusive

Kwento reveals the private agony behind the celebrity sperm scandal that has rocked the world.

By Alyssia Moran

'When they told me what had happened, I literally couldn't believe it. I mean, it's mad, right? Like a body snatcher coming into your home and then farming you out, like some prize stud, over the Internet.'

Kwento's understandably still fuming. He had no idea anything was wrong until a friend sent him a link on social media: a picture of a cute baby boy, with the caption, 'My mini-Kwento'.

The 'parent', who can't be named for legal reasons, claimed the baby was biologically Kwento's and that she'd purchased 'Kwento sperm' to get pregnant. But Kwento has never been a sperm donor.

Kwento went straight to the police. What the National Crime Agency's cybercrime unit unearthed next rocked the world.

Their investigation revealed that Kwento's hairdresser had been storing samples of Kwento's hair and secretly selling them on to a fertility clinic.

The clinic, believed to be a front for an organised-crime gang, used these samples to manufacture sperm cells using a pioneering new fertility treatment called in vitro gametogenesis (IVG). The DNA extracted from Kwento's hair follicles was reprogrammed to produce stem cells, which in turn, were turned into sperm. Samples of Kwento's sperm were then sold on the black market for thousands of dollars.

It's still not clear how many Kwento babies have actually been born, but investigations have uncovered more illicit celebrity donor sites, trading not just sperm, but eggs too.

So how does Kwento feel about these babies?

'I mean, it's not the babies' fault, what happened. But what kind of parent are you, if you're happy to steal part of another human being to have their child? The point is, I never gave consent. But, biologically, those kids are still mine.'

181

35
Zurel

Grammar is important.

We are told this, in English, but the others mostly fidget and yawn, counting the minutes until the bell.

Words can be slippery, like fish. Especially when grown-ups use them. But grammar has to follow rules.

Nouns are people, places or things.

Exclamation marks show emotion or surprise.

The subjunctive suggests something isn't true.

Grammar does what it says. That's why I like it.

It doesn't pretend to be something it's not.

★ ★ ★

'Right, you should have finished your simulations, so screens down, please.'

Mrs Crowther plants her hands on her hips. Her shirt tugs at its buttons like a trapped sail.

'Who can tell me the difference between the active and passive voice?'

Everyone looks down, even Lara. I focus on the shapes Mrs Crowther's mouth is making.

She turns to the e-board:

Danny kicked the ball.

Her e-pen hovers, like a wand. 'How could we change this sentence into the passive voice?'

Passive voice: my speciality. My eyes drop to my desk, in case she's thinking the same thing.

I catch Amy mouthing at Jodi, our class bot, who's perched by the window. Jodi will pick up a whisper, even on standby. But Mrs Crowther's too savvy for that. She only uses Jodi for small group work; the rest of the time she's offline. I'm pretty sure if it was up to Mrs Crowther, she wouldn't use Jodi at all.

Mrs Crowther's tongue presses against her teeth and makes a tutting sound. My throat locks; the answer's there, on my tongue. Already throttled.

'I wonder who might be able to help us with this one?'

My head sinks lower. She hasn't said my name, but it's her high, cheery voice, just for me. Most people have one. I think of Lola with a twist of envy, snuggled up in her bed at home.

Whispers trade behind hands. Gary Baker yawns like a walrus and coughs: 'Squirrel!'

That's his nickname for me; it nearly rhymes. That's what you get for having a stupid name.

I smear my palms over my skirt and start to write. The e-pen loops over the screen, the letters bumping up against each other. I show Mrs Crowther my answer and fix my eyes on her tense, yellow buttons.

— The ball was kicked by Danny.

'The ball was kicked by Danny.' She beams at me. 'Great job, Zurel!'

The heat coils in my belly. You'd think I'd just discovered a new gene.

The bell rips into the room. William and Gary shovel their screens into their bags; an e-pen skids across the floor.

Mrs Crowther raises her eyebrows. 'In a hurry, gentlemen?'

She strolls towards their table, her heels clicking

with a casual menace. "William packed away his screen.' How would you say that in the passive voice, Gary?'

Gary Baker's revolting bottom slides down further. He's had detention twice for farting, although Mrs Crowther never uses that word. She prefers 'trouser cough', which I think's worse.

Gary glances at William, but William is staring at a bear-shaped stain on his sleeve. Gary's face is cherry red. If he were an octopus he'd be furious.

Gary opens his mouth and closes it as Mrs Crowther's shiny pink nails circle his desk.

'The screen . . . ' His eyes dart to hers and instantly rush back. He swallows.

There's a whisper from the back: 'Get on with it.' Even form loyalties crack under the strain of missing break.

Gary starts to rock a little. 'The screen . . . got packed away —'

'*Got?*' Mrs Crowther barks. I actually see him flinch.

'*Was.*' He clenches his fists. 'Was packed away.'

Mrs Crowther eyes him carefully. 'And who did the packing?'

Gary glares at his table mate. William's shoulders hunch a little tighter. 'William.'

'That's correct. Thank you, Gary.' She opens her arms like the vicar does at the end of assembly, and smiles. 'You may go.'

Bio-plastic feet shriek against tiles. I reach the door, but Mrs Crowther's voice flies to catch me:

'Zurel? Could you stay behind, please? It won't take long.'

My heart sinks. I hang back, let the rest file past, avoiding their gaze. My nose wrinkles: damp hair and

184

sweat.

'Take a seat, Zurel.' She crosses her legs. 'I just wanted to have a little . . . To check in with you.'

I focus on her hands, which seem older than the rest of her. She has two rings on her fourth finger: a plain silver band, and one with a circle of blue stones. I imagine a younger Mrs Crowther at the altar, her brand-new husband slipping on those rings.

She takes a breath. 'How are your meetings going, with Mr Thomson?'

Mr Thomson is the special needs teacher. I don't mean he's got special needs. Well, not that I'm aware of. Although he does nod a lot. It's his job to deal with the hypers and the ones who throw things, or fidget. Or can't talk, like me.

— Fine.

'That's good.' She's trying very hard not to look at me directly. 'Is Mr Thomson helping you . . . work through things?'

I nod, because I like Mr Thomson, and I think that's what she wants to hear.

Mr Thomson doesn't nag or rush me. He doesn't play tricks, or pretend he knows what's wrong.

'Excellent.' Mrs Crowther flashes an uncertain smile. Sometimes, I get the feeling she thinks this is her fault.

'And you had a good session with the speech therapist? I've heard she's very nice.'

I keep my eyes on the screen.

— Yes. She is.

'I know things must seem hard at the moment, Zurel. But they will get easier.'

She blinks. Twice. People blink a lot, I've noticed, when they're waiting for you to speak.

'It can be an anxious time, your last year at primary. Moving up to secondary.'

My cheek twitches. *Not that again.*

'Those feelings are entirely normal.' She catches my gaze, then remembers she shouldn't. 'Still, it can help to . . . get your worries out into the open.' She takes another breath. 'You understand what I'm saying?'

I twist my fingers into my skirt and nod.

'If you ever want to t — '

She stops herself before she says it: the dreaded t-word.

'. . . *share* anything. I'm always here. You know that, don't you?'

— Yes. Thank you.

'Good.' She slaps her knees and sighs. I think she finds this as hard as I do. 'Very good. Right then. Off you go.'

I grab my coat and scurry out the door, weaving through the other kids who are bombing around the playground, their breath panting out in white curls. I head towards the lower block, behind the canteen. I sneak out my phone and open the GoggleWoof app. Camera two.

Lola's lying on her back, in her favourite sleep position: a furry bundle of black, copper and cream. Her hind legs are splayed, exposing her pale belly, her front paws lolling mid-air.

I activate my ear imps, and the screams and shouts are replaced by the gentle sigh of her breathing.

One eye half opens: a slit of amber, as if she's winking at me.

I lean back against the wall and smile.

36
Susan

'Good day, love?

Zurel stares at the windscreen. I hear the distant thump of drums. Those blooming implants; you can't even tell they're wearing them, unless the light catches them. I wish we could go back to clunky headsets or earbuds. At least you knew when someone had zoned out.

I reach across and squeeze her hand. She startles. I point at my ear. She frowns, and the music stops.

'Good day?'

She nods.

'Anything exciting happen?'

She shakes her head. Her eyes veer back to the road.

'I've made pancakes for tea. Your favourite,' I add, as if she needs reminding.

Her lips approach a smile. She writes:

— Thanks.

Polite but aloof. As if we're not really family — she's just lodging with us. I'd rather she swore.

I have a sudden urge to tell her how much I love her, how remarkable she is. I used to say these things. When she was a baby, I'd sit by her cot for hours, watching the dreams dance behind her eyes.

The car accelerates onto the dual carriageway. Spiky hedgerows of hawthorn and bramble blur past.

Zurel's eyes narrow.

— Where are we going?

187

I ponder how best to break it to her. She never used to mind the lab visits, but lately she's become more difficult about them, refusing to go.

'A very important scientist happens to be over for a conference. You may remember him. His name is Professor Stakhovsky.'

Her mouth twists.

— Not the creepy Russian guy?

'Ukrainian.' I bite my tongue. 'Zurel, he's a very clever man who's — '

She swipes off her screen and glares straight ahead.

I swallow: ' . . . who's taken an interest in you. He may be able to help with your . . . '

She turns, daring me to say it. I don't.

'He won't do any tests today, if that's what's concerning you.'

Her head swivels back round. Drums thump into the car.

Don't cry. Do not cry.

I study her silent profile with a wrench of love. Deep-auburn hair scraped into a ponytail, a dusting of freckles, thick lashes curtaining her eyes. The hollows underneath are new. The little, prawn-shaped girl that used to clamour for cuddles has vanished. She's growing up. And we're growing apart.

The car brakes and turns onto the bypass. Stakhovsky will know what to do; he has to. He's a man with a reputation to uphold. Since Zurel was born, he's been nominated for awards, elected to countless boards, and now he's heading up his own fertility chain. I told Steve I'd signed us up to a research project studying the home's impact on changes in children's genes; Stakhovsky's brainwave, of course. Nothing too intrusive, medically speaking: a few

188

rudimentary health checks and interviews. Stakhovsky gets his research data, and I get peace of mind. At least, I used to.

Eventually, we reach the entrance to the science park. Zurel scowls at the sign:

Zendter Biolabs

Above the silver letters is an outline of two adults and a baby, joined together in the shape of a heart. We park up and walk along the path to the glass doors.

Zendter Biolabs are trying hard to look natural. Mycelium bricks support panels of microalgae quietly generating energy for the labs. A vertical garden extends through the middle of each floor; more plants clamber over the balconies. It reminds me of a Mayan temple I once visited, whose ruins had been reclaimed by jungle. A pregnant woman guards the entrance, bronze arms raised above her head, her swollen belly decorated with leaves. Opposite her stands a vast double helix: nanofibre spirals cross-sectioned with bars.

We scan ourselves in and head to reception. I sit on a beech futon with plenty of room, but Zurel chooses a seat next to a mossy wall. I clasp my hands on my knees and wait.

I spot him trotting down the stairs, lithe as ever. Stakhovsky doesn't seem to age. A tinge of grey around his hairline only makes him more distinguished, accentuating that sparkle in his eyes.

'Susan! You look well.' He pumps my hand. 'And, as for you, young lady . . . ' His eyes skim over Zurel. 'You're growing up fast.'

Zurel bites her lip and looks past him, no attempt at a smile.

He leads us into one of the treatment rooms and shuts the door.

'I'm not doing any medical checks today, Zurel; just a few questions. Some with the three of us together, and some separately, with your mum, if that's OK?'

Zurel picks at the skin on her fingers.

'Zurel?' I give her an encouraging smile. She tilts her chin in a nod, and I glimpse that thin, pale scar.

There's a knock and the door opens. 'Ah, perfect timing. Here's Magda with your snack.'

A black-haired assistant bot with stunning green eyes deposits a tray on the table. Zurel's gaze sweeps over her; machines aren't as intimidating as people, and she won't have seen this model before.

'Thank you, Magda,' says Stakhovsky. 'Perhaps you'd like to stay a while, keep Zurel entertained?'

Magda lavishes Zurel with a smile. Magda looks, to all intents and purposes, human. Embedded under that smooth, latex skin are sensors to make her touch-responsive; she reacts to facial expressions as well as words, and even simulates breathing.

Stakhovsky turns to me. 'Shall we go through?'

I squeeze Zurel's arm: 'We're just next door.' I notice a gleam of sweat on her forehead.

He takes a seat behind the desk. 'So: how's she doing?'

I inhale. 'Well, the screen's working well, so I suppose that's something.' I look at my hands. 'She's still hiding herself away most of the time.'

'Hmm.' He rests his elbows on the table. 'She's at that difficult in-between stage: almost a teenager, but not quite . . . What does the speech therapist say?'

' 'It's still early days, we can't rush it.' 'Every child is different.'' I drag my hand through my hair. 'Zurel's what they call a stage three. She'll respond to questions through non-vocal means, like gestures or writing. But she makes no audible sounds.' My foot is jiggling. I make it stop. 'Not even a laugh.'

'How's she coping at school?'

'Her form teacher's very supportive. And she's seeing the special educational needs lead each lunchtime. He's working on a 'small steps plan'.' I swallow. 'From what I can make out, though, she's lost most of her friends. I don't think they're being mean or anything; it isn't as if they haven't tried.' My eyes meet his. 'She *wants* to be alone.'

'What about her language processing? How are her literacy scores?'

'Oh, she devours books. Strong on reading comprehension and spelling; her teacher says her writing is especially good. No surprise, really; her profile flagged strong literacy skills.'

I think of that story Mrs Crowther showed me, about a world ruled entirely by children. The details were painfully vivid. Right down to the macabre punishments inflicted for breaking the law.

'So, have they given you any indication as to what they think's going on?'

'They've tested her for autism and ADHD. I mean, we already knew that wasn't it. So now they're exploring other areas.' I sigh. 'They've mentioned a clinical psychologist. Apparently, a child usually has one trusted person they'll communicate with; normally a parent. But it could be someone at school.'

'Perhaps the dog is her trusted companion. Wasn't that what your school lead suggested? Haven't there been animal-assisted cases before?'

'Hmm.' I clench my fingers. I don't want Lola to be her trusted companion, I want it to be me. 'The speech therapist kept asking about our family

191

history . . . Whether there'd been any traumatic incidents that may have triggered a . . . response.' I shift in my seat. 'She asked if anyone in the family suffered from anxiety.' I bark a laugh that takes me by surprise. 'As if the school hadn't already figured that one out . . . I think that's where they're going with it . . . There's no *physical* problem, as such. It's some kind of . . . anxiety disorder.'

Stakhovsky gives a slow nod. I hope he's building to something. Because I have a few questions of my own.

'I consulted a colleague who works in this area, Susan. He told me that social anxiety is a key factor. As you know, anxiety can be genetic, but not in Zurel's case; it never showed up on any of our screening. There are, however, environmental triggers.'

He doesn't say it but I know what he's thinking: I don't carry any risk factors for anxiety either, and look at me.

I run my tongue over my lips. 'I read that a foetus can experience trauma in the womb. That the mother's emotions can be transmitted to her baby . . . And that can affect how the child responds to events after they are born.' My eyes catch his. 'Do you think this could be some kind of delayed reaction? I mean, I was under so much stress in those early weeks of pregnancy. That could have had an impact, couldn't it? All that cortisol rushing round my body, into hers . . .'

He reaches out a hand. 'You must stop blaming yourself, Susan. You went through so much to have this baby. And you gave birth to a fine, healthy daughter.' He smiles. 'You're a wonderful, caring mother, but even the best parent in the world can't protect their child from everything. There could be triggers you don't know about . . . Friends, or school —'

'What about the interventions?' It blurts out: I can no longer contain it.

He hesitates. 'You're still worried that Zurel's condition may have some . . . *genetic* basis?'

It feels dangerous, saying it. 'Well, to be honest, yes.' I force myself to meet his stare. 'This wasn't what I . . . expected.'

His eyes slide over me. 'I *totally* understand your concerns . . . But only a fraction of speech and voice disorders have genetic causes, and none of the tests to date have flagged any of those markers in Zurel.'

'Yes, I realise that, but . . . ' I feel my cheeks colouring. 'Could this be happening as an indirect result of the edits? Some kind of . . . change that might have presented symptoms later . . . ? A — what do you call it — 'off-target effect'?'

His mask cracks, just for a second. He clears his throat. 'I would say that's highly unlikely. If there had been any neurological damage, any biochemical imbalances, we would have picked them up by now.'

My heart plummets. He has no answer waiting for me, no miracle cure. Which means it's down to nurture, not nature. My failure, as a mother, right from the off.

Tears threaten, and the old Stakhovsky, the professional empathiser, steps in.

'Susan, listen to me. We may not know what's caused this, but the important thing to remember is, it's not permanent.' He leans forward. 'There's nothing *physically* wrong with Zurel. Things will improve.'

That's what everyone keeps telling me: I pray they're right.

Because, if not, after everything I've been through,

everything I've done . . .

I glance through the glass panel at my daughter. She's bestowing a smile I would die for on a robot.

I'm not sure I can live with it.

37

Zurel

I like the Peace Pod. It's basically a shed with lots of glass, but they've made it cosy, with its yellow walls and perky blue-and-green chairs. It's away from the main buildings, on the edge of the playing fields, by the house that belongs to the grumpy lady next door. It reminds me a bit of those glass boxes they put snakes and stick insects in . . . What are they called? Vivariums, that's it. You can slide around by yourself unnoticed, while everyone outside gets on with their day.

Another sparrow hops onto the feeder; I've counted eight so far. Mum says that sparrows are social birds, with quite complicated families, although it's the females who call the shots. Probably why she feeds them.

I'm waiting for Mr Thomson. Every lunch break, after I've eaten, I meet him here. The first time, I was sick with worry; I'd only ever seen him at assembly or striding around school. But it turns out the deputy head isn't as scary as I'd thought. Sometimes, he brings in old board games. I'm sure it's some kind of test, but it beats stomping around the playground on my own.

Mr Thomson's smart, too. In our last session, he asked me to draw a picture: my favourite place to relax. I thought it was a bit babyish, but I did it anyway. He said he had some marking to do, so while he scrolled down his screen, I sketched my bedroom. I drew every detail: the blinds on the windows, the pattern on the rug. Even the photo screen on my desk. And, of course, sprawled on the floor: Lola.

He looked at that picture for a long time. I mean, it wasn't *that* interesting. So, of course, he spotted it. He didn't say one word; he just wrote:

What's that, under the bed?

I'd only drawn a thin grey line: you could barely see it.

I twirled my e-pen.

— My phone.

He nodded. I could see his thoughts turning, under all that hair.

Why's it under your bed?

I was going to write 'because I like chilling on the rug with Lola', which is true. But the words just popped into my head:

— Because it keeps secrets.

He didn't write anything else. Just smiled.

Here he comes now, loping along the path. My eyes fall to my screen.

'Hi, Zurel. Sorry I'm late.' He swings through the door with a blast of cold air.

He's always rushing from some meeting or other. That's why he told me the key-safe code, even though he's not supposed to, so I can let myself in. I love that little box, it's like going back in time. This must be the only building I know that still uses an actual key.

'Now, where shall I sit today? Over here?'

He chooses a chair on the opposite side of the table. That's another thing I like about him. He doesn't get in my space.

'How's your day going?' He curls his fingers into his

196

palm and holds up his thumbs. Then flips them over. I angle mine in a straight line, towards each other, like the poles of two magnets. 'Ah, it's like that, is it? Well, let's see what we can do.'

He pulls a battered blue box out of his satchel, with yellow and red words on the front.

'I thought we'd try a different game, today. If you're up for it.' He smiles. 'It's called Yes, No.'

A faint memory stirs. I think I played this with Dad, years back. I think I was pretty good.

He pulls a stack of cards out of the box and a round silver bell. It looks like something from an old film, the kind they used to have on hotel receptions.

He shuffles the cards. 'I don't know if you've ever played this, but it's fairly easy to pick up.'

I keep my eyes on my screen.

'Basically, you have to answer questions, but you can't say yes or no. Sounds easy, but there are some tricky ones, I'm warning you.'

Good. I like a challenge.

'If one of us does say yes or no, the other person gets to ring the bell and take their card.' He smacks the little black stopper, which makes a cheery *ding*, and suddenly I'm desperate to ring it, too.

My eyes flick to his.

'Go on, then.' He smiles.

I give it a tap. *Ding!* And another. *Ding!*

'So, the person with the most cards wins. Sound OK?'

I give him a thumbs-up.

'Great. So, shall I start, or you?'

I point at him. He picks up a card.

'OK . . . what month is your birthday?'

— December.

197

'Did you say December?'

I nod.

'You have to write your answer . . . '

— I did.

'Does December have thirty days?'

I hesitate.

— It doesn't.

'Does January have thirty days?'

— It doesn't.

'What month has thirty days?'

— September.

Did you say September?

— Ye —

His hand jumps to the bell, but he doesn't ring it.
My pulse races as I delete the letters.

— I did.

He chuckles. 'Nearly . . . '

Actually, this is fun.

He picks up another card. 'Ready?'

I nod.

'Do you like cats?'

— I do not.

'Do you like dogs?'

I grin.

— I love dogs.

'I know you do. How's Lola, by the way?'

— Great!

'Is she naughty?'

I catch myself. That was sneaky.

— She can be.

'Is she as naughty as Gary Baker?'

I smother my smile with my hand.

— You're not asking proper questions.

'Hmm, maybe. OK, last chance. Here goes.' He

turns over another card. 'Do you like school?'

I check his face. He's looking at the screen, not at me.

— Sometimes.

'Do you like homework?'

— Not really.

'Do you like home?'

I hesitate. Such a simple question. I glance at the birds on the feeder.

My fingers race to catch up.

— I like my bedroom.

I swallow.

— Is it my turn now?

'Yes, you're up.'

I slam the bell, and hold out my hand for his card.

He raises an eyebrow and pushes the stack towards me. 'I can see I'm going to have to up my game.'

His eyes narrow. 'Zurel, are you *sure* you haven't played this before?'

China Denies Secret IQ Enhancement Program

Czech source claims China's much-lauded Disease Immunity Program has a covert objective: to make the next generation of Chinese babies smarter.

By Ivan Tagorsky, Health Editor,
News International

China's ambitious Disease Immunity Program, launched three years ago, offers prospective parents the opportunity to protect their embryos from life-threatening diseases using genetic screening and editing during IVF. These include types of dementia, blood disorders, heart disease, diabetes and cancer.

Unsurprisingly, with costs subsidised by the Chinese state, a large percentage of parents have signed up. Last year, twenty percent of births were opted in: that equates to nearly four million babies. But a respected Czech expert is claiming the program's goals extend far beyond disease immunity.

'My research investigates treatments for certain kinds of dementia,' said Eva Smirnova, a professor of neurology at the First Faculty of Medicine at Charles University, in Prague. 'There's been strong interest from the Chinese in our work. Five years ago, we made an interesting discovery. We found that the alteration or removal of certain genes associated with dementia can improve memory formation and cognitive function in healthy people, too. We did not pursue this line of research as it was contrary to agreed protocols.'

So when Smirnova bumped into a fellow researcher who used to work at Tsinghua University in Beijing, she couldn't believe what she heard. The scientist told her that China's Disease Immunity Program incorporated genetic edits linked to her research, with the explicit goal of boosting memory and learning from early childhood.

If Smirnova's claims are correct, China has contravened international protocols agreed under the United Nations Framework Convention on Governance of the Genome (UNFCGG) which prohibit human genetic enhancements. However, the treaty is not legally binding.

The Chinese Health Ministry has denied these reports, calling them a 'miscellany of lies' and another example of 'Czech fake news'.

38
Susan

'The usual?'

'The usual.'

Carmel grabs a bottle of Cabernet Sauvignon from her extensive wine rack. I've been drinking more red since they edited the yeast to ramp up some compound that's anti-cancer and anti-inflammatory. It's supposed to eliminate hangovers, too. It's finally been proven: drinking wine is good for you.

'Come on, then. Judging from your face, I assume this isn't a celebration.'

I sprawl onto the sofa. 'No. It isn't.'

Rain slides down the patio doors. 'I got my hopes up, like a fool. Stakhovsky doesn't have any more of a clue than the rest of them. And he's certainly not taking any responsibility.'

Carmel sticks her head round a cupboard. 'You're not serious?'

'Deadly.'

She twists out the cork. 'But . . . Didn't he have *anything* to say?'

'Nurture, not nature, allegedly. He says I'm overthinking it, that it's just a phase and things will improve with time. Meanwhile, Zurel's getting more aloof by the minute.' I sigh. 'She's only eleven, for goodness sake: this shouldn't be happening for another two years.'

Carmel slugs some wine into a glass. 'Well, what

did you expect, calling her after a visionary tulip . . . ?'
She hands me the glass and smiles. 'I believe 'independent and determined' were two of the flower's traits . . . '

I take a large gulp. I'm suddenly desperate to change the subject. 'How are things with Leo?'

'Oh, you know . . . TBS: teenage boy syndrome.'

She gives a theatrical wave, but there's something in her tone that catches.

She slumps down next to me. 'Moody, monosyllabic and mostly in another world.'

That used to be a metaphor; now it's reality. Gaming implants mean all they need is Wi-Fi and they can play anytime, anywhere . . . The brain is the new console.

I eye her over the rim of my glass. She takes a swig. And another.

'Hey, are you OK?'

'Yeah, it's nothing . . . I'm probably just being paranoid.'

'I think you'll find that's my department.' I nudge her. 'Go on . . . '

She twists the stem between her fingers. 'I think there could be more to it than TBS. Leo's changed, over the past year.'

'Changed, how?'

She frowns. 'He's so . . . lacklustre, all the time. He's not eating properly. I don't think he's sleeping properly either. It's like he's cutting himself off. Not just from us: everyone, even his friends.' She sighs. 'If I didn't know better, I'd say he was . . . ' Her voice trails off.

'What?'

She grinds a tooth over her lip. 'Depressed.'

I don't react, not immediately. That was one of the 'corrections' Carmel had done.

I watch a granite cloud scud past.

'Have you spoken to anybody about it?'

'I mean, Barry, obviously. But he isn't good with this kind of thing.'

'What about Leo's school? Have they noticed anything?'

'His form tutor called me. They suggested he spoke to the school counsellor. Well, I tried to have a conversation with Leo about it, but he point blank refuses. Says there isn't a problem and I should 'butt out'.' She exhales. 'He'll be taking his exams next year. We need to get this sorted.'

I swallow. 'Can't you schedule an e-pointment with his doctor? Get some professional help?'

She shakes her head. 'Not a chance. Not while he's like this.' Her jaw tightens. 'I keep thinking about the clinic. Asking them to run another test. Maybe whatever they were supposed to disable, has somehow . . . reactivated.' She glances at me. 'Or maybe they switched off the wrong genes in the first place . . . '

'I'm sure there'll be an explanation. I mean, this kind of thing, it's not unusual, is it, in adolescence? Lots of teenagers struggle. Their brains are remodelling themselves; they're a hotbed of impulse and emotion.'

I've been reading up after my conversation with Stakhovsky. Stats can be reassuring.

'And then there are the social pressures . . . Hormonal changes . . . ' I exhale. 'Some of them just can't cope.'

Carmel's mouth twists. 'I know, but I didn't think . . . I mean, the whole point of paying vast

204

sums of money was to *protect* Leo. To give us some guarantees . . .'

My chest tightens. I think of Zurel. The changes Leo had are nothing compared to what she went through.

'There's something else.' Carmel sets her empty glass on the table. 'Have you heard what's happening in China?' I shake my head. 'They're trying to hush it all up as usual, but I've a friend out there.' She takes a breath. 'Apparently, there's been a spate of teenage deaths.'

I stiffen. 'What?'

'The government are denying it, but . . .' She hesitates. 'They're all suicides.'

Suicides? I comb my brain for news snippets, posts, anything that might compute.

'Different ages, different parts of the country. Seemingly unconnected, until . . .' She swallows. 'One of them posted on social media, before they . . . did it. Turns out there was a secret forum. But the thing is, Susan . . .' Her lip quivers.

'Carmel?' I've never seen her like this. 'Carmel, what is it?'

Her eyes lift to mine. 'They were all . . . They all underwent certain . . . procedures. During IVF.'

'What? What do you mean?'

But I already know what she means. A chill runs the length of my spine.

'Gene edits. For mental-health disorders. Like anxiety and . . . depression.'

My stomach thuds.

'And now there's pressure building, for the government to launch an investigation.'

Jesus. *Jesus.*

'Have you spoken to your consultant?'

'I've been on the brink of calling the clinic at least a dozen times.'

'Why haven't you?'

'Because I'm frightened of what they might say.'

The Carmel I know doesn't baulk at anything.

I grab her hand. 'Listen to me, Carmel. We're talking China, here. You know the pressure those children are under, the competition to perform . . . I mean, they've been screening those kids since conception to determine what they're good at. Then hothousing them in schools and sports academies where they're expected to shine . . . ' I swallow. 'There could be any number of reasons for those deaths. And even if there is some link to genetic procedures, things are different over there. It's not regulated the same way.'

She nods, and wipes her eyes.

'Don't assume this has anything to do with Leo. Don't go to that place. Not until you know more.'

She holds my gaze, but it's as if she's looking through me. 'I've been telling myself the same thing all week. I know I'm being illogical, but when it comes to Leo it's not logic that prevails.'

I put my arm around her, reassure her we'll get advice and that things will be OK.

But even as I speak the words, I feel it seeping through my veins: an insidious dread.

My instincts are with Carmel's. That this is just the start.

39

Zurel

'Hey, Daughter!'

Dad looks up from his screen and opens his arms wide. He's home early.

I lean into him for a hug and breathe in that spicy coffee smell I love.

He plants a kiss on top of my head. 'Good day?'

I nod.

'Where's your mum? Let me guess: Carmel's?'

I nod again. He rolls his eyes.

Dad doesn't like Carmel. I think it may be something to do with the amount of time Mum spends with her, although Mum says that's a 'drop in the ocean' compared to the hours Dad spends on his screen at home, doing work.

Lola arrives with a scatter of paws and barrels into our legs, fearful of missing out.

'Well, hello, there!' Dad bends down to stroke her. 'How are you, Trouble? Been a good girl?'

When Lola's excited, her whole body wags, not just her tail. She flattens her ears and stretches her mouth into a wolfish grin.

'What d'you reckon, Zurel, do you think she deserves a treat?'

Lola instantly sits, gazing at Dad with bright, amber eyes. She understands everything. She doesn't need her own words.

Dad slips a biscuit out of the jar and sighs. 'If only

humans were this easy to please.'

Lola is a German Shepherd-collie hybrid. I wanted a natural pup, but it was a deal-breaker for Mum. Only two modifications: a year-round coat with no shedding — Mum's main objection — and fur that gives off a lavender smell when wet. Lola got off lightly compared to some. Next door's Chihuahua has fur that glows in the dark, and Dad told me a guy from his office just ordered a Labrador that changes colour according to its mood.

Dad shoves his head in the fridge. 'So, did you see Mr Thomson again today?'

He knows I did; I see him every day.

'What did you do? Games? Drawing?'

Both Mum and Dad seem very interested in my lunchtimes with Mr Thomson.

— A fun game. And he asked me what books I like.

Dad pours himself some water and smiles. 'It'd be quicker to say what books you don't like. I'll bet you've read more than all the other kids put together.' He glances at me. 'Maybe we could read something together later.'

— Sure.

We haven't done that in ages. Usually, if Dad's back before bedtime, his phone rings, or Mum needs to talk to him about something, or he gets 'sucked into his screen'.

— Mum took me to the lab again yesterday.

'Did she?' He frowns at Lola, who's sniffing his trousers, piecing together the puzzle of where he's been.

— Do I have to go?

Dad looks up. 'Well, your mum think it's a good idea. To do our bit, you know. For research. Why,

208

don't you want to?'

— Not really.

He sucks in his lips. 'Why's that, then?'

I shrug. I can feel Dad's eyes on me, trying to work me out, but he's not a dog. He's not as good with non-verbal cues.

'Have you raised it with your mother?'

I nod.

'I take it she's not a fan of stopping.'

I shake my head.

'Well, if it's really bothering you, I could have a chat with her, if you like. See if we can maybe put the visits on hold.'

My pen flies across the screen.

— That would be great, thanks!

If *he* asks her, maybe she'll listen. I just hope he doesn't forget.

— I'm taking Lola up to the woodland now.

'In this?' Dad looks out of the window, horrified.

— I like the rain.

A wet snout prods my hand in agreement.

'OK . . . Well, make sure you wear a coat. Your mother will kill me if you come back soaked.'

I head into the hall, Lola trotting alongside. I grab my jacket from the hook and pull on my boots. As I open the door, rain fizzes in my face and Lola's nose starts twitching like mad. Dogs' noses are amazing. They use each nostril separately so it's like they smell in 3-D. They can even smell and breathe at the same time.

I keep her on the lead until we reach the gate to the woodland. Before my fingers even touch the latch she bundles underneath and races into the trees.

I skid along the muddy track after her; the rain

makes odd spattering sounds on the leaves. I notice little hoof marks in the mud where deer have quietly stepped. The ground is still bare: only the occasional primrose; the bluebells are still asleep. I tip my face up and open my mouth. Drops fall on my tongue, fresh and sweet.

A buzzard's cry echoes in the branches. I grab my phone and swipe the audio app, facing the mic up, towards the sky. I shield the screen with one hand and keep very still. Lola scurries back and forth, nose to the earth, and gives something a tentative sniff. The buzzard calls again, right on cue. That should be a good one, as long as the rain doesn't drown it out. I file it under 'Birds' and catch up with Lola.

I smell it before I spot it. A sweet, musky odour, washed with damp. The lifeless eyes of what used to be a rabbit gaze at me; its paws are outstretched, as if it's still trying to get away. The once soft, grey body is now a muddy husk, ripped open and scooped out. I know it's natural, but there's a violence to it that makes me shiver. I grab Lola's collar and yank her off.

I take two photos and cover the carcass with leaves. They go in the 'Sad' album. As I scroll down the list, my eye lingers on an audio file. It feels as if someone's hollowing out my insides, too.

I lean against the trunk of an old tree. The air presses in, cold and clammy, filling up my mouth like a sponge.

It's just a stupid recording.

I don't even know what it means.

Lola is watching me, head tilted, eyes gleaming like wet stones. She gives a low wag and nudges me with her nose. I squat down and bury my face in her soggy fur. I think of the Peace Pod, with its cosy yellow walls.

We could stow away, the two of us: curl up under a table together, like two little snakes.

As her heart beats against my cheek, I wonder if Mr Thomson has a dog.

I should ask him, next time we meet.

MOKOSH FERTILITY CLINICS

We're here for you. No matter who you are.
Because everyone has the right to conceive.

Mokosh Fertility Clinics have been helping people of all ages, genders and nationalities embark on the journey to parenthood for over forty years.

We are proud of our reputation for pioneering safe new fertility treatments, because we believe everyone deserves the opportunity to have a baby.

'We invest in research at the cutting edge of reprogenetics so we can bring the most advanced reproduction services to our clients.'

— Mokosh Fertility Director,
Professor Viktor Stakhovsky

One of our newest treatments: in vitro gameto-genesis (IVG) has opened up even more possibilities for those previously denied the chance to have their own biological child: partners in same-sex relationships, trans* clients, post-menopausal women and those whose fertility has been affected by medical intervention or disease.

At Mokosh Clinics, everyone has equal access to our services. Book a consultation, and we'll tailor a plan just for you.

Conception is a right, not a wish.

Exercise your right today.

40

Zurel

'So, Zurel, I thought we'd do something creative today.'

I give Mr Thomson a sideways glance. He doesn't have dogs — I checked. Which is a pity.

'You like cartoons, right?'

I nod.

'And stories?' He knows I do. 'Well, today, we're going to make up one of our own.'

A slant of sun lights up his face, and I notice a small patch of stubble that he's missed. Mum would never let Dad go out like that.

'So, the way this works is a bit like role play. One of us thinks of a couple of characters, in a particular setting, and the other one draws what happens. We have to choose someone from real life, not some vlogger or robo-celeb. Then the other person sketches some scenes with what they say and think. Sound OK?'

I feel a flutter in my belly. But I give him a thumbs-up.

'Why don't we start with me? You think of something I might be doing, at home or here.'

My eyes drop to his hands. He has nice fingers, I think. Long, with short, clean nails: not too hairy. Not like Mr Chase's, next door.

'Anything you like.' Mr Thomson smiles. 'Within reason.'

My mind has gone blank. It's hard to imagine Mr Thomson doing anything apart from striding around school. Then I remember the stubble.

— You have a row with your wife.

He lifts one eyebrow. My breath catches.

Did I cross a line?

'No wife, I'm afraid. Will a partner do?'

I nod, flushed with this jewel of knowledge. Not married after all.

He picks up his e-pen. A little stick man appears with spiky hair. I cover my smile.

Mr Thomson shifts his screen so I can't see. 'Patience, Zurel . . .'

I stare past him, to the garden. The feeder's empty; no wonder there aren't any birds. Maybe Mr Thomson will let me fill it up again; it's sort of become my job. I watch him out of the corner of my eye. He always wears that wristband: three leather strips woven like a plait of hair. It better not be from a real animal. Maybe his partner bought it for him.

'Right. Here we go.' His stick figures have coloured bubbles coming out of their heads and mouths. 'You see the different colours? They represent emotions. Perhaps you can figure them out.'

The first speech bubble, his partner's, is red: *You haven't washed up again!* Red thought bubble: *I have to do everything!*

Mr Thomson's speech bubble is also red. *I'm tired, OK?* But his thought is blue. *I'm having such a bad day.*

His partner's next thought is yellow: *He doesn't seem himself.* Speech also yellow: *Is everything OK?*

Now Mr Thomson's speech bubble turns blue: *My boss shouted at me again.*

His partner's thought is yellow: *I feel bad. He's upset.* Her speech bubble turns green: *Sorry, I didn't realise.*

I'll make us a cup of tea.

Mr Thomson sits back. 'So . . . high drama in the Thomson household.' He folds his arms. 'What d'you reckon?'

I twirl my e-pen, unsure.

— Mrs Hanberry shouldn't shout at you. That's against school rules.

He chuckles. 'Quite right.' He leans closer. 'She doesn't really shout . . . Well, not at me, anyway. What else?'

— Maybe you should get a house bot.

'Ha, on my salary? I'd love to, but I can't afford one. What about these colours?'

I roll my eyes. Child's play.

— Red, angry. Blue, sad. Green, happy. Not happy . . . The opposite of angry.

I sigh.

— Not sure about yellow. Maybe . . . worried?

'Full marks. I knew you'd get the hang of it.' He nods at my screen. 'Now it's your turn.'

The flutter in my tummy returns.

'It's your first day at secondary. Your mum's taken you in the car and she's about to drop you off.'

Something sinks inside. They're all obsessed with this secondary thing. I thought Mr Thomson knew better.

I scowl and pick up my screen.

'Doesn't have to be long. What's interesting is the difference between what people *think* and what people *say*. Or write.'

I glance at him, but now he's the one looking out of the window.

My e-pen hangs, mid-air. This is hard. I frown. Really hard.

215

I draw the figures first, with their bubbles. Then I add the colours.

'Nearly there, Zurel?'

I angle my screen away from him, suddenly unsure. 'Don't worry, I'm no artist. As you can tell.'

I'm about to delete the last scene when he stretches out his hand. 'Can I see?'

I bite my lip and push the screen towards him, my face growing hotter by the second.

My stick avatar is in the passenger seat, with a ponytail. Mum's behind the wheel with strangely puffed-up hair. I cringe. A year one could have done better.

Don't be nervous, says stick Mum, in yellow letters. *You'll be fine.* Her thought bubble is also yellow: *I hope she's OK.*

My thought is red: *Stop fussing!*

Mum, yellow again: *You can make new friends.*

My thought is blue: *Like that's going to happen.* My screen words are red: *I don't want new friends.*

Mum's speech is yellow: *Please, Zurel. Just try.*

Mum's final thought is also red: *Why can't she be normal?*

But mine is blue: *I wish I was normal. But I'm not.*

Mr Thomson doesn't say anything. I realise all my bubbles are either angry or sad. I dig my e-pen into my palm, slowly dying.

He slides my screen back. 'Thank you for sharing that, Zurel. That was really honest. Well done.'

I keep my eyes fixed on the table.

He takes a breath. 'I'm interested in what you wrote about being normal. Everyone's different, to some extent, Zurel. We each have our own characters. Our own habits. That's what makes us an individual — who we are.' He pauses. 'And often, it's those differences that are the things other people love best.'

I carve the e-pen deeper.

'You've actually reminded me of a quote by a famous African-American writer. Do you know what she said?'

My head gives the slightest shake. More of a twitch.

"If you are always trying to be normal, you will never know how amazing you can be." He taps my screen and smiles. 'And lots of people here think you're pretty amazing, Zurel. I know for a fact Mrs Crowther does.'

The heat surges up my neck to my face. I can barely breathe. It's terrible, and wonderful, at the same time.

'You have friends here who care about you. I know, because I've seen it.' He nods. 'I tell you what. How about you find me a film clip or a story you like, about being different? And bring it in one lunchtime. How does that sound?'

I dip my head.

'Great. Well, we'd better stop there as I think we may have run a bit over. If I don't get you back to class, Mrs Crowther will have my guts for garters.'

I scrape back my chair and grab my bag; I manage a small wave as I leave.

The playground is empty. I must be late if everyone's already inside. I hurry past my classroom, round the back of the canteen. The window's open, and the smell of boiled vegetables makes my stomach loop. I sneak out my phone and swipe the audio app. Hold it close to my mouth.

At first, there's only the sound of my breathing mixed with the banging of pots and trays.

I swallow. 'Today . . . ' My eyes dart back up the path. 'Today, Mr Thomson said I was amazing.' The words rush out in a low whisper. I snatch a breath. "If you're always wanting to be normal, you'll never know how amazing you can be."

I file it under 'Special'.

41

Susan

No one really knows what causes selective mutism. Despite all our artifice and technology, we still haven't deciphered it. As with most conditions, there are many factors. Emotional. Psychological. Social. But at its core is anxiety. That's the only genetic piece: most sufferers have a genetic predisposition to excessive worrying. Selective mutism can stem from, or lead to, other problems, such as sensory-processing disorders or language impairment. Once it sets in, if not treated, it can last for years.

Most children with this disorder speak in at least one setting, usually the home. But there is another form of mutism, where a child who had no difficulty speaking previously, suddenly stops talking. As if their voice has been stolen, like the Little Mermaid's. This is normally linked to the child witnessing or experiencing a traumatic event.

They haven't said it in so many words, but this is what they think's happened with Zurel. That's why they want her to see a psychologist. She stopped talking three months before her eleventh birthday. No one has any idea why.

Apart from me.

★ ★ ★

219

Steve shrugs off his coat and pecks me on the cheek. 'How was your day?'

'Apart from the sensory Lego, not bad.' I shake my head. 'It's always the same when something new arrives — sharing goes out the window. They revert to good old tug and slap.'

Steve slumps into a chair. 'Zurel upstairs? Or out with the dog?'

I give the soup a stir. 'She's out.'

'How was she today?'

I don't answer. If I start, I'm not sure I'll be able to stop. I think of the silent ride home, my desperate questions. And now this message from school . . . I wonder whether I should tell him.

He glances at me and frowns. 'What is it?'

I take a breath. 'I don't know . . . Things are getting worse, Steve. She barely *looks* at me, let alone speaks to me. It's like there's this . . . wall of anger — '

'They said that was normal — an inability to self-regulate. It's her frustrations, building up through the day. Like all parents, we get the brunt of it.'

'I suppose . . . I just miss that chattering little girl who used to leap on our bed every morning . . . '

'I know.' He sighs. 'She's the same with me. They did warn us it wouldn't be easy. Though, as it happens, we did have something approaching a conversation yesterday. I meant to tell you. She was asking about those research sessions.'

I keep my eyes on the pan.

'She's not that keen on going. She said she'd mentioned it to you.'

'Yes. She did.' I clench the spoon. 'Did she say why?'

'No, not specifically . . . '

'Hmm. Me neither.'

220

'Maybe you should give them a miss for a while. You know, until we start to make headway. If she doesn't feel comfortable . . .'

I stir the soup in slow circles. 'Yeah, it's just we made a commitment . . . I'd hate to mess things up for them.'

'I'm sure they'd understand. You don't have to can it, just . . . put it on hold.'

My back stiffens. I can't stop going, particularly now, with this China scandal. Those tests are what's keeping Zurel safe.

'I'll have a chat with them, see what they say.' I clatter two bowls onto the table and change the subject. 'I had a message today. From Zurel's SEND lead.'

'Oh, really? Mr . . . What's his name?'

'Thomson.' I swallow. 'He wants to see me, tomorrow. Sounded rather . . . officious.'

'It's their job to sound officious.'

I glance at Steve. 'Do you ever wonder what they do in those meetings? Him and Zurel?'

'Play games, mostly, from what I can gather.' Steve blows on his soup.

'Yeah, but there's more to it than that, isn't there? He's trying to get to know her, build trust. So she opens up.'

'Well, makes sense, I guess. If he's going to help her.'

'Feels a bit weird, though. Someone outside the family spending that much time with her. Alone.' My foot starts to jiggle. I make it stop. 'He wants to make a home visit.'

Steve frowns. 'A *home* visit?'

'Yeah. He said it was to get a better understanding of her environment.'

221

Steve's cheek twitches. 'I thought we'd already done that. Jeez, the speech therapist asked enough questions. Felt like I was in therapy, at one point.' He takes another spoonful and swallows. 'What time is this meeting?'

'Two.'

'I can't make it. Not this short notice.'

I shake my head. 'It's OK, he'll probably just ask the same old things. Have a nose around.'

Steve narrows his eyes. 'I don't know . . . Maybe I should be there . . . '

'No, no, honestly, I can handle it.' I sigh. 'It's just . . . no matter how many times they tell you it isn't your fault, you can't help feeling it is.'

Steve reaches across and takes my hand. 'Hey, come on . . . We'll get through this.'

'I know . . . ' I force a smile, but a memory stabs me. 'You know what? I don't care what they say. I still think it could have been the scooter.'

His face falls. 'We've been over that a thousand times. That was six years ago. They don't believe tha — '

I brandish my palm. 'It was *my* hand on her back, pushing her along . . . ' My eyes screw shut as the image presses in. 'Her poor little chin.' Tears burst into my eyes. 'The look that nurse gave me — '

'Susan, you've got to stop it, this . . . incessant guilt-tripping. Children have accidents every day; that's normal. The shit some kids have to deal with — Zurel's one of the lucky ones.' He exhales. 'I tell you something I *would* be worried about: what's been happening to those teenagers in China.'

An icy finger glides up my spine.

'You must have seen it? Kids jumping off buildings,

in front of trains. Well, now they've finally admitted it. Those children were messed with.'

I have to force the words into my mouth. 'When you say, 'messed with' . . . ?'

'Genetic edits. Not the regulated kind, either. They were basically guinea pigs for that immunity programme. Some of the parents had been on at them for 'not living up to expectations': can you believe it? '

My spoon slides out of my hand.

'They reckon those underground clinics were doing edits for all kinds of stuff: autism, ADHD, addiction, you name it. I mean, it's bordering on eugenics. Plus, this was well over a decade ago. We're only just getting a handle on the genetics behind those conditions now.'

'God, that's . . . that's terrible.' I grab my phone and start frantically searching. It doesn't take long for a barrage of headlines to appear:

'Suicide Toll Climbs. China Under Pressure To Probe Unlicensed Fertility Treatments.'

"Robbed of My Right To Be Me.' Chinese Son's Suicide Note Blames Parents.'

Steve wipes his chin. 'It's really kicking off now — hundreds of families coming forward. They say there are riots. You can imagine how the Chinese authorities are responding.'

My eyes zoom in on a comment by some professor at UCL:

'We don't have any information on the mutations they're finding in these children because they haven't existed before. Mental-health conditions such as schizophrenia and mood or substance-use disorders involve the interaction of hundreds, possibly thousands, of different genes. The way these genes interact is extremely complex, both within our bodies and with the environment around us. Altering them without fully comprehending their place and function in the human genome is both foolhardy and dangerous.'

I have to call Carmel. And Stakhovsky. I have to speak to them, right away.

I shove back my chair. 'You know what? I think I may jump in the bath. Have a quick soak.'

Steve looks at my bowl and frowns. 'You've hardly touched your soup.'

'I had a big lunch.' I stand up. 'I'll eat later. You carry on, don't mind me.'

I drag my feet upstairs. My hand is shaking as I lock the bathroom door.

I crank the taps on full blast and dial Carmel.

42

Zurel

'How are you getting on? Everyone chosen their back-drops? Have you got your sprites moving?'

A few of us nod. My dog sprite is chasing a stripy cat over a purple mountain range.

'Good. Now I'd like you to try adding some speech and sounds.'

Mrs Crowther covers a yawn with her hand. I'm not sure coding is really her thing. I suppose it is pretty pointless, given machines do it all these days.

I drag some blocks over and type my script. Add a few miaows and barks.

I like coding. No talking, no questions, you just bring your own ideas to life on screen. This story is going to end well. Because today has been a good day. A very good day indeed.

At break, I played HumanHunt with Tulya.

At lunch, I pulled off my plan.

I suspect Mr Thomson may have had a hand in HumanHunt. Tulya had kind of given up on me; she'd tried enough times. But when she strolled over with that big, lopsided grin, for some reason, I went along with it. There are no words in HumanHunt. There's quite a lot of squealing though. The rules are simple: you run like crazy, make it to the safe zone, and don't get caught by the bots. It actually felt good, being part of something, racing around with the others. Maybe that's what set me up for later.

I brought in a film for our session, like Mr Thomson asked. A clip from a movie I'd found on PixFlix Vintage. I chose the scene where David, a robot boy, is abandoned by his human mother. Mr Thomson didn't say anything while it played, but I swear his eyes went a bit gooey. That made me glad, because when I first saw it, I blubbed, too. Even watching it third time around I had to blink and pinch my hand.

Afterwards he asked me, just like I knew he would, why I'd chosen that particular scene. My heart was clattering like Lola's paws on the kitchen tiles. I never thought I'd manage to go through with it. I mean, I'd planned it all out and everything, but I was pretty sure, when it came to it, I'd chicken out.

— Are you on ConnectApp?

He tipped his head to one side, a bit like that other robot in the film, who makes women happy. 'Sure. Why, d'you want to message me?'

I nodded, blushing like an idiot.

— It's my answer. To your question.

'Oh, OK. Great idea. I've a work number I can ping you.'

I hesitated.

— It's an audio clip I made.

I don't know what he thought to that, because I didn't dare look.

— I don't want you to listen to it until I've gone.

'Right. OK.'

— And I don't want you to share it with anyone else.

Only then did I risk a peek.

'You have my word, Zurel.'

He looked so calm. As though it wasn't a big deal at all.

I turned away from him while I sent it and waited

for the little ping on his phone.

— Can I go now?

'If you want to.' I made for the door. 'Oh, Zurel? One question.' I stopped. 'Can I message you back?'

I hadn't thought about that.

I dipped my chin in a nod.

'Are we nearly there?'

Mrs Crowther yanks me back to attention. She's prowling the room like a hungry wolf.

'Anyone need some help?'

Predictably, two arms shoot up, at Hellie and Mikey's table. She'll be stuck there a while. I decide to risk it and sneak out my phone.

One new message.

My heart leaps. And falls. It's Mum:

Don't forget to bring your PE kit home! See you later x

My dog sprite jiggles back and forth, tongue lolling, waiting for its next move.

And I remember Lola. With so much going on, I haven't checked on her today.

Mrs Crowther is frowning at Hellie's screen. My finger slides to the GoggleWoof app and activates my imps.

I select camera two. Not there. I switch to camera one. And freeze.

It's *him*: Mr Thomson. In our kitchen. On a stool.

Lola panting at his feet.

As he bends to pat Lola, Mum appears and hands him a mug.

It feels as if I've swallowed something very hot that's scalding me all the way down to my tummy.

He didn't mention anything about coming to our house.

He didn't say one word.

My finger plunges, about to swipe, when he says: 'She's doing great, you know.'

I hesitate.

No good comes of snooping. You know that . . .

'It was a real breakthrough today.'

He must have played her the audio file. That's why he's there.

I'm squeezing my phone so hard it hurts.

The girl next to me, Carol, taps my shoulder and whispers something. I scowl at her and shake my head.

Whatever Mum just said must have been important, because Mr Thomson shifts in his seat and frowns. I nudge the volume a little higher.

'I can't. I'm sorry.' He looks at her. 'That would be a betrayal of trust.'

Mum's jaw stiffens. I can't tell whether she's about to shout at him or cry.

'*Please*, Marty . . .'

Marty?

Mr Thomson shakes his head. 'I'm sorry, I know how hard this must be, Susan. Give it time.'

Mum's mouth twists into a bitter smile. 'Patience never was my strong point.'

I hear the clop of Mrs Crowther's shoes and slip my phone into my pocket. Carol throws me an anxious look. My fingers scurry across the keys, sending my cat flying up a cactus.

I detect a scent of something flowery.

'My, aren't we busy, Zurel?'

It's Mrs Crowther's assembly voice, the one you need to watch out for.

I keep my eyes on the monitor and stretch my mouth into a smile.

Her breath tickles my neck. 'Hmm. Just as well

228

you're a fast worker.'

I complete my project, not really conscious of what I'm doing, randomly selecting and dragging blocks.

Mr Thomson is like the robot boy, David. He doesn't tell lies.

Unlike David's mum.

43

Susan

'So, they *definitely* don't think Leo's condition has anything to do with — '

'No. No they do not.' Carmel puts down her fork and folds her napkin. 'It's like you said. That whole China fiasco, it's another world. You can't compare.'

The Chinese edits scandal is getting worse by the day. The latest reports suggest that far from lowering the risk for certain mental-health conditions or behavioural disorders, the genetic changes have increased anxiety levels, triggering severe mood disorders in a growing number of children.

'My consultant explained it to me,' she continues. 'Some of these so-called 'clinics' are literally operating out of residential flats: no permits, unlicensed staff, no proper qualifications. There are hundreds of them. And the numbers they're getting through . . . ' She shivers. 'Lining them up like the old factory farms. Nothing like the clinics we used. It's no coincidence they call China 'The Wild East' of assisted reproduction.'

I pick up my fork. Shreds of cultured chicken nestle into sprigs of rocket. They're almost *too* flesh-like, as if some kind of murder's been committed. I put my fork back down.

'Stakhovsky told me pretty much the same. I got the impression he'd had a few calls.'

'Well, at least they're on the same page, which is

230

reassuring.'

Carmel sounds more confident than I am. I wonder if she still has doubts.

'All this media attention is a worry, though. What if Zurel starts asking questions?' My mouth goes dry, just at the thought. 'Would you tell Leo about the treatments?'

'He already knows about the Huntington's edit. We told him the lengths we went to, to stop him inheriting that awful disease. But as for the rest . . . now I'm not sure.'

I am silent. It's different for me. I can never tell.

'So, you mentioned you'd got Leo to see someone.'

Carmel dabs her mouth with a napkin. 'As you know, that was quite the battle. But, in the end, he relented.'

'How did it go?'

'It's early days, but they think . . .' She looks round and lowers her voice. 'They think he may have some kind of sensory-processing disorder. Where the brain struggles to process its environment. Apparently it's like a sensory overload.' Carmel leans closer. 'But get this: it can affect their sleep. Make them feel anxious. Isolated. Even depressed.'

I nod. 'I've had a few kids over the years who've been diagnosed with that. It was one of the things they considered with Zurel. Some children can be over-sensitive to certain things, and under-sensitive to others.'

She exhales. 'I tell you, just knowing what it is makes me feel so much better. At least we can work with it. Get Leo the right therapy and medication.'

I feel a twist of envy. As usual, Carmel's on her way to fixing her problems. Unlike me.

The service bot whose nametag says Estan arrives with our drinks and a wide smile.

'Is everything to your satisfaction, ladies?'

Carmel beams. 'Absolutely glorious, thank you.'

Personally, I find these models a little too fawning. Maybe it's because, underneath that smiling silicon exterior, you know the microchips couldn't give a damn.

It gives a slight bow. 'Do let me know if I can enhance your dining experience in any way.'

'Oh, believe me, Estan,' says Carmel. 'I will.'

'Jesus. Now you're flirting with a robot,' I whisper, as it glides off to another table.

'I'm just messing,' she laughs. 'Anyway . . .' her voice drops an octave '. . . there are much better models you can hire for *that*.'

I shake my head and catch sight of myself in one of the many pub mirrors. It's a little disconcerting, seeing your reflection everywhere you turn.

Carmel wags her fork at me. 'Talking of which, when, exactly, were you going to come clean about this SEND guy?'

My heart thuds. 'I honestly didn't think it was material.'

'Are you kidding me?' Her fork clangs onto her plate. 'Of all the people in the world, Zurel ends up in session with her actual — '

'Shhhh!' We may be secreted in a corner, but Carmel still manages to make an elderly couple at the other end of the room look round. 'Jesus, Carmel. Why don't you just get up on the table and make an announcement?'

'Well, I'm sorry but . . .' She expels a breath. 'Any *normal* person would have said something straight

232

away.'

'Yeah, well.' I take a slug of wine. 'Normality is overrated.'

Carmel stabs a wedge of aubergine. 'So, come on. Details. How long has your Italian stallion been at her school?'

I wince. This is exactly why I didn't tell her before. But after that meeting, I caved.

'A bit over a year.'

'A *year*? You didn't tell me for a whole year? God, what kind of friend are you?'

'Look, it's not as if I've seen him or anything. Not until Zurel stopped talking.' I push some croutons around my plate. 'We had the odd conversation, you know, over the toy stall or at a parent assembly. We hadn't been in touch for ages. If you remember, he left while I was still on maternity leave. But then, just my luck, he shows up at Zurel's school.'

I feel that same twist in my gut that I felt when I found out they'd hired him. I couldn't believe it. I wondered if Mokosh was having a last laugh.

I hesitate. 'I'm worried Zurel's forming some kind of attachment to him.'

'Really?'

'She's pretty vague about their lunchtime sessions, but it's obvious she enjoys them. And, as far as I know, it's the first time in months that she's let anyone hear her voice.'

'Well, I guess that's progress, right? What did she say?'

I pinch the stem of the glass. 'I don't know, because I haven't been allowed to listen to it.'

Carmel's eyes widen. 'Ouch. Not sure I'd cope too well with that.'

I swallow. 'No. Well, I'm not sure I am. It's a 'trust' thing, apparently.'

I think back to the meeting. My silent fury that Marty wouldn't share the recording with me. Thank God Steve wasn't there.

'He kept asking questions about my relationship with Zurel. As if there's some kind of . . . issue. '

Carmel frowns. 'Like, what?'

'I don't know, exactly.' I bite my lip. 'He implied that Zurel felt isolated. Beyond the speech problems, I mean. That she felt she wasn't like other children, in some undefined way.'

'Hey.' Carmel reaches over the table. 'Come on, all kinds of weird stuff happens when they hit puberty. Isn't that what you told me? They go through their own mini-identity crisis.'

'Yeah. But most don't stop talking.'

Carmel's mouth flattens. We both take another sip.

'So, what are you going to do, Susan?'

'What can I do? Just let them work through their little plan. Until Zurel feels ready to communicate with me.'

'Actually, I didn't mean that.' Her eyebrows arch. 'Do you honestly think you can keep up this pretence? Playing teacher and parent?'

'Carmel, it was more than a decade ago. All that is history.'

'For you, maybe. Don't you think it's interesting that Zurel's made a connection with him? Aren't you the slightest bit intrigued?'

I ignore the flapping in my chest. 'He's the SEND lead, Carmel. They meet daily; she doesn't have much choice.' My lips tighten. 'And no, I'm not remotely intrigued.'

Carmel's eyes twinkle at me over her glass.
Wisely, she decides not to push it.

44

Zurel

I watch them: line after line of women, dressed in white. Some hold poles attached to cloth banners printed with elegant black symbols I don't understand. Others clutch white flags that flutter in the breeze. Like me, these women are silent. One of them looks as if she is sleepwalking: her dark eyes stare but don't see. They march past grey-and-brown tower blocks that remind me of Dad's Lego bricks; their feet sound like rain against glass. Two walls of men in black uniforms stand in the road either side; the badges on their jackets glint in the dull sun. Behind them are soldiers in bulky body suits, and helmets with the visors pulled down.

Who are these women? Why are they so dangerous?

All they have are signs.

My screen auto-translates the symbols on one of the banners:

Justice for our children!

This must be about those teenagers I read about in China. The ones doctors did things to, before they were put in their mothers' tummies. And now the families are angry. But mostly sad. They're sad that the doctors hurt their babies; they're sad that no one is doing anything about it, but most of all, they're sad that their children are never coming home.

I wonder if that woman with the faraway eyes lost a son, or a daughter.

I search for her amongst the rows of mothers. But she has melted into the white throng.

★ ★ ★

I thought it might be difficult, seeing Mr Thomson. After I sent him the file.

'Zurel. Good to see you.'

But it isn't.

He wrestles out of his jacket and drops into a chair. His face is slightly flushed. 'Good weekend?' I smell a pulse of spice.

— OK.

I'm tempted to ask what he thought of Lola, but I think better of it.

'Did you get my message?'

I nod. He thanked me for sharing my recording. Assured me it would go no further. Which, of course, I already knew.

'What you said about the film . . . Very interesting.'

My gaze veers to his shirt, which is a deep blue. Like the sky at the end of a sunny day.

'I thought we might just touch on it, now.' He leans back and crosses his legs. 'If that's OK?'

— Can I ask you something?

'Sure. Go ahead.'

— What made those teenagers in China kill themselves?

His face goes a bit stiff. 'Ah . . . I suppose you saw it on the news?'

I nod.

— The mothers' march.

He uncrosses his legs and sighs. 'So tragic.' He shakes his head. 'Those children were suffering with

237

mental-health problems, Zurel. And they didn't get the help they needed.'

— I read that doctors made them ill. When they were babies.

'Well, that's what they're *saying* might have happened, yes.'

— Is it true?

His tongue pushes into his cheek. 'We don't know yet, for sure. There's going to be an investigation.'

I think carefully about my next question.

— What did the doctors do to them?

His eyes lift, for a second. 'You *really* want to know this stuff?'

The way he says it makes me think he doesn't want to tell me. But I need to know.

I nod.

'OK.' He clears his throat. 'Well, as you may be aware, when a couple want to have a baby, they often need help. From a special doctor.'

Sex-ed simulations slide into my mind. I hope Mr Thomson doesn't go over *that*.

'The doctor does various checks when the baby is only a few days old, to make sure it's healthy.' I blink at him. 'Sometimes, if there's a problem, they may make changes, to stop it getting a disease. Does that make sense?'

I nod again.

'Well, in this case, they made some changes. But the doctors didn't realise that by changing one thing over here . . . ' He taps the table. 'It might affect another thing over there.' He moves his finger across, towards me. 'Our bodies are very complicated. We still don't fully understand how everything fits together. And we knew a lot less fourteen years ago, which is when a lot of this took place.'

— Do special doctors still do those things? Make changes?'

'For certain conditions, yes.' He leans forward. 'But there are strict laws that govern what can or can't be done in this country. It's highly regulated. Mistakes like that would never happen here.'

— I think my mum saw a doctor like that.

His mouth tightens. 'Oh, really?'

I swallow. I'm taking a risk, but Dad hasn't said anything more about the visits, and neither has Mum. I don't even know if he's spoken to her.

— We still see him, sometimes. My finger hovers over the screen. — Unfortunately.

Mr Thomson raises an eyebrow. 'Doesn't sound like you're a fan.'

I shake my head.

— He asks too many questions. It's not always him, though. Sometimes there are others.

Mr Thomson stares at me then remembers to drop his eyes. 'Other doctors, you mean?'

— Yeah. They take my blood, weigh me, check my height and stuff. And ask more questions.

If Mr Thomson had a thought bubble, it would be yellow.

— Maybe they're worried I'll get sick, too.

I force a smile, although my thoughts are very, very yellow. Before he can say anything, my fingers fly across the keys:

— Do you want to talk about the film now?

He runs his tongue over his lip. 'If you want to. Sure. Let's do that.'

So I write about the clip, and why I like it, even though it's sad. I tell him how David knows he is different, that he's 'mecha' — a machine — but all he wants is to be human, so his mother will love him. Even though he's much nicer than his brother, who is a real, human boy.

Mr Thomson listens, but I can tell he's thinking about what I said before. Which is OK. Because I'm still thinking about what he said to me.

'Zurel?' he says, when our time's almost up. 'I need to finish a little early today. But, before you go, I'd like to make a request.'

— OK.

'Would you consider doing another recording?' His finger taps the desk. 'For me, or . . . your mum?'

It's not like Mr Thomson to pressure me. Mum must have given him serious heat.

I drop my eyes.

— I'll think about it.

I don't like to be pushed.

45
Susan

I thrust my hands in my pockets and stomp across the playground, breath smoking from my mouth. It's nearly the end of March, but you wouldn't know it; spring must be loitering elsewhere. The children are not deterred; coated and booted, they plunge across the playing field, swinging themselves over climbing nets, yelling with glee. I scan for trouble, and spot a girl alone on the bench by the pergola, two pigtails sticking out from her head like twigs. I don't recognise her: she must be new.

'Hello, there. Do you mind if I join you?'

She shivers slightly and yanks a toggle on her coat.

'I'm Mrs Rawlins. I teach the year ones. Are you in Mrs Achebe's class?' She nods, blotches of red breaking out across her face. 'What's your name?'

She fixes her eyes on her shoe. I have a fleeting memory of Zurel at this age, hopping from foot to foot, barraging me with questions.

I hunker down on my haunches. 'I tell you what, let's play a little game. I like games, don't you?' She gives the smallest of nods. 'I'll try to guess your name. When I get the first letter right, you have to nod, OK?'

She drags one tooth over her lip. Her gloveless hands are red raw.

'So, here we go: A, a.' I repeat each letter phonetically. 'B, b. C, c.' I pause but she doesn't stir. 'D, d . . . E, e.'

She tilts her head.

'Was that a yes?' She nods. I clap my hands. 'Elizabeth?' She shakes her head. 'Emily?' She shakes it again. 'No? How about emu?' I flatten my hand in an approximation of a beak. She smiles. 'Or . . . elephant?' I wave my arm in front of my nose and trumpet.

She slips her hand over her mouth and giggles. 'Elephant isn't a name. I'm Ellie!'

'Well, I was nearly right then, wasn't I? So, Ellie, have you ever played 'it'?'

She shakes her head.

'You see those girls over there?' She eyes the bodies hurtling across the netball court, wielding hula hoops. Fluorescent patterns shimmer round the hoops as they run. 'Well, they're playing a special version called 'Hula-It'. Looks fun, don't you think?' Her smile wilts. 'How about we take a closer look?'

She lets me take her hand. Her skin is soft, with little pucker marks over her knuckles, as if the bones are still growing into their skin. Just like Zurel's used to have.

I wave discreetly at one of the hula girls with an unruly mop of curls. She jogs over.

'Amber, this is Ellie. She's new. Would you show her how to play your game?'

Amber proffers a hand. Ellie glances at me. I smile. 'Go on. Give it a try.'

The two of them trot off, just as my phone rings. We're not supposed to take calls on duty, not unless they're urgent.

Then I see the name.

I wave at Francis, the other teacher on duty, and point at my phone. She gives me a thumbs-up. I move to a more secluded spot, under the pergola.

'Marty, hi.' I try to keep it casual as the blood thuds in my ears.

'Hello, Susan. I just need a quick word. Can you talk?'

'Sure.' No precursory chat: must be serious. 'Has something happened?'

'Not exactly ... Well, nothing you need to worry about. It's just that ... ' He expels a breath. 'Zurel was asking lots of questions about what's been going on in China — '

'*China?*'

'Yes: the suicides.'

I swallow. 'Right. Wow. I'll have to check her filters. It's not exactly viewing material for an eleven-year-old.'

'It did take me a little by surprise. Understandably, it's made quite an impact on her. I tried to reassure her, but you may want to discuss things with her yourself.'

'OK. Thanks, I will. I don't want her fretting.'

There's a pause that makes me think there's more.

'She made a couple of comments about what the doctors did ... ' He hesitates. 'She seemed to think that you'd undergone some kind of similar procedure during your pregnancy with her.'

I freeze.

'Well, I don't know where she got that idea from,' I splutter. 'She wasn't even an IVF baby.'

I wait for him to respond, ignoring the sparks at the edges of my eyes.

'At this stage, I don't know whether she actually *believes* what she's saying' — he's choosing his words carefully — 'or whether this is her way of processing fears that feel very real to her, based on what she's seen . . . But she implied that she was having medical check-ups on a regular basis. By the doctor that treated you.'

I pinch the skin on my thigh.

Where has she got all this? How can she know?

He exhales. 'Look, Susan, I appreciate this kind of information is private . . . I just wanted to follow up, in case there was anything that might be pertinent to her condition. That might help us, if we know.'

'Ah, hang on, I think I know where this might have come from.' I run my tongue over my lips. 'You see, I signed us both up to a research study. On epigenetics. The impact of the home environment on the child.' I swallow. 'We have quarterly meetings. They interview us both, and carry out a few basic checks on Zurel. I think she must be getting it all confused.'

'Ah . . .' His breath rushes down the phone. 'Well, that explains it, then. I have to say, it did all sound a little . . . odd.'

I force some jollity into my voice. 'My daughter's always had a vivid imagination. You should see some of the stories she writes for Mrs Crowther.' I think of that last one. Then again, maybe he shouldn't.

'Well, I'm sorry to have bothered you, Susan. Thanks for clearing that up. If you could maybe follow up with Zurel.'

'Absolutely, don't you worry, I will.'

'Great. I'd better let you get back.'

I drop onto the bench and breathe. Shouts echo in the playground.

I need to find out what Zurel knows. Or thinks she knows.

Fast.

46

Susan

Steve's whispering at the door. I shut my eyes and pretend I'm asleep, even though I've been awake for hours. We all have our part to play in this day, and mine is to lie here and be pampered, but my mind won't stop turning. I still haven't got to the bottom of what Zurel told Marty; when I asked her about it, she was decidedly elusive. Then she started on about the lab visits again. Maybe I should postpone them, just while she's seeing Marty. Assuming, of course, that this China thing settles down. At least I was able to put Zurel's mind at rest about that. I think I did, anyway. These days, it's hard to tell.

I hear the clink of crockery. The curtains whine open. Yellow and red spots drift behind my eyes.

'Morning, Mummy,' says Steve. 'Did you have a nice lie-in?'

I stretch my arms over my head and yawn. 'Lovely, thanks.'

Zurel inches towards me, gripping a tray, her mouth tight with concentration. She looks like a cuddly squirrel in that furry onesie; no wonder Lola can't leave her alone. A mug of coffee slides towards my passange juice, thankfully buttressed by a plate of toast.

'What a treat.' I push myself up and hold out my arms. 'Thank you, darling.'

Passange is my latest craze: orange crossed with

245

passionfruit, incorporating all the recommended daily vitamins. I take a sip. 'Mmm, delicious.'

Steve nods at Zurel. 'Freshly squeezed by your daughter's fair hands.'

I smile at her and pat the bed. As Zurel clambers over the duvet, I think again how stunning she is, with her fiery hair and cobalt eyes.

She arranges herself on the pillows next to me. I seize the opportunity for a hug, but as my arm encircles her, she stiffens. She thrusts a card at me.

I make a fuss of opening it, trying not to mind.

Purple and white paper petals fold out: the colours of a Zurel tulip. Underneath, in alternating gold and purple letters, she's written:

Happy Mother's Day, Mum!
Love Zurel xxx

My throat constricts. Zurel is watching me, a pinch in her face. I should be happy: Steve and I here, with our daughter, on this special day. The day I used to dread.

I swallow. 'Thank you, Zurel. It's beautiful.'

Steve smiles at us. 'Happy Mother's Day, Susan.' He nods at her.

Zurel hands me a bag.

My present has been meticulously wrapped. I unpick the tape, careful not to rip the paper, and slide out a picture frame. Mounted on gold paper are three portraits: purple silhouettes, in profile. The faces are unmistakeable, even with our features blanked out.

'Zurel did those herself,' says Steve. 'It was all her idea.'

She tentatively holds up her screen.

— Do you like them?

I take a breath and lift my gaze to hers. 'I *love* them!'

And it's true: I do love them, but they instil a slow ache in my heart.

I know these faces so well, but their expressions are hidden from me.

Like Zurel, they are unreadable. Silent.

★ ★ ★

The drive to the cemetery is quiet, so I put on some music. Zurel has never been fazed by the dead, not like some children. Maybe it's because she's been coming here ever since she was born. When Mum died, it was early days for alkaline hydrolysis, or dissolution, as it's now known, but she'd appreciated the cleaning connotations in the blurb: 'imagine you're a greasy plate in the dishwasher'. When we explained to Zurel what the big glass building was for, she wanted to know every last detail. After that, whenever we visited, Zurel would point at it and say: 'That's where Grandma and Grandpa dissolved.'

She used to say lots of things like that. Things that made us laugh.

I go to lift the bulbs out of the boot, and Zurel follows me round.

— Shall I carry some?

'Thanks.' I hand her two pots. 'I thought I'd try a new variety this year: tulip crossed with hyacinth. What do you reckon?'

She eyes the pink-and-silver clusters on the label and gives me a thumbs-up.

We walk under the old yews, sunlight filtering onto rows of plaques below. Zurel stops by a small headstone with a stone cat curled at its base. That's new. When she presses the screen, a young girl with blonde ringlets flicks across the display.

— Why did she die so young?

I peer at the screen. 'I'm not sure; it doesn't say.'

I don't let on what I'm really thinking. That perhaps her parents were anti-intervention.

— Did the doctors make her ill?

I freeze. Steve glances at her and then at me. I haven't told him about our China conversation.

'No, Zurel.' He frowns. 'Doctors make people better, as a rule. She probably had some kind of accident.'

Zurel continues scrolling; birthday parties flash past, school photos, family holidays: the highlights of a truncated life. I resist the urge to grab her hand and make her stop.

Eventually, she picks up the pots and we walk on.

My pace slows as I spot the flint-grey granite.

In Loving Memory of Betty Cookson
Most precious wife and mother
To live in the hearts of those we love is not to die

The baby daffodils and purple crocuses I planted last year have already poked their heads through. Seeing them on Mum's grave calms me.

I wipe down the stone, yanking out some weeds at the edges. 'OK,' I say. 'Let's get to work.'

Zurel digs the holes, careful not to disturb the other flowers, as she's been taught. Steve hands me a bulb, and I massage the soil around its roots. A robin flits onto a plaque and cocks its head, regarding us with bright, beady eyes.

'You're doing a great job, Zurel.' I smile at her as she trowels. 'Grandma would have been proud.'

I think of that tub I found in the greenhouse, after

248

Mum died: Viridiflora Spring Green, labelled in her small, neat letters. She must have dug up the bulbs, as she always did, and packed them in paper. I wonder if she knew she wouldn't be around to plant them out. It was me who found them, one frosty morning, wrapped in an old pot like a forgotten present. I hacked away at the ground until there were fifteen holes. When those creamy white-and-green petals pushed up the next spring, I sat in the garden and cried.

We're on to the last two bulbs when my phone rings: Carmel. I ignore it. She's probably in some swanky restaurant with Leo and Barry, quaffing wine and tiramisu.

A second later, it rings again. Steve rolls his eyes.

'Sorry, I'd better take it.'

I clap the earth off my hands and move to a safe distance. 'Carmel, now's not real —'

'I'm at A&E.' Her voice is shrill. 'I found Leo on the floor in his bedroom . . .' A siren wails in the background. 'He's OD'ed, Susan. He's OD'ed!'

Sudden rise in childhood leukaemia may be due to 'catastrophic' gene interventions. Leaked EU report says Kremlin is 'sitting on the facts'

Maya Tholsberg, Health Reporter for Independent Online in Moscow

An EU report has revealed the Kremlin ordered a top-secret investigation into a surge in cases of chronic myeloid leukaemia (CML) in young adults and children across Russia, Georgia and Ukraine.

Doctors believe the genetic abnormalities that caused the cancer were triggered by 'catastrophic edits' of the babies' genomes. These interventions were part of a government-authorised genetic optimisation scheme to foster future athletes.

According to the report, parents were encouraged to consent to 'routine edits' during IVF which, they were told, would make their children 'healthier and fitter'.

'They told us it would make Valery's muscles even stronger. Increase his stamina,' said one father of a thirteen-year-old boy with CML. 'They told us it was safe. If those changes gave my son this disease, I'll never forgive myself, or those specialists.'

47

Zurel

Another bad thing has happened.

As soon as I see Mum's face, I know. It has that tight, distant look — a bit like those Chinese mothers. I've barely fastened my seatbelt, when the car sets off, charging past the children running out of school. A couple of the mums who are chatting by the kerb turn and frown. We're going quite fast. Too fast for a pick-up zone. I glance at Mum. Her fingers are gripping the wheel so tightly all the blood has squeezed out.

She doesn't ask me about my day.

She doesn't speak at all.

And that's when I realise: Mum's switched the auto-function off. She's driving the car herself.

I scan the pavement and the gaps between parked cars where buggies and prams are being folded into boots. Mum's eyes are fixed on the road. Suddenly, her foot jams the brake. My body flops forward, straining against the belt.

'Sorry.' She glances at me. 'Junction came up a bit fast.'

'Sorry,' she says again, and turns left.

We should be turning right.

I swallow my fear and hold up my screen.

— Is Leo OK?

Her eyes dart to the screen and back to the road. 'They think he should pull through, don't worry. He's

251

getting lots of support.'

— Are we going to the hospital to see him?

'No.'

My face drops.

'Look, I need to focus, Zurel. Sorry.'

I turn up my music as the road flies past; I already have a hunch where we're going. Sure enough, we pull off the dual carriageway, and my heart sinks. I thought, after Mr Thomson spoke to her, things would change.

Mum slows a little for the roundabouts, but it's still jerky, and I feel a bit sick as my body sways left and right. As we pass the Zendter Biolabs sign, I see red graffiti scrawled over it. Mum's so intent on getting there she doesn't notice. It looks like it says *Murder*.

No. That can't be right.

The car swings into a parking bay. I spot a crowd outside the entrance to the lab. Mum spots them too. Her face pinches even tighter, and she swears under her breath.

Maybe the fire alarm's gone off, and they've had to evacuate the building. Maybe we won't have to go, after all.

Mum puts one hand on her door.

I tap her arm.

— Is it a drill?

She frowns at me and rummages on the back seat. 'No.'

She grabs her hat. 'Listen carefully, Zurel.' Her voice is hushed, but I recognise the tone; it's even more frightening as a whisper. 'I'm sorry you have to see this, but I have an urgent meeting. We *have* to go in.'

I start writing another question, but she presses her hand over mine.

252

'They're not nice people, Zurel. I mean, what they're *doing* isn't nice . . . They're . . . misguided. But they may say some horrid things.' She squeezes my arm. '*Don't* listen to them. Don't read any of their signs, or touch anything they try to give you. Just walk straight past. And keep hold of my hand. OK?'

My mind explodes with questions. Is this something to do with Leo? Are they protestors, like the ones on the news?

'Did you hear me, Zurel?'

I nod, wide-eyed. It feels like I have fireworks going off inside.

'Good.' She attempts a smile. It stretches across her mouth and sinks. 'Now get out of the car.'

She pulls her hat down low and yanks up my hood, even though it's not raining. 'Keep that up, in case they're filming.'

Filming?

She grips my hand. 'Right. Let's go.'

She marches towards the labs. The nearer we get, the tighter my throat becomes. Mum's breathing is deep and slow, as if she's gearing up for a race.

I want to get back in the car.

They've put up barriers either side of the statues; the security bots are lined up in front, struggling to keep back the crowd, who are chanting something.

As we get closer, I notice some of the protestors have prosthetic limbs or are in auto-chairs. A woman with long grey hair and a flowery dress is singing a song that's vaguely familiar. I know I'm not supposed to look at her sign, but I can't help it:

Behold, children are a heritage from the Lord, ALL fruit of the womb a reward.

It sounds like something the vicar would read out

at school.

One group of people are wearing white T-shirts with a red circle on the front and a line through it. In the circle is a dish and a knife. They're all staring at us; it's not a good stare. Mum's grip tightens.

We make it into the narrow tunnel between the barriers. The chanting is loud now:

'*NOT* YOUR RIGHT TO CHOOSE, *NOT* YOUR RIGHT TO CHOOSE!'

My heart is skittering in my chest. A girl in an auto-chair, who looks about my age, holds up her poster and smiles:

Unscreened, unedited and happy to be alive.

The woman next to her doesn't look very happy. At least, not with me.

We trample over a carpet of red-and-white pamphlets. I think about picking one up. Maybe it has the answers I need.

A man lunges forward and tries to give one of them to Mum. As she bats him away, another woman presses something small and hard into my hand. I hesitate then slip it into my pocket before Mum sees.

Words pound my ears. I'm finding it hard to breathe.

Mum shoves her hand over someone's phone. They shout at her as a little boy with round brown eyes and a tiny nose squeezes through the barriers. He seems totally unfazed, swaying from side to side with his tongue poking out, clutching a blue-and-white sign that says:

PGD? NO, I'M PERFECT, THANKS.

A security guard ushers him back through and steers us towards the door.

Mum tugs my wrist: 'Come on!'

The doors slide open, and we practically fall into

reception. Mum pulls me further inside. She's sweating. So am I.

She clasps both hands around my face. 'Are you OK, darling?'

I can't stop trembling. I eye the windows, but luckily, they've pulled all the blinds.

'I'm so sorry, Zurel. That was horrible.' She pulls me to her. My arms flop around her neck like a doll's.

'Mrs Rawlins?' It's the security guard. Mum ignores her. 'Mrs Rawlins? He'll see you, now.'

Mum hugs me tight and pushes herself up. I grip my e-pen and force my fingers to write. The letters loop desperately across the screen.

— What were they saying, those people? What did they mean about 'choosing'?

She pats down her skirt and smooths her hair. 'We'll speak about it later, Zurel. Now's not the time.'

Something inside me breaks. I ram her with my hands.

She staggers back, into the security guard. Her face goes white.

'Zurel . . . ' She drops to a crouch and grips my shoulders. 'I know this must be frightening, and you have questions. But you have to understand, these people . . . The things they're angry about . . . It's like those families in China. They don't concern you.'

I glare at her.

— Then why are we here?

The guard steps forward. 'Is there a problem?'

Mum doesn't answer.

She swallows. 'The research we're doing, it's linked. I will explain it to you. But not here.'

The guard looks at her then at me. Something in Mum's face makes me back down.

We're taken down a different corridor to usual. Eventually, we reach a wooden door. The guard waits outside and knocks.

'Come in.'

It's the older doctor, with the grey moustache, not the slimy one. He scurries out from behind his desk.

'Mrs Rawlins. So sorry about all that. If I'd known you were coming this aft —'

'I left *several* messages, Dr Stringley. I assume you read the news?'

She gives him the kind of look that would make me shiver. Judging by his face, I think he is. She glances at me. 'We need somewhere private. Before you do the tests.'

What? I clench my fists. She never mentioned more tests. Why does she always treat me like a baby, keeping things from me, like I can't understand?

'Of course.' Dr Stringley gives Mum a nervous smile. 'I thought Zurel might like to wait for us next door.'

I don't even look at her when we leave. He leads me into another room and winks at me. 'We won't be long. And Magda's dropping by with something tasty.'

As questions swirl round my head, I suddenly remember the thing the woman gave me. I sneak it out of my pocket. It's a tiny bioplastic baby, so small it fits in the palm of my hand. Its eyes are shut, arms clasped tight around its body, as if it's cold. I notice a label on its belly:

Squeeze me.

My fingers can't resist.

The baby's eyes open:

'Mummy, please don't change me. I'm perfect, as I am.'

256

I gasp; it slips through my fingers, bounces and skids under a chair.

The voice: it's just like David's. From the film.

And that's when the idea comes to me.

It steals in so easily. Like a burglar climbing through an open window.

I kneel down and pick the baby up. Its brown eyes slowly close.

48
Susan

'How's he doing?'

I listen to Carmel's breath, stuttering down the phone.

'We're past the worst. They don't think there'll be long-term damage.'

Her voice doesn't sound like hers. It sounds like an eighty-year-old version of Carmel.

'He hasn't spoken, yet. Not to Barry. Or me.'

I stare at the smiley animal circles on the rug where we do story time. 'Did they manage to ID it? The drug, I mean?'

'Yeah. Some customised synthetic. Designed to max out his brain receptors.' Her voice hardens. 'They better track down the bastards that sold it.'

'God, I'm so sorry.' I exhale. 'Look, can I bring you anything? Change of clothes, food? I could nip out now, I've got planning and prep time after lunch.'

'No, I'm sorting all that. I need to keep busy. What I'm desperate for is answers. And you can't help with those.'

I watch the children chasing each other around the playground.

It doesn't seem fair.

I hesitate. 'Have they told you anything?'

'Not yet. But they're screening him for . . . mutations.' She spits out the word and lowers her voice: 'They interviewed us, you know.'

'Who?'

'The doctors. And someone official-looking, from the hospital.'

'Shit, really?'

Bertie, our class bot, swivels round.

'Hang on, Carmel.' I march over and switch him off. We're told they don't listen in, but I don't believe a word of it. How else do machines self-learn?

'Sorry about that. What did they ask?'

'They wanted my whole fertility history. Where I went, what I had done.' She sighs. 'At first, they seemed supportive, you know? Until the conversation moved on from Huntington's.'

My eyes widen. 'You told them? About the other edits?'

'What choice did I have? They've requested access to my records. I could hardly say no. I've instructed the clinic to release them.'

'So, what exactly did they say?'

'Nothing. That was the worst part. I kept telling them my consultant assured me it was safe, but I could see it in their eyes. I know what they were thinking . . .' Her voice cracks. "How could you? How could you take that risk, with your own baby?"

'Listen, Carmel, I saw Stringley yesterday. I confronted him, after the whole Russia thing blew up.' I don't mention the protests. 'According to him, there's no definitive proof of any link between these illnesses and genetic optimisation. He says spontaneous mutations naturally occur, and it's still speculation at this stage.'

'It doesn't feel like bloody speculation, I can tell you. Not when you're sitting across a table with three doctors interrogating you.' She sniffs. 'They're

259

comparing Leo's DNA with ours. To pinpoint specific changes that might have been caused by the edits.'

Worry gnaws at me. Will Zurel's test results reveal similar problems? If they only occur years later, how will we know?

'There's stuff all over social media,' Carmel continues. 'More cases coming out of the woodwork every day. Barry is freaking out.'

I try to summon something positive to say.

My phone vibrates: it's Marty. God, what now?

'Listen, Carmel, I'm really sorry, but I'm going to have to take another call — it's Zurel's school.'

'I should probably go back in, anyway. I'll call you later.'

'OK. You'll get through this. All of you. And remember, I'm here for you. Whenever, whatever . . .'

I answer Marty on the sixth ring. 'Hi, Marty.'

There's a pause. 'Hello, Mrs Rawlins.'

Each word has its own emphasis. If they were typed, they would all be bold.

'We need to talk.'

★ ★ ★

I check the cloakroom, make sure no kids are loitering by the door. But it's just the usual pandemonium of coats, bags and shoes.

'You sound terribly stern, Marty. What's this all a —?'

'I'm going to play you an audio file. That Zurel sent me.'

All the other worries drop out of my head.

The teens contracting cancer or trying to kill themselves; Zurel's test results; Carmel and Leo . . . all of them fade, for an instant, as if these things are inconsequential. Compared to what's coming.

'Susan?'

'Yes, I . . . Sorry. Go on.'

I close my eyes, train all my senses on what I'm about to hear.

There's a brief silence, then:

'. . . Zurel's doing extremely well, we're very pleased with her.'

My skin goes cold.

'Bloods still good. Mutations continue to be within the acceptable range. Genetically speaking, to all intents and purposes, she's completely normal. Remarkable, really. Given the extent of her edits.'

'So, you have no concerns?'

I shudder as I hear myself speak.

'No. Do you?'

I clench my jaw. Willing these next words to stay unspoken.

'Only . . . What happens, if . . . ? If someone finds out?'

Hearing Stakhovsky's chuckle makes me want to stab him.

'The only way that will happen, Susan, is if you tell them. Which, as we've agreed, you won't.'

Sound waves have no weight, but silence does.

It's Marty who eventually breaks it.

'So, are you going to tell me what the *hell* is going on?'

49
Susan

We arrange to meet at a park, in a village between our two schools. On the drive over, I replay that recording in my head, again and again; picture Zurel listening to it, swamped with confusion and fear.

I remember that visit. It was the last time Stakhovsky came to our house. I thought Zurel was upstairs, in her room. We were sitting in the kitchen, discussing her latest screening results. Stakhovsky had been elated.

Tears spring to my eyes. How could I have been so blind? No wonder she doesn't want to see him. It must only have been a matter of weeks before she stopped talking.

Marty's already there, waiting. I glance at the swings idling on their chains; the rubber seat lolling from the zip wire. A cartoon duck grimaces at me from a crisp packet in the dirt. The playground is bereft of children — no feet to light up the springers, or stamp out tunes on the jumping stones; no fists to summon the climbing towers' virtual spaceship destroyers. The only sound is the desolate squawk of crows.

'Shall we sit?' Marty's huddled in a black sports coat, collar pulled up round his ears.

I take a deep breath. 'Sure.'

Instead of the bench, he heads for the swings. I push my feet against the ground and sway slowly back and forth.

'So, then.' I manage to keep the tremor out of my

voice. 'I imagine you have questions.'

'Just a few.' His legs stretch out in front of him, heels digging into the mulch.

'Did you . . . discuss it?'

'Zurel sent it at the end of our session. She didn't ask me not to share it.' He scuffs his shoe. 'I think this is her way of asking me for help.'

It's a stake through my heart.

Can I blame her?

Marty turns. 'The man. On the recording. Who was he?'

'A specialist in assisted reproduction.'

His jaw sets. 'The last time we spoke, you said you hadn't had IVF.'

'I hadn't.' My mind is spinning so fast, I'm worried all my thoughts will fly out. 'The changes he referred to, they came later.'

Marty frowns. 'What do you mean?'

'Later in my pregnancy.'

He stares at me. 'You mean you had genetic intervention, *after* you became pregnant? I thought that was only allowed in a very few cases.'

'Over here, it is.'

His mouth opens and closes. He swallows. 'The conversation implies the edits were significant.'

I lock my fingers into the chains. 'They were to stop her inheriting certain conditions. It was a reputable clinic and she has regular checks. We didn't use some backstreet shop in China.'

'I appreciate that, but those parents thought their kids were safe, too. And it's not just China anymore.' His voice rises. 'I'm sorry, but I don't think you appreciate how serious this is. Apart from the edits, it's quite possible what she overheard triggered her mutism.'

I don't acknowledge it. My heart thuds a little harder.

'What did you have done, Susan?'

I dig my foot in the dirt. 'I can't tell you the details. I'm sure you understand. It's private.'

'So private, your own daughter doesn't know?'

'She doesn't need to!' The words blurt out before I can stop them.

His eyes narrow. 'If these changes are as harmless as you say, what are you scared of?'

'I'm sorry, Marty,' I shake my head. 'I can't go into it. Look, I'll talk to Zurel, when the time is right — '

He swerves round. 'Susan, she's looking at those newsfeeds about dead teens and thinking she could be next.' He takes a breath. 'Zurel's wellbeing is my responsibility. My duty is to *her*. So, if there's any risk, I have a duty to inform the relevant agencies.'

Is that a threat?

I try to summon an answer, as the pounding in my head intensifies.

'Do you understand, Susan? It's Zurel's right to know what happened to her. And to get help, if she needs it.' His brown eyes bore into mine. 'Let me speak plainly: if you don't do something about this, then I will.'

MailOnline

Britain facing 'hidden health crisis' from damaged embryos conceived in foreign clinics, watchdog warns

By Tracey Baxter, Health Correspondent

The NHS may soon have to treat hundreds of children whose genes have been damaged during botched fertility treatments abroad, the country's top regulator has warned.

Mary Chasmeyer, chief executive of the Human Fertilisation and Embryology Authority (HFEA), said hospitals were dealing with a worrying number of young patients suffering from sudden onsets of mental-health disorders and types of cancer similar to those being investigated in China and Russia. The children had been conceived in fertility tourism destinations over the past two decades and had undergone certain genetic procedures that were banned in the UK. This is despite the regulator's repeated warnings about attending poorly regulated clinics abroad.

'Currently, UK citizens are free to travel wherever they choose and select from a range of ART (assisted reproductive technology) procedures, including genetic optimisation. The trouble is, not every country has the same safety standards and scientific rigour as the UK.'

She added: 'We are already seeing a small

but significant number of hospital admissions for children with a range of unexpected conditions. What these cases have in common is that further investigation has shown evidence of genetic 'rearrangements' most likely caused by genetic edits.'

Campaigners against genetic intervention have called on Sonja Avesbury, the health secretary, to introduce an outright ban on travelling to countries for ART.

'We believe the time is right to stop the wealthy undergoing risky and discriminatory procedures abroad, and protect the safety and wellbeing of their future children,' said Suzy Trainer, a campaigner with protest group Genome Defence Alliance (GDA). 'We cannot expect an already overburdened NHS to have to pick up the pieces. We need to ban this appalling trade.'

However, pro-choice campaigners insist it would be wrong for the government to take away parents' rights to have their own healthy biological baby. Kim Streetly, thirty-one, from Wellingborough, who travelled to the Czech Republic for treatment last year, said:

'Since when was it OK to deny people their basic human right to have a family? These parents aren't breaking any laws. Instead of vilifying the unfortunate victims of fertility scams, we should be offering them and their children help and support.'

266

50

Susan

The afternoon drags, second by second. Just as well I'm not teaching. My mind is in two places: here, in the classroom, mechanically marking; and back in the park, reeling from Marty's words. I can't stop thinking about Zurel. All the questions she's asked me. All the lies I've told.

Spidery digraphs and lopsided phonemes swim past my eyes.

ch-ur-ch
s-t-ar-t
l-ie-s

I have twenty-four hours. That's all Marty gave me. One day before he blows the whole thing loose.

I wish Carmel was here with her fixer skills, spinning me solutions. I picture her, eyeing me over her glass, picking through my web of untruths. What would her advice be?

Look at the bare facts. Weigh honesty against damage limitation. Figure out what does and does not need to be said.

I take a breath.

I got pregnant on a one-night-stand. With an ex-colleague who is now my daughter's SEND lead.

I never told my husband. I hid my pregnancy from him for weeks.

I tried an untested procedure on my unborn child. A procedure which may be putting her life in danger.

A whine pierces my skull. Is this me?

Am I really this monster?

I take refuge in a phonics simulation. The children have to fill in the blanks to reveal where the pirates stashed their gold.

As I map the clues to the treasure, thoughts surface:

1. The only edits I can mention are the medical ones. The rest must stay buried.
2. Zurel will be difficult. But Steve will be worse.
3. Before I say anything, I must speak with Stakhovsky.

And get Zurel's results.

* * *

Stakhovsky's mobile goes straight to voicemail. I dial Mokosh Clinic. A holograph of their receptionist shimmers into view:

'Thank you for calling Mokosh Clinic. I'm afraid our clinicians are all busy at the moment, so if you'd like to leave your details we'll be in touch as soon as we can . . .'

I frown and hang up. That's never happened before; someone always picks up.

I try Stakhovsky again, even though he's probably in surgery. If he sees two missed calls, he'll know it's urgent.

I make futile attempts at lesson plans. I redial the clinic, leave my details and explain it's critical that someone returns my call.

But they don't.

I try the clinic two more times. When the hologram appears for the fourth time, I slam my phone down so hard I crack the screen.

I glance at the clock: nearly three. I need to leave soon, to pick up Zurel.

And then I remember the other number Stakhovsky gave me when I was pregnant, his personal mobile, only for emergencies. It doesn't take long to find it.

The phone rings six times. I'm about to give up when the dial tone stops. There's a pause.

'Susan?'

It must be Stakhovsky, but it doesn't sound like him.

I falter: 'Yes.' There's a rustling sound, like papers being shuffled. 'I need to speak to you, about Zur —'

'It's really not a good time.' He's breathing hard. 'As I'm sure you'll appreciate. All I can tell you is, we're doing everything we can.'

A cold sweat sweeps over me.

They've found something in her blood. Something terrible.

'If it was ransomware, believe me, we'd have paid it.'

My brain screams to a halt.

'The programme must have been *really* smart, I mean super-intelligent.' He exhales. 'The cyber-defence systems we use are military spec AI.'

I try to unpick his words, but it's as if he's speaking another language.

'This was machine hacking machine.'

The penny drops: 'Oh, God . . . You've had a breach!'

There's a heavy silence. 'I assumed Carmel had told you. All our investors were briefed a week ago.'

Investors?

I blink at the phone.

'How bad is it?' My voice is a whisper.

He sighs. 'The worst kind of bad. They got it all: every patient record. And we're not the only ones.'

Jesus. *Jesus!* I have to stop myself screaming it out loud.

Why didn't Carmel tell me, if she knew? Does she have some kind of stake in this?

'Nine other clinics in the chain have been hit,' he continues. 'Zendter, too. It's a coordinated, global attack.'

'But . . . who? Who would do this?'

'Too early to know for sure. They've not demanded money. Not yet, anyway. Security don't think it's the cybercrime syndicates, and doxing on this scale is rare. But I did hear that —'

There's a barrage of words in Ukrainian. Stakhovsky reels something off in reply.

'Sorry, I've got to go now, Susan —'

'Wait!' It's a shriek. 'Please, Viktor. What's 'doxing'? What do you know?'

He sighs. 'Look, it's just a rumour. Nothing confirmed yet, so don't quote me. Doxing is when online vigilantes publish personal data they've hacked. This could be the work of some anti-intervention radical.' My chest tightens. 'If so, I'm afraid it's not good. Those criminals aren't interested in putting a price on your data. They want to name and shame. Make sure everybody knows.'

'But, my details . . . You put extra security in place —'

'That's of no consequence, I'm afraid. They took it all.'

My eyes clamp shut.

'I was careful, with your record, Susan. Everything pertaining to the samples was anonymised. But, given

270

the . . . sensitive nature of your treatment, it's probably best if we don't contact each other. Not until this blows over.'

I claw my hair. 'What about Zurel, and her tests? And my contact details? They're on those records.'

'All treatments are suspended. We're about to send out instructions to our clients recommending they take immediate security precautions. We had hoped we could salvage this, but it's clear we're beyond that now.' He exhales. 'I'm truly sorry, Susan. Best of luck.'

He ends the call.

I stare at my hand, gripping the phone. It shimmers slightly.

Nothing is permanent or contained. We can shear off and float loose at any moment.

I dial Zendter BioLabs.

As expected, it goes straight to a hologram.

51
Susan

I sit in the car, a crucible of emotions. Carmel picks up on my third call.

'Hey, Susan. I can't really speak on the ward, they don't li — '

'Why didn't you tell me?'

There's a pause.

I stare at the white van racing along in front of me. Could that be one of them? The vigilantes?

'Sorry, babe, I — '

'I just got off a call with Stakhovsky.'

'Ah.' Her breath rushes down the phone. 'This is about the hack.'

'Not just the hack, Carmel.' I press on, before her fixer skills have time to scramble. 'Turns out you have money in the game. Who'd have thought? Is that why you persuaded me to do it? Because you wanted a little bump on your investment?'

'OK, stop right there. I don't know what Viktor said, but it wasn't like that . . . '

'*Viktor*'? That says it all.

'Well, what was it like, then?' I slam the steering wheel and the car judders to self-correct.

'It's just a fund, OK?' Her tone changes. 'That Barry manages. New fertility products, chain expansion — '

'Is that what I was? A 'new product'?'

'No. Of course not.'

'You hadn't even heard of Stakhovsky before that

272

first meeting. You fed Barry the intel, didn't you? On his ambitions? You primed him about those new procedures, using *me* — '

'No, look, I . . . The only details I gave up were purely scientific.' She's breathing harder. 'The technology behind his fertility solutions. It was all in the strictest confiden — '

'I listened to you. I *trusted* you.'

I think back to that first conversation, in Carmel's kitchen.

There'll always be scaremongering when something's new, Susan . . .

PGO is practically routine . . . Barry says all the funds are investing in it . . .

'God, I'm so stupid.' I brace my head in my hands. 'No wonder you went to such lengths to convince me . . . Shooting off to London; getting the green light for Kyiv with Steve.'

'Because I genuinely thought Stakhovsky was your best bet, Susan. Because he assured us it was safe — '

' "Safe"?' I give a bitter laugh. 'What do you know about 'safe'? All this time I've been feeling so bad for you about Leo . . . Are there other kids dying in your investment portfolio? Or are you and *Viktor* covering that up, too?'

'No! You have to believe me: I would never do anything to hurt you or Zurel.'

'Why didn't you warn me about the breach? You were told a week ago. What could it possibly have cost you to let me know?'

She sighs. 'We were hoping they could either pay the hackers off or arrest them, and save everyone the stress. I didn't want to burden you.'

'Was your clinic hacked?'

'Yes.'

'So, they have your data, then, too?'

'I assume so.'

My hands clench. 'Well, you better pray they don't publish those files. Or it won't just be Barry's bonus going down the pan.'

'Susan, let me come over. We can talk this through . . . '

'I'm a bit busy right now, putting out fires.'

'Please, Susan — '

'Go to hell, Carmel. And Barry, too.'

I hang up. She immediately rings back.

I dismiss the call, and block her number.

52

Zurel

The car turns down a narrow lane with hawthorn hedges on either side. I hug my screen and risk a glance at Mum. She hasn't mentioned the recording but her leg's been jiggling ever since we set off. We're only sitting a few centimetres apart, but it feels like there's a mile of unsaid words between us.

The lines around Mum's mouth deepen. 'I thought we might go for a walk.' She's lightened her voice, trying to make up for her face.

— With Lola?

'No. Just us.'

My stomach tingles.

I've wanted answers for so long. Now, I'm not sure.

A pheasant darts out in front of us, and the car brakes. The sun catches the bird's feathers with a flash of green.

— Are you angry?

'Not with you, no.' Her thumb kneads the skin behind her knuckles. 'Are you?'

I bite my lip.

We stop at the junction and turn left towards the common. We snake round the double bend, over the railway bridge with the spiky green railings, past the lone tree where red kites nested last summer. The car pulls into a bumpy layby and stops.

I stare at my feet. I wish Mr Thomson was here.

— My school shoes will get muddy.

She opens her door. 'Don't worry about your shoes.'

As we go through the gate, a buzzard streaks past; it trills high then low. Mum thrusts her hands in her pockets and sets off at her usual pace. I scurry along beside her, trying to avoid the rabbit holes.

'You know, cows grazed here for centuries.' She gazes across the empty meadow. 'There was one breed, completely white, the name escapes me . . . Huge, woolly heads and soft, pink mouths. They had this mane of curls that flopped between their ears . . .' She stops and her eyes go all misty. 'I know the vats are more humane and better for emissions, but I miss seeing cattle in the fields.'

She takes the lower path, by the grassy slope with craters of rabbit warrens. That's where Lola would be, if she'd come, stuffing her nose down each hole.

I wish she was here, too.

Mum heads for a log a few metres on, and we sit. The wood's slightly damp so I tug my coat underneath me.

She takes a breath. 'I spoke with Mr Thomson.'

I keep my eyes on my shoes. Watch them crush the grass.

Maybe it's him she's angry with.

'I'm so sorry, Zurel.' Her voice wobbles. 'I want to explain things, properly. Things I probably should have explained before.'

She swallows.

'D'you remember, before we got Lola, we talked about the different breeds of dog? And how some breeds used to inherit certain illnesses?'

Only because we interfered with them. Mrs Crowther showed us a simulation about that, in bio. The way we bred dogs weakened them, because the ones with dodgy joints and hearts that wouldn't have survived naturally still did. She said it was a lesson in unnatural selection.

I don't write that, though.

'Well, as we've discussed, some illnesses pass down through humans, too. But we know how to avoid a lot of them.' She glances at me. 'We were so thrilled when I got pregnant, your dad and I. The last thing I wanted was to pass on anything bad. So I had a little procedure. To make you as healthy as you could be.'

My face falls. I knew it. She's been lying to me, all along.

I grip my pen:

— You said those Chinese children had nothing to do with me.

'They don't . . . ' Her eyes flash. 'This was an entirely different procedure, carried out by professional doctors who were highly qualified.'

A plane flies past, its engine throbbing.

— How did you know I would get ill?

'Well, there's this test they do during pregnancy, where they analyse a little bit of your blood, and it shows the baby's risk for different diseases.' She clears her throat. 'You only had two risk areas. One was a condition that can affect your heart, which they corrected. The one your dad takes pills for. The other was a type of . . . compulsive behaviour that . . . that you'd be better off without.'

I dig my fingers into the wood and prise off a strip.

— What's 'compulsive behaviour'?

'It means that you can't stop doing something, even if it's bad for you. You have no control over it.'

I do things I have no control over all the time. Like going to school. Wiping my cutlery before I use it.

277

Remembering things I really want to forget.

Genetically speaking, to all intents and purposes, she's completely normal . . .

Mum touches my arm. 'Zurel, I don't want you worrying about this. Like I said, the clinic I went to is nothing like the ones those other parents used.'

I think of those mothers, on their silent march. And I remember what Mr Thomson said, about what went wrong.

— What if they changed things that aren't supposed to be changed? How do you know I won't get sick, too?

She rests her hands on my shoulders. 'Listen to me. The doctors did lots of checks to make sure you were well. They're still doing them now. That's the real reason we visit the lab, as you've probably worked out.' I manage to meet her gaze for a second. 'They're taking care of you, making sure everything is exactly as it should be. And it is, Zurel. You're fit and strong.'

I think of the campaigners outside the lab, waving their signs:

NOT YOUR RIGHT TO CHOOSE!

The little girl in the auto-chair.

— But . . . what if they changed who I was meant to be?

Mum blinks. 'I'm sorry, I'm not sure I follow . . . ?'

— Maybe I would have been different. Better. Even with those things.

Mum doesn't say anything. Her eyes glisten.

'I . . .' She fiddles with her fingers and sighs. It's the kind of sigh that Mrs Crowther does sometimes. 'I just wanted the best for you, Zurel. I wanted us to be happy.'

I stare at the river below and see a perfect reflection of the sky. The sun is hiding behind the clouds, shimmering at their edges.

— Why didn't you just tell me?

'Well, it's quite a complex thing to get your head around . . . You're still young, I didn't want you to worry . . . ' She pauses. 'And, to be honest, your father and I didn't agree.'

I look up.

— About telling me, you mean?

She twists her shoe in the grass. 'No . . . ' Her other foot starts to jiggle. 'The thing is, Zurel, your dad . . . ' She looks at her shoe, then at me. 'Your dad didn't know either.'

She swallows. 'The decision was mine.'

53

Susan

I grip the edges of the counter, try to steady myself. It feels as if I'm caught in my own cyclone, being sucked into the eye of the storm. I glance at the fridge. Not long, until Steve gets home. I'd absolutely kill for a drink, but I need a clear head. This nightmare is only just beginning.

My eye lingers on the poem pinned up with fridge magnets. Totems of happier times. A winking puffin Zurel chose in Northumberland; the smiley whale shark from Cornwall.

Zurel wrote the poem last year. She got a head's award for it.

HOPE IS . . .
Hope is the belief in yourself,
It's the lucky charm in your pocket,
It is the first beat your heart ever made.
Hope is the first light that finally comes,
To your eyes,
It's the tap of your first step,
And the sound of your first word.
It's the first page of your favourite book,
Your first friend.

It breaks me. I'd managed not to cry all day.

I think about her, up in her room. I gave her as much honesty as I could. As for the rest . . . Until I know her test results, and what the hackers intend to do next, I have to at least attempt to shield her.

I remember that dating site that was breached: the one for married people who wanted to have affairs. Must be two decades ago now. When their server was hacked, millions of account holders were exposed. It crushed marriages and destroyed careers, as blackmail threats spiralled. Some users couldn't face the public disintegration of their lives, so ended them.

I prepare the vegetables on autopilot, my hands robotically peeling and chopping. Every few minutes I check for messages and news. They say the longer you keep a secret, the worse it gets. Deception acquires a moral density over time, the agony of its unveiling only magnified by years of complex cover-ups and mounting lies.

I know my husband, and how high this hurdle will be.

I cannot possibly jump it. And nor can he.

I think about all the other universes out there: clones of me pottering about their kitchens, preparing dinner, just like any other day. But in my cosmos, an irreparable tear is looming. A before, and an after.

As I reach for my glass, a news alert flashes up, on my phone.

And I hear the first rip.

★ ★ ★

The hackers have published a statement:

The time for peaceful protest is over. The time for action is now.

For decades, campaign groups have warned of the abuses perpetrated by fertility clinics in the name of

281

reproduction. The discriminatory interventions and abhorrent alteration of babies that have led to escalating inequality and the destruction of innocent lives.

These warnings have been ignored.

And now we see the consequences of commodifying God's children: the corruption of our natural genome by the wanton experiments of a wealthy elite. What started in the name of disease prevention has become reckless eugenics. We must stand up for the rights of the unborn child and protect our lineage, while we still can.

Tomorrow, we will post the records of three hundred thousand patients from two hundred fertility clinics across the world. We will name and shame those parents and doctors who must answer for their actions.

We call upon all governments to ban this immoral trade in humanity now.

I lurch to the sink and gag.

★   ★   ★

The door bangs.
I strain for the usual greeting. It refuses to come.
I mark the seconds before the blast.
The thump of his bag in the hallway.
The stagger of feet; a sigh.
I wet my lips. 'Tough day, love?'
I look at him and try not to cry.
Steve pulls his hand through his hair and nods.
It's about to get a lot tougher.

54

Susan

My fingers tighten around the fork. 'I need to tell you something.'

Six words. That's all it takes to wreck a marriage.

Steve carries on chewing. I study his face: those deep blue eyes I lost myself in, the slightly crooked nose, a token of old rugby days.

'Steve?'

The way I say it makes him look.

He frowns, knife mid-air. 'What?'

I've rehearsed this in so many ways, but each version ends the same.

I think of Zurel — music on, door shut. 'Dad and I need time to talk,' I told her.

But it isn't really time that Steve and I need. Unless we can travel back in it.

I take a breath. 'I got pregnant with Zurel after a one-night stand.'

I run my tongue over my lips. 'Then I had a procedure. A genetic procedure. To make her yours.'

His eyes tighten to a squint. 'What *are* you talking about?'

'I . . . I didn't know. Not at first. I took a test. And it said . . . ' I steady my hands. 'It said, you weren't the father.'

The knife clatters onto the plate. He barks a noise like a laugh and pushes back from the table. His mouth makes little puffing sounds — the starts, or

283

ends, of words.

'Is this some kind of joke?'

'I'm sorry. It was the one and only time.' I force a breath. It feels as if my lungs are collapsing. 'I never meant to hurt you.'

His eyes widen. I notice a tiny red thread across the corner of his left eye.

'Are you saying . . . ?' His voice slows. The disbelief is ebbing, as his universe upends, too. 'Are you *actually* telling me . . . that Zurel . . . isn't mine?'

I try to remember the phrase I'd planned to use, but my mind has frozen. 'She *is* yours. Now. But she wasn't. When I conceived.'

He stands up suddenly; the chair flips back and crashes on the floor. He leans over the table, his breath in my face.

'You'd better bloody start making sense, Susan, or I swear — '

'I had a procedure. At a clinic.' My voice is shrill. 'When I was ten weeks' pregnant. They changed the paternal DNA to yours.' I cannot meet his stare. 'I . . . I know it sounds crazy, but I was so desperate to keep her.' Tears prick. 'And this . . . this was the only way, for the three of us to be a fami — '

He holds up his hand: 'Shh . . . Stop . . . ' He's shaking his head, as if he's trying to dislodge my words. 'Look, Susan, I don't know if this is your anxiety playing out, but I'm telling you, you need to see a profess — '

I jump up and slam the table. 'They're going to publish it. Those hackers. Don't you understand? They've stolen records from two hundred fertility clinics, and they're going to publicly expose every patient who had edits. And I'm on their list.'

He blinks.

'You really mean it, don't you? You actually did that, to your own child . . . ' He gazes at me, aghast. 'Whose is she, then?' His question is dangerously quiet. 'Who were you seeing?'

'No one, I swear. It was the night before Mother's Day. I was upset, I wasn't thinking straight, and things just got . . . out of hand.'

'*Out of hand?*' His lip curls. 'You're telling me, after everything we've been through, all the paranoid shit I've put up with, you slept with someone else?' He gives a derisive laugh. 'Jesus, who was he? One of your teacher friends? They're always sniffing round you. Was it one of them?'

The way he's looking at me makes my skin crawl. Like I'm nothing. Worse than nothing.

'Please, Steve. It didn't mean anything.' I reach for his hand, but he snatches it away.

'God, I must have been a real bastard in a previous life, because every wife I have *fucks* me over.'

His eyes shoot up to the ceiling. 'Does Zurel know?'

'No. I had to speak to you first.' I dig my nails into my thigh. 'I told her about some medical edits. She doesn't know the rest.'

"Medical edits'?'

I swallow. 'To prevent Long QT Syndrome and . . . ' he glares at me ' . . . alcohol use disorder . . . '

He rubs his face. 'How is something like that possible? Let alone legal? I should report you. Yeah, let's call the cops. Because they should *lock you up* for what you've done.'

His shout is a bomb blast.

'Steve, *please*. Zurel's in her room. Listen, I — '

'No. No, *you* listen. I need to get out of this house.

285

I need to get as far away from you as possible while I try to work out what's real.' He thrusts his finger in my face. 'I don't know what you did to our little girl . . . Christ, I don't even know who she *is* anymore . . . ' He gulps back a sob. 'I do understand one thing, though. You're not fit to be a mother.'

He pushes past me into the hall, grabs his bag and stops at the foot of the stairs. His head turns towards Zurel's room, and I wonder if he has it in him. But he trudges to the door.

I brace myself for the slam, but it still rocks me. I creep up four steps and my last flicker of strength snuffs out.

Zurel's door is open.

**Not everything about making
babies is guaranteed.
But the standard of your
treatment should be.**

Assisted reproduction is emotionally and physically challenging. If things don't work out the way you expected, it can be hugely distressing for you and your family.

If you have experienced negligent care during your treatment, or if your clinic has committed serious errors that come to light before or after your treatment ends, then you may be entitled to compensation.

While we understand that not all reproductive procedures can guarantee a successful pregnancy, you should feel confident that you and your baby are getting the right standard of care, with the health outcomes that you were promised.

At Charlton-Fuller's, our experienced specialists have in-depth knowledge in all areas of reproductive medical negligence, so if preventable mistakes have been made, our experts will help you get the compensation you deserve.

Contact us for a free consultation today.

55

Zurel

I can't stop picking at my nails; I wish Mr Thomson would hurry up. I distract myself with the birds, flitting on and off the feeder — tiny blurs of brown, yellow and blue. My head has been spinning all night. I dreamed that Mum was standing outside the house, with one of those banners, and I was locked inside with Dad. He refused to let her in.

The birds dart for cover as Mr Thomson marches up the path.

'Morning, Zurel.' His smile looks a bit tired. He drops into a chair and sighs. 'How are you doing? It's been a difficult week.'

I'm not sure what to say, so I shrug.

His face softens. 'If you want to talk about the audio file, we can. Or not. It's entirely up to you.'

My gaze swerves to my screen. Secrets are dangerous. Particularly other people's.

— I didn't listen on purpose.

'It's fine, Zurel. You don't have to explain yourself.'

I look at the sparrows. That's what the words feel like. Fluttering around my throat.

— I was recording the birds in our garden. And I heard this bumblebee. It had crawled inside one of those bell-shaped flowers. It was so huge, it sounded like a plane.

He smiles.

— I knelt down to get closer, and ... I heard my name. The kitchen window was open. I didn't mean to

288

listen. But I just . . . froze. And it carried on recording.

My e-pen hovers over the screen.

— I didn't know what the words meant. But I had this feeling . . . like I'd swallowed something bad.

Mr Thomson takes a deep breath. 'Did you tell your mum that?'

I shake my head.

— It was hard. Talking about it.

He exhales. 'Yes. I imagine it was.'

My eyes flick up to his and down again.

— She told me about the changes. To stop me getting ill.

'Right.'

— She said I shouldn't worry.

He nods, slowly. 'And how did that make you feel?'

I twist the e-pen round and round.

— I don't know. I don't know what I feel.

Which isn't completely true. Because it feels like I'm carrying something dangerous inside me. No matter what Mum says.

Mr Thomson rests his elbows on the table. 'It's very hard when we discover things that have been kept secret from us, Zurel. Even if it was with the best intentions. It's perfectly normal to feel confused. Upset. Even angry.'

Not as angry as Dad.

That shout. It made me jump, even with my music on. That's what made me check. I've never heard them fight like that before. Then Dad stormed out, and Mum appeared, with her red face and swollen eyes, trying to convince me everything's going to be alright.

I stare at Mr Thomson's boots — polished and shiny, laces neatly tied. Those funny green socks hugging

his ankles. Everything about him seems . . . reliable.
Honest.

— There's something else.

'OK.'

I grip the e-pen. — Last night, Mum and Dad had a
row. Dad got really mad.

I hesitate.

— Those changes. Mum never told him. He didn't
know.

Mr Thomson's eyes grow really wide. As though
he's seen an avalanche rolling down a hill towards us.

'I'm so sorry, Zurel.' And he really does sound sorry.
'I can't imagine how . . . unsettling this all must feel.'

He reaches across and touches my arm, ever so
lightly.

'You know I'm always available. If you need me.'

I have to blink really hard.

'Not just at school. You can message me anytime.'

And in that moment, I feel closer to him than I do
to any other human.

I suck in a breath. 'If . . . ' It comes out more like a
growl. 'If these changes were so important . . . '

I daren't look at him, but I sense it: a spark of surprise.

' . . . why didn't Dad know?'

Mr Thomson's fingers must be gripping that table
hard because his nails have turned white.

'I can't answer that, I'm afraid, Zurel.' He swallows.
'The only person who can is your mum.'

★ ★ ★

I spot Mum on the pavement, right outside the gates. Her hair has that frizzy look it gets when she hasn't brushed it, and there are black marks under her eyes.

'Zurel!'

She waves at me, as if she's not obvious enough. Usually she waits in the car.

I stomp through the gate, my face burning. She clamps one hand on my shoulder, like I'm an infant, and ploughs through the children and prams like a ball hurtling down a bowling lane. I try to shrug her off, but she's gripping me so tight, she's actually pinching. I notice some of the parents are staring at us, leaning their heads together and whispering like catty year fives.

A woman in a pale-pink coat and bright lipstick steps out in front of us.

'Hello, there. It's Susan, isn't it?' She smiles at Mum. 'Susan Rawlins?'

I recognise her: she's Gary's mum.

Mum's mouth flattens. 'Sorry, I'm in a bit of a rush.' She tries to barge past, but the woman blocks her, as if they're on the netball court.

'I'll bet you are.' Her smile vanishes. She lifts her arm and points at us. 'She's one of *them*. From the list.' Her voice rings out, as if she's making an announcement. 'One of those gene fiddlers.'

I glance at Mum, who's still trying to elbow her way through.

A few of the parents quickly turn and leave, the others just stare. Their children peer up at them, unsure.

Gary's mum swivels round. "Significant genetic alterations, most of which are illegal in the UK.' That's what it said on the app. You can check for yourselves. This so-called 'mother' went abroad and genetically

291

redesigned her unborn child. And now the rest of us have to live with the consequences.'

My throat tightens. There must be something monstrous in me, after all.

'Just ignore them, Zurel. Don't listen,' hisses Mum.

Everyone's glaring at me as though I've done something wrong.

They start talking about me as if I'm not there:

'No wonder she's top of the class.'

'Is that why she doesn't speak?'

'She looks normal on the outside.'

Mum rams past Gary's mother, almost knocking her over. She hauls me along the pavement, and we make it to the car, just as a different woman appears.

'Hello, Susan.' A silver cross glitters on her throat.

Mum takes a sharp breath. 'Get in the car, Zurel. Now.'

Fear is choking me. I cannot move.

"Deliver me, O LORD, from lying lips, from a deceitful tongue." The woman shakes her head and sighs. 'That was quite the story you engineered, all those years ago.'

'Leave us alone.' Mum steps in front of me, shielding me with her hands.

The woman's lip curls. 'How *could* you? Adulterate your own child?'

'You have no idea what you're talking abou — '

'I know you made changes to a perfectly healthy baby. Well, now your sins are exposed for all to see.' The woman's eyes drop to me. 'I'm just sorry for your daughter. It's always the innocent who suffer.'

'Destroying other people's lives won't bring back your son, Helen,' Mum spits.

The woman smiles. 'Oh, Susan. This is nothing.

This is just the start.'

'What's going on here?'

A voice booms through the crowd. Everybody turns. It's Mr Thomson. I'm so relieved, tears rush into my eyes.

The woman nods at Gary's mum and strides off.

'In case you'd forgotten, our school values are love and tolerance. I don't see much evidence of that here. What's more, you're obstructing the pavement and causing a safety hazard. Everybody, please, go home.'

'Well, I hope the school are going to step up and do something,' says Gary's mum. 'We can't have naturals and unnaturals in the same class. It wouldn't be fair. Anyway, our kids might catch something.'

'Mrs Baker, take your son home,' bellows Mr Thomson. I've never heard him speak to an adult like that before. 'This school does not accept discrimination or harassment of *any* sort.' He turns. 'That goes for all of you. If it continues, there will be consequences.'

The remaining parents mutter to each other and shuffle off. Mum folds me into the passenger seat and hurries round to her door. Her fingers tremble over the control panel.

My window whines down, and Mr Thomson leans in. 'Are you OK, Zurel?'

I gulp, and nod.

He squeezes my shoulder as his gaze shifts to Mum. He looks like a storm cloud about to burst.

'Mrs Rawlins. You and I need a talk.'

56

Susan

Zurel knots her hands together as the afternoon sun picks out bronze and copper glints in her hair. A solitary tear runs down her cheek. It spears me. I'm her mother; it's my job to keep her safe.

'I can't begin to tell you how sorry I am, Zurel.'

I brush her arm. She flinches.

'Those people . . . they don't know what they're saying. They know nothing about you.'

Her eyes glitter as her e-pen flies across the screen.

— They know more than I do.

She hasn't looked at me since she got in.

— When is Dad coming home?

'I . . . I don't know. Maybe later.' I haven't heard from Steve all day.

Zurel clenches her screen.

— Who was that woman?

I exhale. 'Someone I met a long time ago. When I was pregnant with you. She belongs to a protest group. They're against all genetic procedures. Even when they save lives.'

Zurel's face darkens.

— Is that what I am — 'unnatural'?

'No, of course not. It's just a phrase ignorant people use. Don't take any notice of them.'

— Stop saying that, I'm not stupid.

Her chest heaves.

— You can't keep fobbing me off with your lies.

294

'I promise, Zurel, everything I told you yesterday is true.' I swallow. 'There *is* more that I need to explain . . . I just have to speak with Mr Thomson and then we — '

She twists her head in one resolute shake.

— I don't believe you. I don't believe anything you say.

She swipes her screen and turns her back. Drums and bass beat out the rhythm of my failure.

I have to rescue this; rescue her.

But I have no idea how.

* * *

'So, she's up in her room?' Marty drums a finger on the counter.

'Yes. With the dog. She doesn't want to see me. She's still very upset.'

'Well that's understandable.' He shakes his head and sighs. 'Shall I go and speak to her?'

My eyes flick up to his and instantly bounce back, as if he's switched on some kind of force field. 'You and I should probably talk first.'

He looks at me then. The kind of look that burns me to the core.

'No more bullshit, Susan. Is Zurel at risk? From these . . . edits?'

'Not according to her doctors. Although I'm still waiting for her latest results.' I bury my face in my mug. 'You've been on it, then? The 'hack app'?'

He grimaces. 'Why on earth would I do that?'

'I just thought . . . after you heard . . .' I squeeze the cup. 'It's only my name on there. With links, for those that want to burrow into the gory details. The entire world can read about what diseases run in our family, what our risk factors are. Not that any of *that* matters.'

For the uninitiated, the procedure looks like a three-parent baby, using a sperm donor. Except this intervention took place after fertilisation.

He frowns. 'You should have called the school and warned us. We could have taken Zurel out early, kept her away from that . . . mob.'

'The app only went live after lunch. They must have farmed it out to their networks beforehand. Mobilised all their vicious little troops.'

Marty trudges to the window. 'Was it worth it, all this trouble? Whatever's on there?'

I bite my lip. I almost wish he *had* gone on the app. So I didn't have to be the one to tell him.

'One moment.' I tiptoe into the hall and check the stairs. Zurel's door is closed. I pad back into the kitchen and shut the door.

'I told Zurel about the medical edits yesterday. As we agreed.'

'Yes. She said.'

I meet his cool gaze. 'But that's not where it ends.'

He shoves his hands in his pockets. 'I figured.'

I take a breath. 'Before I start, I want you to understand, this was about becoming a mother. Saving my marriage. I didn't mean to . . . ' My voice falters. 'I don't expect you to forgive me . . . '

'Shall I make it easier for you?' His tone sharpens. 'Is Steve really Zurel's father?'

I stare at him. 'How did you — ?'

'The tech may have moved on, Susan, but as far as I know, pregnancy still lasts nine months.'

I swallow. 'How long have you known?'

296

'I had my suspicions, when you first told me, in the canteen. I dismissed them. Now it feels like a part of me has always known.'

'I'm sorry, Marty. Truly, I am ——'

He cuts me off with a violent shake of his head. 'You should have asked me. Instead of using me like that. Like some . . . unofficial sperm donor.'

'It wasn't like that, I swear ——'

'Oh, come on, Susan. You never spoke about it, but it was obvious. I saw the way you looked at the other mums. There was a sadness to you. You wore it like a coat, it was strangely alluring.' His eyes meet mine. 'I never mentioned it because I figured it was too painful. As ever, I took your cue.'

Blood rushes into my face. 'Marty, you cannot think . . . I would *never* do that. It wasn't planned, I promise you.'

His shoulders slump. 'I don't know what to think, Susan.' He sighs. 'It's such a mess. What I still don't understand is what you did to her.'

I press my palm into the cold granite. Millions, maybe billions of years ago this worktop was magma, bubbling under the earth's crust. No humans, no bonobo chimpanzees. Not even barnacles. Just worms, sponges and jellyfish. Living short, uncomplicated lives.

'The consultant . . . the one you heard, on Zurel's recording . . . ' My voice is barely more than a whisper. 'He made changes, to the paternal genes. To make her Steve's biological daughter.'

Marty doesn't stir. I want him to shout at me. I want him to rage.

A breath erupts. 'You *hacked* me? My DNA?'

'I didn't know if I'd ever get pregnant again. Steve

refused to get help. All I wanted was for us to be a family.'

'*Family?*' Now the anger comes. 'Is that what you call it?' He steps closer. 'Look around you, Susan. Where's your family now?'

I blink, hard. 'I'm going to tell Zurel the truth. All of it.'

'Well, you don't have much choice, do you?' he says bitterly. 'Soon, everyone will know.'

I shake my head. 'Your name isn't on any of the records. Nor is Steve's.'

'It doesn't matter; they'll figure it out somehow. And Zurel will blame me, even though I never knew.' His mouth stiffens. 'Just when she'd laid her trust in me. She'll be stranded. Again.'

We lapse into silence. The clock ticks off seconds. Maybe hours.

'Will you stay, while I speak to her?'

He doesn't look at me but gives a slow nod. 'For her sake.'

'Thank you.'

I traipse upstairs. My legs get heavier with each step. I wait outside her door and knock.

'Zurel? Can I come in?'

I gently push it open.

Her room is empty.

She's gone.

57

Susan

I call Zurel's phone; it goes straight to voicemail. We search the house, but I already know it's pointless. I try the location app, check Lola's tracker, but she's disabled both. I dash off a message:

Zurel, I love you. Just let me know you're safe.

'Can you try, Marty? She might respond, if it's from you.'

'Sure.'

I call Steve, for the tenth time. That goes straight to voicemail too. I suspect he's blocked my number.

'Where d'you think she's gone?' asks Marty.

I massage my brow. 'The woodland's a possibility . . .' I glance outside. 'Come on. We've two hours until it gets dark.'

As I grab my coat, I notice a leaflet on the doormat. I frown. The picture looks like the dissected parts of a chick that's hatched too soon.

Murdered at six days old.

'Behold, children are a heritage from the Lord, the fruit of the womb a reward.'

Marty peers over my shoulder. 'What's that?'

'Nothing.' I screw it up and shove it in my pocket.

We head out into the rain. The sky is leaden, blanketed by clouds the colour of dirty paintbrush water. My mind breaks loose, firing through my fears:

Zurel, cornered by protestors, haranguing her about her genes.

Zurel, collapsed in a country lane, cars speeding past.

We reach the gate to the woodland. The trees loom, dark and silent.

'Zurel? Lola?'

I whistle for the dog and wait, praying for the quick pant, the scatter of paws.

Nothing. Only rain, spitting on leaves.

We squelch along the path, heads bowed. A boot thuds; Marty lurches forward and swears.

We reach the hazel fence panels by a small enclosure of ash and oak. I whistle again. A blackbird raises its rat-a-tat alarm.

We both check our phones.

Marty glances up. 'Which way?'

'Well, we can do a shorter circuit in the lower woodland. Or take a longer route round the edge.' I frown. 'The shorter one probably makes sense — we've a chance of catching her. Assuming she's here.'

The rain's coming down heavier now, and muddy rivulets stream down the path. All of a sudden there's a patter of feet racing towards us. I scan the trees. A silver retriever flies past, tongue lolling; its owner sloshes along behind.

'Excuse me? You haven't seen a young girl, have you? Walking a copper-cream collie cross?'

The owner looks up. She has a kind face, keen brown eyes. She shakes her head. 'Sorry, haven't seen a single person since I set off. Is she lost?'

Such a simple question. It robs me of breath.

'Not lost, exactly.' Marty steps in. 'What we call 'an unauthorised absence'.'

Marty gives her his contact details and we press on.

After a few minutes, he clears his throat. 'She spoke

to me, you know. Zurel.'

I spin round. 'Really? When?'

'This afternoon. At the end of our session. Just a couple of sentences, but still . . .'

'That's . . . incredible.' Despite everything, my heart lifts.

He takes a breath. 'Did it ever cross your mind that I might want a relationship with her? Or Zurel with me?'

My eyes drop to my feet. 'It wasn't possible, Marty. You know that.'

'Not then, maybe. But now everything's changed.'

I don't say anything.

'I could apply to the courts, you know.'

My head swerves.

'I was her biological father. And we had sex; it wasn't some test tube job. I'm pretty sure that gives me a case.'

'You wouldn't . . . would you?'

His voice is deceptively calm. 'Given what she's gone through, me having a more active role in her life might be a good idea.'

I clench my fingers. 'Even if I say yes, Steve will never agree.'

'It may not be his decision.'

I stop dead. 'What?'

'You have no idea, do you? About the legal repercussions of what you've done?'

The rain blasts my face.

'We had a situation with a family at school, so I became quite the expert. If Steve didn't know about your treatment, or give consent, then he arguably has no legal obligation to Zurel. And unless ours was some private donor arrangement, which you

301

categorically deny, I've no legal status either, without a fight.' He pauses. 'What you've effectively done, in the eyes of the law, is make her fatherless.'

I try to process Marty's words. Steve wouldn't abandon his responsibilities, would he? I think of him, hovering by the banister. Such anguish in his face.

Marty sighs. 'Look, Susan, I'm not interested in a protracted court battle. That's the last thing Zurel needs. I want what's best for her. And whatever *she* wants.'

We finish the loop without seeing another soul. The light is beginning to fade. Mossy logs morph into the skeletons of long-dead creatures. Knots and burrs on bark become the symbols of a forgotten tribe.

Marty checks his phone. 'Still nothing. What now?'

'Home. And if she's not there . . . the police.'

We wander back in silence. But as the house comes into view, my heart skips.

'The lights are on.'

I sprint to the door, finger trembling over the sensor.

'Zurel? Zurel, where are you?'

I kick off my boots and rush into the kitchen. There's a dull thump upstairs. I dash to the landing.

Steve appears in our bedroom doorway. I swallow.

'I thought Zurel was with you.' His words are sullen. 'She's not answering her phone.'

I shake my head. 'I . . . I tried calling you. I left messages — '

'I turned off my phone after I saw that post.' He glowers at me. 'I just turned it back on, and it went mental.'

I try to meet his gaze. His love has congealed into an icy, matt blue.

302

'There was an incident at pick-up. With another parent. It wasn't pleasant.'

He exhales. 'Jesus . . .'

'And now Zurel's taken off with the dog, Lord knows where. We've been up in the woodland looking for her.'

"We'?'

Steve peers down the stairs. Marty's sitting on a chair in the hall, wiping the mud off his boots.

Steve frowns. 'Isn't that the SEND guy?'

Marty looks up. His face stiffens.

'Yes.' Somehow, I find the words. 'He's the man I slept with.'

58
Zurel

It was much further than I thought, on foot; we're both drenched. Not that Lola minded, of course. To her this is one big adventure. But not all adventures end well. I've never left home before. I've never broken in anywhere, either.

I glance at the rickety stone wall. It shouldn't be that difficult; it's not very high. The hard part will be sneaking up that woman's drive — the one who scowls at you if you so much as look at her. There's a big yellow moon, so at least I can see where I'm going. But so can she. And that gravel won't help.

I tread carefully, spreading my weight, but Lola is pulling, keen to investigate new smells. A security light comes on, blinding me, and I sprint to the shadows, Lola racing alongside. I make it round the side of the house and onto the lawn at the back.

The wall looks a lot higher from this side.

Lola jumps first; she clears it easily. As I clamber over, the stones rattle like marbles in a jar; my rucksack catches and one thuds to the ground. I drop to a crouch. Lola's panting at me, ears pricking up and then flattening back down, unsure if this is a game. I stroke her neck and whisper to her.

I inch along the wall, count to three and make a dash for the key safe. I spin the dials to match the numbers to the code and press the button. The lid flips open.

We're in.

I knew Lola would like the Peace Pod.

She commences a thorough inspection, sniffing every table and chair, while I try to find the setting for the heating. I can't stop shivering: I wish I could have brought my duvet, but there wasn't room. I set to work on our den, sliding the chairs to the walls and pushing the tables together. I lay a small blanket and towel underneath and scatter a few biscuits for Lola. My stomach rumbles. Sadly, only one of us has snacks; the kitchen was out of bounds.

Lola polishes off her food and snuggles into me: a furry hot water bottle. I bury my arm in her ruff and think of those women outside school. Even now, Mum can't tell me the truth. They were looking at me as if I had some kind of infectious disease. My chest tightens. It feels like a can of pop, all shaken up, that's about to explode.

I wish Dad was here. I called him earlier, but it went to voicemail. She's ruined that, too.

I switch on my phone. Fifteen missed calls and five messages. I ignore the ones from Mum and play Dad's:

'Where are you, Zurel? We're worried. Message me, as soon as you get this.'

He still sounds a bit angry.

I skip to Mr Thomson's:

'Zurel, I've spoken with your mum. None of this is your fault. We just need to know you're safe. We'll find a way through this.'

My fingers hover over the screen.

Dad? Or Mr Thomson?

— I'm at the Peace Pod. Don't bring Mum. Please. Come alone.

59
Zurel

I hear Mr Thomson before I see him. The quiet knock breaks into my dream. It's only when Lola scurries to her feet with a low woof that I wake. I sit bolt upright and bang my head on the table. A tall grey shape is looming against the glass. My heart thuds. Then I remember. It thuds again.

I scramble out and unlock the door.

He holds up his hand. 'Hey, Zurel.'

His gaze drops to Lola, who bundles into his legs. 'Well, I've heard of cat burglars, but this is new.' He ruffles her head. 'Mind if I turn on the lights?'

He flicks a switch and squints at me. I notice a purply-red swelling, under his right eye.

He surveys our table-den. 'You've certainly made it homely. Maybe we should try it this way one lunch-time, what do you reckon?'

He gazes at me with a strange intensity. His smile fades.

On instinct, I pull out my screen. And put it down.

He takes a breath. 'Your mum's worried sick, you know.' He pauses. 'And your dad. I should ring them. Just to let them know you're safe.'

I squeeze my fingers and notice a line of dirt trapped under my nails. 'Did she tell you? What really happened to me?'

His mouth tightens. 'Yes.'

'All of it?'

'I believe so.'

'Am I going to die?' My voice sounds very small.

He leans forward. 'No, Zurel.'

'How do you know?'

He exhales, long and slow. 'Because you have regular checks and that's what the doctors told her.'

'But what if they're lying? Or she is?' Now I'm blinking back tears.

'I don't think she is lying, Zurel. Not about that.' He swallows.

I pull Lola closer. 'Will you tell me? About the other changes?'

His face screws up, as if he's in pain. 'I think your mum has to be the one to do that.'

I shake my head. 'I don't want to see her.'

He puts his hand on my arm. 'I know. I understand how difficult this is, Zurel. But it's important you hear what she has to say. You don't need to respond. Just listen.'

I shake my head again. 'It's always her version of things. Never the whole truth.'

'It will be this time. I give you my word.'

I glare at him. It's not really a glare, though, my eyes are too tired.

'I'll be right here. She doesn't even need to come in. And, once your mum's finished, there are a few things I'd like to say, too.' His face pinches.

It really must be bad.

'What do you say, then, Zurel?'

Lola sniffs me and licks my face.

'She'll stay outside?' He nods. 'I don't even have to look at her?'

'Not if you don't want to.'

I stare at my hands. They may be a bit grubby, but

they look like any other girl's.

'Alright.'

* * *

Mr Thomson sits on one of the chairs by the wall. I hunch next to Lola on the floor. She stretches her jaws wide in a yawn, no clue of what's to come. Mr Thomson dials Mum who picks up on the first ring. He talks quietly to her, explaining where we are, and what we've agreed. I hear the shape of her questions, breathy and urgent.

Then Mr Thomson says: 'You're where?' and stands up, and my heart beats even faster.

He turns away from me, and his shoulders rise and fall. He hisses: 'For God's sake, Susan,' and glances at me. Then he says: 'OK, I'll talk to her.'

He pockets his phone and frowns. 'Turns out your mother has been playing detective. Despite explicit instructions to wait at home for my call, unbeknownst to me, she followed me here.'

I bite down on my lip.

'And now she's stuck outside, by the gates.'

My eyes meet his. He shakes his head, and something about his expression and how ridiculous this is collides with how nervous I am, and almost makes me laugh.

Almost.

He sighs. 'So. Shall I go and get her?'

I squeeze Lola and nod.

'Zurel, I . . . ' He stops. 'Whatever happens, I want you to know . . . I really do think you are amazing.'

And there it is again, that look. As if he's the one that's been hurt.

308

A tear escapes, and I turn away.

The door closes softly behind him.

★ ★ ★

Lola hears them before I do. Her ears prick up and she shoots to her feet.

Then I hear Mr Thomson's voice: stern and low: 'Remember what I said. *Don't* come in unless Zurel says so.'

The door opens with a blast of cold air. I keep my back turned. I can hear Mum panting, as if she's been running; the whip of Lola's tail against a chair.

'Everything's as we agreed, Zurel. Your mum's just outside.' Mr Thomson squeezes my arm and takes a seat by the wall. Lola stares expectantly at the door.

I hug my knees and think of the sparrow families, all snug in their nests.

She starts with things I already know. How she longed for a baby, and how difficult it was. How all she ever wanted was a family. Her voice reminds me of the time I fell off my scooter, her words desperately trying to reassure me, but her fear blazing through.

And then she tells me about the night she met somebody else. The night she forgot she was married. My breath goes still. And she says that this was the moment I was created. And before it even has time to sink in, she tells me that Dad isn't my real dad, not my first dad, but the creepy doctor made him into my father, before I was born.

And it's as if she's pushed me out of a very high window, and I've hit the ground and am shattering into tiny pieces.

I don't hear anything after that. Just static. A signal,

309

about to drop.

And then she's saying how sorry she is, and how much she loves me and Dad, and how this doesn't change anything. But it already has. I think she's crying. And even though I'm desperate to turn round, I don't.

And then she tells me the man she met that night, the man who made me, was Mr Thomson.

And I think I'm going to be sick.

★ ★ ★

Everything I thought I knew is un-known. Everything I am or was, is a lie.

My dad wasn't my real dad.

Mr Thomson was. But now isn't.

And *he* did it. She let that doctor loose on me.

My mother — the person supposed to love you best of all.

I am a freak. An experiment.

Nobody can ever love me because I will never be a normal child.

★ ★ ★

'Zurel? Zurel: please, listen to me.'

Just the sound of his voice makes my skin crawl. Lola gives a high-pitched whine and paws at me.

I cling to the window ledge and gulp the cool night air. My eyes are wide, like the cows in those films about the old days, before they fired bolts into their heads and cut their throats.

'Your mother only told me this afternoon. I didn't know, I promise you. I didn't know.'

I can't look at him. I can't look at either of them.

Mum's still pleading with me; I think she's come in. He snaps at her: 'Susan, *please*. Just give us a minute.'

I stare at the shadow girl in the glass. I watch her bring her hand to her face and pinch her cheek. I wait for it to hurt. To feel something.

Maybe I am one of those cows. Maybe they fired a bolt into my head so it wouldn't hurt when they did this.

Lola nudges my palm with her nose.

'Zurel, I know you're confused right now. I know you're upset, and I don't blame you.' He takes one step closer. 'The dad who's loved you and looked after you since you were born — he's still your dad, that doesn't change. But there's a connection between us, you and me. It's always been there. I've felt it. Haven't you?'

There's a sharp twinge in my chest. It swells to a throb.

'What I'm trying to say is, it doesn't matter what some doctor may have done. The girl we all care about is standing right here. That girl, Zurel, is you.'

Now the tears start, and they won't stop.

We can't have naturals and unnaturals in the same class . . .

Who is the real Zurel?

The one she was in the beginning? Or the one she is now?

Genetically speaking, to all intents and purposes, she's completely normal . . .

My hands tingle, as if they've been out in the snow.

Lola's whines become fainter as the buzzing in my head builds to a roar.

Remarkable, really. Given the extent of the edits.

I can't catch my breath.
Stick drawings of Mr Thomson flash past.
The baby photo of me in Mum and Dad's room.
That doctor's face, looming over mine.
I'm trapped beneath the ice . . .
Sinking down with the fishes.
Until there's no light. No air.
No sound.
Nothing, at all.

Heathrow flights grounded as protests spread.

Demonstrations by anti-interventionists step up after fertility clinic hacks.

Sonia Iqbal, Science Correspondent, *Guardian* Online

Protestors against genetic intervention have caused transport chaos across Britain and other European countries, closing motorways and grounding flights.

Just after 5am this morning, demonstrators invaded the M4 near Heathrow, chaining themselves to crash barriers and setting up tents on the carriageway to prevent passengers reaching the airport. Shortly afterwards, a drone was seen flying across Heathrow's perimeter fence, towing a banner reading 'Eugenics airlines — you're grounded'.

All flights in and out of Heathrow were immediately suspended. The protestors were part of the anti-intervention network Genome Defence Alliance (GDA).

Meanwhile, a separate group, Fruit of the Womb, tried to block the M56 near Manchester airport just before 8am, but retreated after a lorry and two cars collided as they swerved to avoid drones that the demonstrators had set off. Four people travelling in the vehicles were injured, none seriously.

The actions mark

the start of a world-wide 'week of protest' in response to the worsening health crisis attributed to unsafe fertility treatments. Protests have struck more than one hundred cities across Europe and America, with campaigners mainly targeting transport hubs and fertility clinics. The GDA claims many more protests are planned, sparked by yesterday's illegal publication of stolen patient records, including personal details and treatment histories for an estimated forty thousand patients resident in the UK.

Cybercrime units in police forces globally are trying to track down the hackers who are believed to have links to a far-right anti-interventionist group. Meanwhile, fears grow for the privacy and safety of patients and their families.

60

Zurel

Noises slide in and out.

Beeping.

The rattle of wheels.

A baby, crying.

My eyes open, just a crack. Wild creatures wander along the walls: spotted giraffes with long eyelashes, grinning hippos with shiny teeth. A train of elephants hold each other's tails in their trunks.

I shut my eyes, but the animals march on through the jungle, changing colours as they trot.

'Hey, Zurel. Good morning.'

A woman's voice I don't recognise.

'If you can hear me, just squeeze my finger.'

Warm skin on my hand. A scent of something bitter. I squeeze, ever so lightly.

'That's great.' She puts something in my lap. 'I've brought you a screen. So you can let us know how you're doing. If there's anything you want.'

How am I doing? I might float off into that jungle any second, with the giraffes.

'You're probably still feeling a little woozy. We gave you some medicine to help you rest.'

The bed sags.

'Can you open your eyes for me, Zurel?'

I'm not sure I can.

My eyelids flutter against the light. A woman with twinkly blue eyes smiles at me. She's wearing a

315

pale-blue shirt and trousers. I peer past her at a long, bright room full of beds, separated by curtains. In each bed lies a child.

'You're in the children's hospital, Zurel. You were brought in last night.'

Some of them are talking to adults, some are on screens, some are still asleep. Wiggly lines and numbers flash on monitors above their heads.

The nurse rests her hand over mine. 'I want you to know that you're completely safe here. We're going to look after you until you feel better.'

A few beds have metal stands holding bags attached to tubes that curl under the bedcovers like monkey tails.

'We think you had something called a panic attack. Have you ever had one of those before?'

I look at her and shake my head.

'Don't worry, panic attacks don't cause you any lasting harm, but they can feel very frightening. Your body moves into a sort of emergency mode. Shuts down certain functions, a bit like a computer. You might feel dizzy, or a little sick. It can affect your breathing.' She smiles. 'The good news is they don't last long.'

A loud wail pierces the ward, followed by a crash. My eyes shoot round. It came from a cubicle with all the curtains pulled.

'It's alright,' she whispers. 'Routine injection. Some of the kids are better with needles than others.'

A cleaning bot glides towards it with a sanitation trolley.

The nurse squints at the monitor. 'How are you feeling now?' She does a thumbs-up or thumbs-down, like Mr Thomson does.

And I remember.

I turn my face into the pillow and grip the sheet.

'Not great, huh?'

A python from that jungle has wrapped itself around my body and is squeezing, tighter and tighter. Any second now, there will be a sharp crack.

'OK, Zurel, let's do some breathing exercises together. I'll count, and you breathe with me, OK?'

She tells me to inhale while she counts for four, then to hold for two, then exhale for four. We do this five times.

'Is that a bit better?'

Nothing is better. But I can breathe.

'That's a little exercise you can do by yourself, if you feel anxious. It just slows everything down.'

She touches my hand. 'The doctors will be round later. They're just running a few more tests to make sure everything's back to normal before we discharge you. And then your parents can take you home.'

I seize the screen.

— Just Dad. I only want to see my dad. Not anyone else.

Apart from Lola, that is. But I'm pretty sure dogs aren't allowed in hospitals.

— Do you know where my dog is? She was with me last night.

The nurse smiles. 'Is that Lola?' I nod. 'Your teacher told us you'd ask. He said not to worry; he dropped Lola with his girlfriend on the way to the hospital. I think your mum is going to pick her up later.'

I think of Lola with Mr Thomson. Then I think of Mum with Mr Thomson, and the sickness wells back up.

'Zurel, a woman from children's services is going to

317

visit you this morning. She just wants to ask you a few questions. To see if she might be able to help.'

I stare at the curtains. Tigers pounce across a blue forest. I imagine I'm there, with Lola, stalking through the trees. Away from people. And hospitals. And schools.

'Now, how about some breakfast? Cereal? Toast? What about a chocolate muffin?' She waggles her eyebrows. 'No? I tell you what, I'll pop one on your tray with some juice, in case you feel like it later. Back in a jiffy.'

My eyes skitter to the girl opposite, who is wolfing down her cereal, eyes glued to a screen. On her table is a hand-drawn card saying: *Get Well Soon.*

I think of my Mother's Day card.

The faces I drew, again and again, trying to get them just right.

All this time, I worried about having some terrible illness. But this is worse.

Because diseases can be cured.

61
Susan

We sit across the table from each other, stiff with silence. I stare into my cup. Carmel stirs her coffee.

'How many hours d'you reckon we've spent in this kitchen?' The spoon tinkles against her glass. 'Must add up to a good few months.' She sniffs. 'Maybe years.'

I wrap the dressing gown a little tighter. Not much point getting dressed.

Her eyes dart to mine. 'You must be exhausted; I can't believe you're up.'

I exhale a long, slow breath. 'Couldn't sleep.'

They were waiting for me outside the hospital last night, the media vultures. I had to shunt my way through with my jacket over my head while they shouted obscene questions and rammed their mics in my face. They'd even sent in a drone cam. It was Carmel who rescued me: she'd seen the posts. I asked her to drop me at a hotel, but she insisted on bringing me back here. I couldn't go home. Not with Steve.

'Anyway, I need to call the hospital. Once the doctors have made their rounds.'

I think of Zurel's hunched back, and my eyes clamp shut. I have to breathe through it, the pain. It's like someone's hollowing me out with a molten spoon, lump by lump.

Carmel runs her tongue over her lip. 'Did they tell you anything last night?'

'Only that Zurel must have had extreme anxiety to trigger an attack like that.' I blink hard. 'The final tribute to my mothering skills: I've medically traumatised my daughter.'

Carmel opens her mouth and closes it.

'I know this doesn't help, Susan, but I really am so sorry.' Her forehead creases. 'I never thought . . . I didn't mean to . . .' Her words collapse. 'I know what I did is unforgiveable. I should never have betrayed your trust.'

A squirrel scampers across the lawn, tail flicking, and I think of those squirrels in the park, before we met Stakhovsky. Carmel, blithely encouraging me, saying I'd be a fool not to take up his offer. Pressing me into the lift.

'So, how come you haven't been outed, then?' I say, bitterly. 'Or are gagging orders another little investor perk?'

She swallows. 'Hardly. I'm sure they'll have a go at some point, once they make the connection. The app may have been taken down but the data's still out there.' She risks a glance. 'We're taking precautions. We used a different name to register Leo for treatment.'

Leo's been admitted to a mental-wellbeing centre. Given the recent surge in cases, he was lucky to get in.

My face thaws. 'How's he doing?'

'We're not over it, not by a long stretch. Whatever 'it' is.' She rubs her forehead. 'But at least he's in the right hands. Under proper supervision.' Her mouth trembles. 'Getting the right care.'

I think of Zurel, alone at the hospital. The agony of watching her collapse.

'I take it you've told the school you're not going in.'

320

I expel a breath. 'No need. My head just messaged me. Suggesting I take a 'temporary leave of absence'.'

Carmel sits up. 'What?'

'Reporters went there this morning, stirred things up. Not that things needed much stirring. I suspect Helen Tomlins had a hand in that. Funnily enough, parents aren't exactly queuing up to have their children taught by 'FrankenMummy'.'

That's what they've dubbed me, the newsfeeds. When I saw the headlines this morning I wept:

FrankenMummy redesigns her ten-week-old baby.

'You mustn't look at those articles, Susan. They're poison. They're not interested in the terminal diseases that have been prevented, the edits that didn't go wrong . . .' She shakes her head. 'We should sue those damned news agencies for defamation. Misuse of private information. Outrageous, the bilge they're putting out.'

'Some of the posts . . .' I shudder. 'They're so full of hatred. The thought of Zurel seeing them — '

'I'm sure the hospital's keeping her away from all that.'

'I really hope so.' I swallow. 'Things were difficult before, but now . . . Now Zurel hates me, too.'

Carmel leans across the table. 'She doesn't hate you, Susan. You're still her mother. She needs time, away from this circus, to process what's happened, work out what she feels.' She sighs. 'I just hope Steve isn't making things worse.'

Another memory ambushes me, and I cringe. 'He actually punched Marty, you know. In the face. I couldn't believe it.'

'Oh my God . . . '

I dig my fingers into my temples. 'He's like this

321

fireball of anger . . . He said I wasn't fit to be a mother. That they might move away, the two of them, somewhere new.'

Carmel jumps up. 'He can't do that. He can't take Zurel away from you.'

'According to him, he can . . . ' My face contorts. 'He told me I'd not only endangered her physically, I'd put her mental health at risk. I could lose her, Carmel. I could lose everything . . . '

Carmel wraps her arm round me. 'But they haven't found anything medically wrong with her, have they? Apart from the anxiety?'

'Not yet, no . . . ' I look at my hands. 'Maybe it's what I deserve. After what I've put them through.'

Carmel scoffs. 'Well, Steve's not exactly a saint, is he?'

'What do you mean?'

She arches her eyebrows. 'If he hadn't been such a control freak, this whole thing might never have happened . . . I mean, he was the one who stopped you getting any help. He put you in an impossible situation. Not to mention that little drink problem . . . '

I twist the belt on the dressing gown. I don't want to go to war.

'Well, when it comes down to it, it'll be Zurel who decides. And, according to Steve, she doesn't even want to spend a minute with me, let alone the rest of her childhood.'

I don't believe you. I don't believe anything you say . . .

'Honey, her whole world just crashed around her. She can't be expected to know what she wants. In any case, she's not old enough, legally, to decide.' Carmel squeezes my hands. 'Come on — you're not going to give up that easily, are you?'

I meet Carmel's gaze. 'It's not a case of giving up, Carmel. I love Zurel, but I've made enough shitty decisions on her behalf. If that's what she really wants, I'll have to respect it.'

Carmel frowns but she holds her tongue.

I think of Mokosh. Did she foresee this, all those years ago, with her empty, white eyes? Did she spin the thread that made this happen?

No.

Not Mokosh. Not Carmel, or Steve. Not even Stakhovsky.

There's only one person to blame.

And that's me.

62
Zurel

Something brushes my hand. My eyes snap open. Dad is leaning over my bed. He's wearing jeans and that baggy old jumper that's a bit scratchy: his weekend clothes. But it's not a weekend.

I lunge at him and fold my arms around his neck. He smells of coffee. And shaving cream. And home.

He gives my back little pats. 'It's OK,' he whispers. 'Daddy's here.'

His voice is crackly, as if he's got a cold. My tears trickle down his neck. He starts to pull away, but I cling tighter. I need him, to stop me spinning. To remind me, who I am.

He peels my arms off his neck and sets me back on the pillow. 'How are you feeling? Better for a rest?'

I scan his face: his eyes look a bit puffy, and there are patches of stubble on his cheeks.

My throat draws tight as I think of the stick drawings.

Mum would never let Dad go out like that . . .

'So, the good news is, all the scans and tests have come back completely normal.' He tries his cheery voice. 'So you don't need to worry, Zurel; there's nothing wrong. I should be able to bring you home today.'

He smiles, but it has cracks in it, like concrete.

I have a sudden urge to point at my hair and my eyes and say: see, Dad? I don't look anything like *him.*

Dad's gaze locks onto the tray-table at the end of my bed.

'As for what your mother told you . . . '

Dad's hands cling to his knees.

' . . . We won't ever mention that again.'

I look at Dad's whiskery face, his sore eyes. We're like those refugees on the news, clutching bits of boats in the ocean. Trying not to drown.

His eyes flick up to mine and away. I notice the dirt still buried in my nails from yesterday.

'You've always been my daughter, Zurel. And you always will be.'

He shifts in his seat and nods. But it's like when Mrs Crowther teaches us about God. She doesn't really believe those stories.

I am a freak. An experiment.

Nobody can ever love me because I will never be a normal child.

63

Susan

There are bad mothers in nature, as well as good ones. There are mothers who eat their own offspring or abandon them from birth. And then there are the mothers who start out caring for their babies but destroy them in other ways.

I clench the table with both hands, digging my fingers into the wood. Steve sits opposite, his face angled away from mine, like dogs do when they pretend the other dog's not there. A wall screen flashes headlines about the latest genetic doping scandal: more Russian and American athletes banned for tampering with their genomes.

It was Steve who suggested the café at the pottery, even though he knows the risk of being out in public. Thankfully, no one's recognised me. Yet. I watch the mothers herding their children along the cake counter and my chest aches. Zurel loves this place, with its homemade pastries and delicate china cups.

It's been three days since I've spoken to her.

I force a breath. 'So. What did they say?'

Steve rolls his tongue around his mouth as if he's about to spit. 'They think she has adjustment disorder.'

I swallow. 'What's that?'

He finally looks at me. 'Basically, PTSD.'

An elderly lady shuffles past with trembling arms, her tray laden with crockery. A service bot rushes to assist her.

'They've suggested she sees a therapist. I've said yes.'

I nod. My eyes are stinging, but I refuse to cry. 'Right. And they're certain there's . . . nothing else?'

'What, like depression? Cancer?' His eyes flare.

'Please, Steve . . . I couldn't get hold of anyone at the hospital.'

His jaw stiffens. 'Luckily for you, no.'

I release the table. Blood flows back into my fingers.

'And what about school?'

'Well, obviously, she's not going back *there*. They break up soon anyway.' He sniffs. 'I've hired a tutor bot for the summer term. Until we work out what's next.'

I run my tongue over my lips. 'It's her last year there . . . She'll want to say goodbye to her friends — '

He swivels round. 'You have no idea, do you? We're virtually prisoners in our own home. I've had to hire a securi-bot to keep the drones away from the house and stop the wackos posting their filth through our door. Even then, they're waiting for us, like bloody hyenas, down the road.'

'I'm so sorry, Steve . . . '

'Yeah, well, I'm taking Zurel away for Easter, somewhere they won't find us. A few days by the sea will do us both good. Give me time to think. Come up with options on the house.'

My heart thuds. 'Steve, we have to talk about this. I agreed to a temporary separation for all our sakes, but this arrangement, it's not permanent.'

His eyes narrow. 'Isn't it?'

'I can't believe that's what she really wants. I'm her

mother, she needs me.'

'Oh, yes. Sorry, I forgot. The mother who slept with another bloke and then let some psycho-doctor inject God knows what into her baby, to cover it up.'

'She's still my daughter. Zurel's only eleven; she's just a child.'

Steve pushes his cup out of the way and leans forward. 'You should have thought of that before, shouldn't you?'

A flock of Canada geese honk past the window in formation, like a swarm of drones.

'Let's just cut to the chase, shall we? I want a divorce and I'm going for custody. And you'd better not fight me, or I'll press charges for DNA theft. Or, should I say, 'thefts'?'

His fists are balled on the table. A woman at a table opposite gives me a worried glance.

I clasp my hands to stop them shaking. 'I know I did a lot of things wrong. I accept that. But do you know why I did them?'

He huffs.

'Because I thought that pregnancy might be our only chance. It didn't matter to you how unhappy I was; you wouldn't let me get help. You insisted we kept trying and failing, over and over.' I swallow. 'And I let you bully me into it.'

His face pushes into mine. 'Oh, so it's my fault now, is it? The one-night-stand? The genetics freak show?' He shakes his head. 'You never could take responsibility for anything.'

The fear of him. It's always been there. But it's nothing compared to the fear of losing Zurel.

I meet his stare. 'I don't care how long it takes. How long I have to try. I will never give up on my daughter.'

328

'Yeah, well, you can tell that to the court.' Steve pushes back his chair. 'Because she doesn't want you in her life. And nor do I.'

He stands up and grabs his coat, but then he turns.

'Oh, I nearly forgot.' He reaches into his pocket. 'I have a gift for you. From Zurel.'

My heart lifts. A crack of light in this hopeless day.

A tiny plastic baby slides across the table. Its eyes open:

'Mummy, please don't change me. I'm perfect, as I am!'

64
Susan

I check the road again. No hacks loitering in the bushes, no drones skimming the pavement. Maybe, now the house is empty, they've finally moved on to some other poor family. In fact, the entire road seems deserted. The neighbours must either be away or cloistered inside.

It's Good Friday, which may or may not be auspicious. Originally a pagan festival, in honour of Eostre, the goddess of fertility, these days Easter symbolises resurrection and rebirth. Which could be what I need.

I slide out of the car and hurry to the door. It's just nine days since I packed my bag, but I already feel like an intruder. The letterbox has been sealed; a new key-operated mailbox juts from the wall. I press my finger to the sensor and the lock clicks back. At least Steve hasn't wiped my prints.

He's taken Zurel to a cottage in Lyme Regis — one of our favourite haunts. It kills me not being there, but hopefully the trip will be a distraction for Zurel. I like to picture her, racing the waves along the Cobb, or hunting for fossils while Lola sniffs for crabs. Quaffing chips from a greasy bag in the stone alcoves followed by ice hockey at the arcades. All the holiday rituals we've nurtured. Happening without me.

I open the door, and nearly topple a bin stuffed with paper. I frown. I fish out a crumpled pamphlet and immediately recognise the grotesque picture, the

330

red print. I think of Zurel innocently picking one up, and rip it into tiny pieces. I can't believe Steve just left them there.

Halfway down the hall, I stop. Something isn't right.

The walls are bare. Empty squares where the photo frames should be.

I try the lounge; only Zurel's school pictures and the photo screen remain. I turn it on and watch the images flick past. None are of me.

I rush upstairs to our bedroom. Zurel's baby portrait is still there, but not the one of the three of us. I look at the wardrobe, hesitate and open it. My clothes are gone. My drawers have been emptied. I've been exorcised from my own home.

I take a breath and open the door to the spare bedroom. My skin prickles. Skirts and shirts are heaped on the bed, tangled together, like bodies in a mass grave. Shoes have fallen at odd angles. A cardboard box is stuffed with underwear and toiletries; beside it is another, full of photo frames. I imagine Steve tearing through the house, ripping out all trace of me. Consigning my possessions to boxes, as if I've died.

I walk across the landing to Zurel's room.

Hers, at least, is as it should be. The little desk by the window laden with precious things she's found; the duvet covered with toys. I open her closet and run my fingers over her clothes. It's a physical pain, her absence. I wonder if she feels it, too.

I slump onto her bed and tears leak into my eyes. Teddy gazes at me.

'So, you didn't get to go, either?'

I cuddle the bear to me, inhaling her smell. I bought him for her fifth birthday, and she used to insist on taking him everywhere.

I curl my knees up to my chest. As I tug her pillow under my cheek, something catches my fingers. I slip my hand underneath and pull out a photo. It's Zurel and I, decorating the Christmas tree, two years ago. I'm holding a bauble she painted specially for me.

I slip the picture back, walk out onto the landing and stare up at the loft hatch. I use the metal pole to open the door and pull down the ladder. I climb the steps with growing trepidation. The loft is Steve's domain, not mine.

I shield my face from the dust with my sleeve. Lights spill onto rows of bio-plastic containers, lined up along the floor like coffins. Each one has a printed label on the front. I shuffle forward on my knees and crawl along the narrow space.

Baby Toys
Children's Books
Dive Gear

Everything is arranged in alphabetical order; Steve is as meticulous about storage as he is about everything else. It's not just the overspill of objects from our marriage; this loft harbours the vestiges of our lives from before. I reach the labels beginning with 'S' but can't see mine. I'm gripped by a sudden fear he's got rid of them, out of spite. I shunt the containers, less careful now, coughing as the dust flies up. And then I spot them. My handwriting, a little faded: *Susan's Things 1* and *Susan's Things 2*. Precious photo albums — of Mum and Dad's wedding, and when I was little. Family heirlooms and other relics that there wasn't room for or I couldn't quite throw away. I haul the boxes to the hatch. I'll ask Carmel if I can stow them at hers, just in case. But these are not why I'm here.

I've already seen it: the container just along from

332

mine. You can tell it's old, because it's made of bad plastic, the kind that never goes away.

Steve's Box.

This is all that remains of Steve's previous life, when he was with Katya. And before.

I remove the lid, and a musty smell seeps into my nostrils. I swallow. I'm crossing another line, but Steve's already violated this taboo.

I start to delve. I recognise a couple of sports trophies. A painting I never liked that used to hang in his flat. Framed photos: his graduation day, a wedding — not his. Old rugby programmes and concert tickets. A stack of digital prints. I flick through pictures of a younger Steve on the ski slopes, on a dive boat, at a conference. None of Katya.

I only ever glimpsed one photo of her with Steve, when we were at one of his friends for dinner: a group skiing shot. I remember how pretty she looked with her tanned face and bright green eyes. Steve broke all ties, wiped all evidence of her from his life. My stomach thuds.

Exactly as he plans to do with me.

I keep searching. It's a long shot, but all I need is one detail: a maiden name, a place of work, an old address. Steve was never one for social media, but I'm guessing she was. I unearth a couple of old passports and flip to the photos. Solemn Steves gaze back at me. I look at the stamps — part curiosity, part nostalgia; every country uses biometrics now. I'm about to put the books back, when I spot the handwriting on the last page. Listed under *Emergencies.*

The first contact details belong to his parents.

The second, to Katya Dabrowski.

65

Susan

The wine bottle sits on the table in front of me. I've only had one glass but I feel giddy. Twenty minutes, that's all it took, trawling social-media sites and search engines, where histories forever circle. Defunct marriages, lost jobs. Deceased people and pets. The only realm where we are eternal.

I grip the phone. It's taking much longer to pluck up the courage to actually call. This resurrection of a bitter past won't be welcome.

I pour a second glass. I'll only allow myself a sip after I've dialled.

It occurs to me, as the phone rings, that 5pm on Good Friday probably isn't the best time to call. Especially with an unrecognised number. She'll think I'm some sales bot, or a voice phisher on a scam. Does she even know Steve remarried?

It rings four times.

'Hello?'

I inhale. 'Er, hi. Is that Katya?'

A breath. 'Who is this?' Very stern.

My mettle wavers. Then I remember the photo under Zurel's pillow.

'My name is Susan. Susan Rawlins.'

A pause. 'Is this a joke? Sonya, is that you?'

'It's no joke. I'm Steve's wife. As in your ex.'

Silence.

I imagine her finger poised over the 'end' button.

So I add: 'But probably not for much longer.'

'How did you get my number?'

'A bit of online investigation. It was pretty easy, actually.' I suddenly realise how that sounds. 'I don't make a habit of it, I assure you.'

'So you're not *the* Susan Rawlins?'

'As it happens, yes. Her, too.'

There's a gasp. She barks a short laugh. 'Shit, maybe there is such a thing as karma.'

I decide to press on. 'I'm sorry to ring you out of the blue like this. You're probably wondering why I've called.'

'Actually, I'm wondering a lot of things. Not least, why you did what you did.'

'I'll get to that.' I swallow. 'But the reason I contacted you is because I intend to fight Steve for custody of my daughter. And I need to ask you some questions. About your marriage.'

She makes a sound between a cough and a laugh. 'Look, I've absolutely no desire to reopen that chapter in my life.' Her voice hardens. 'It took a long time to put it behind me. In any case, why on earth should I help someone like you?'

I bite my lip. 'I realise you owe me nothing . . . And you probably think I'm a monster, like everyone else . . . But there were circumstances people don't know about.'

She doesn't say anything. But she doesn't hang up.

'We had unexplained infertility. We'd been trying for four years . . . ' I squeeze the phone. 'My daughter's so precious to me. If Steve takes her, I don't think I could . . . I just don't know, what I'll do . . . '

She sighs. 'How many cycles did you go through? Before your fling?'

I clench my jaw. 'IVF cycles, you mean? None.'

'Sorry?'

'Steve didn't want to, after what you'd been through. We had to go it alone.'

There's a brief pause. 'But . . . surely, you must have had *some* treatment?'

'Steve wouldn't see any consultants. He was just too scarred by the whole IVF experience. So we were put out to grass.'

She makes another coughing sound. 'That can't be right. He had an issue. He knows he did. With his sperm.'

I frown. 'What? The doctor told us there were no problems in that area. I was there, at the meeting.'

'Hang on, did Steve just have the routine semen analysis?'

'I don't know, I think so . . . Whatever the doctor arranged.'

'So you didn't get referred?'

'No, like I said, Steve refused.'

'Jesus . . . I can't *believe* he did that.'

The hairs on the back of my neck stand up. 'What do you mean?'

'You'd better listen up.' She exhales. 'We started out, just like you. No problems showed up in the preliminary tests, but nothing happened. After two years, we went back and got referred. They did more tests. And that's when they discovered there was a problem with Steve's sperm.'

I stare at my glass.

'Routine analysis just examines the basics: sperm count, movement, shape. But there can be other issues, which only get picked up by more specialised tests.'

336

My hand reaches for the wine. 'Like what?'

'They call it 'sperm function'. Apparently, certain changes need to occur after ejaculation, so the sperm can penetrate and fertilise the egg. In Steve's case, those changes weren't happening. Which meant it was going to be extremely difficult to conceive naturally.'

My fingers tighten around the stem. 'So, you're telling me that Steve *knew* there was a problem all along?'

'Absolutely. It's why we had to use ICSI — you know, where they inject the sperm directly into the egg. I mean, nowadays, they could probably just engineer some healthy new sperm, but not back then.'

I stare at the fridge. Remember my pregnancy note.

'I'm sorry, Susan. Wow, I thought I had it bad.'

'But *why*?' I thump the table as tears spill down my face. 'Why would he do that?'

Katya sighs. 'Maybe he just couldn't face telling you. Going through the humiliation of it all again.' She takes a breath. 'No matter what I said, how often I tried to reassure him, that diagnosis rocked him to the core. I mean, there was stuff going on with both of us — you know how it gets. I never blamed him, though. I used to nag him about joining a men's group, like my fertility forum, to get some support. But he wouldn't. He didn't want to discuss it with anybody. Not even me.'

I think of all those big fat negatives. Steve consoling me, telling me it would happen. When he knew the odds were stacked against us. How could he? How *could* he?

I wipe my face. 'But . . . didn't he want to have a baby?'

'Oh, I think he did, desperately. But only if it was his.'

337

My head throbs.

'After our last round failed,' she continues, 'the consultant asked if we'd consider using a sperm donor. When we got home Steve went off the deep end. He said he'd never use a donor, no matter what. Called the consultant all kinds of names, saying she had no right to bring it up. He said when he had a child, it would be his own, and we just needed to keep trying.'

My hand curls into my fist. I think of my father.

'That was when things really went downhill. I mean, he'd always been a bit over-protective, but he was way worse. It was like he didn't trust me anymore. He started asking me questions about where I was going, what I was spending money on. He got weirdly jealous of my friends. At one point, he even tried to persuade me to jack in my job, saying it was too stressful, and it was affecting our chances.'

A shiver travels down my spine.

All that guilt I've carried. All the risks I took.

'And then, of course, the drinking started. That's when I knew I had to leave.'

I blink at the phone. '*You* left?'

'Well, yeah . . . God, what has he been telling you?'

'He said you started looking into egg donors behind his back. And that was when he knew it was over.'

She mutters an expletive. 'That's bordering on delusional.'

I think of Zurel, stranded with Steve in Lyme. And I know what I must do.

'How did you manage it, Katya? Find the strength to leave?'

'I don't know. It was like, suddenly, the blinkers came off. I realised I didn't want to be with him anymore. Or have his child. So I left. Two years later I met Pete. No pressure, no expectations. Six months after that I was pregnant with Charlie.'

I stare at Zurel's poem.

HOPE IS . . .

For the past ten days, it's felt as if someone's been punching me, continually, inside. And now the bruises are swelling over my organs like purple roses.

I take a long, slow breath. 'So, Katya. Will you help me?'

There's a rush of air. 'Susan, whatever the fuck you need, it's yours.'

66
Zurel

The sea thumps the walls and froths up rocks — a seething surge of green. Its spray whips my face as Lola charges back and forth, chasing gulls on the sand. Blue and white sails race across the harbour as if they're about to smash into the cliffs. As I turn, a wave bursts over the wall and gives me an icy slap. Any other year, I would have dodged it. I spit the salt from my tongue. There's worse things than getting wet.

I found a fossil on the beach yesterday, when we went rock-pooling. It was only small but the pattern was really clear. When we go home, I'm going to put it on my desk, with my collection. Although Dad's been saying the two of us may need to find a new home.

I wander back along the Cobb and clamber down the wonky steps, past the alcoves where families are eating fish and chips. The seagulls eye me warily as they wait.

We usually have chips in those alcoves, when we come.

I wouldn't go outside the first two days, no matter how many ice creams Dad promised. On the third day, I went as far as the sweetshop, but came straight back. At least now, on the fifth day, I can look at people. Because here, they don't stare back.

I hated it.

All those strangers hanging around outside our house, shoving things through our door. Drone cams buzzing my window. Lola hated it too; she wouldn't stop barking. Dad had to hire a security bot which looked like a metal bin, but even then, they didn't give up. I hid in my bedroom with Lola, blinds shut, with my imps turned up high, while Dad ran around, yanking curtains and shouting at his phone.

How could Mum lie like that, to me and Dad?

How could she let that doctor do those things?

But then an uncomfortable thought pops into my head: I wouldn't be here if she hadn't. I'd be someone else. Not Dad's. *His.*

I used to think Mr Thomson was like the robot boy, David, because he kept his word. But actually, he's like the other one: Gigolo Joe.

I glance at the cottages nestled up against each other on the prom and watch the children race across the beach in their swimmers, as if it's a boiling-hot day. Mum always says those houses remind her of fairy cakes because of their colours: pale pinks, yellows and blues.

'Zurel!'

Dad's voice startles me. I thought he was at the beach café. Lola lifts her nose from a clump of seaweed, but I pretend I haven't heard. A girl in a frilly red bikini gallops into the sea, holding hands with her mum. A lump swells in my throat.

But then I remember.

And my heart squeezes shut, like a clam.

'Zurel?' Louder, now. 'Come here, please.'

Lola rushes over, assuming she's the one in trouble. I see Dad, running past the chalets.

Dad never runs.

'I've been calling you,' he pants, all sweaty and red. 'We need to get back to the cottage.'

I frown. I'll bet it's another 'work crisis'. But before I can pull out my screen to object, Dad clasps my hand.

'Come on.'

We march past the dawdlers and the people huddled over their phones. We're nearly at the ice-cream parlour. As we get closer, I see the usual queue at the hatch, but no one seems to be buying ice creams. They're all staring at something inside.

A woman in a blue jacket brings her hand to her mouth and gasps.

I try to wriggle my hand free, but Dad's grip tightens.

'Keep going, Zurel,' he says, in a low whisper, and walks even faster. 'I'll explain when we're back.'

The breath sticks in my throat. Something's happened: I know it.

This is never going to end.

67

Susan

I'm just taking my last swig when the doorbell rings.

My hand freezes, glass against lip.

Have they come back early?

Wine sours on my tongue as the early-evening sun dances leaf patterns across the room.

Idiot. I swallow. As if Steve would ring his own bell...

Now there's a knock.

Two knocks.

'Delivery!'

I lever myself up and squint at the security-cam. A guy in a short-sleeved shirt and navy baseball cap is standing in my porch, clutching a small package. I think of those macabre leaflets in the bin and my stomach tightens. But he looks legit.

Knowing Steve, it's probably some enhanced wearable. I imagine hurling his new Smart Band against one of the empty squares on the wall.

Then again, it could be for Zurel.

I activate the mic: 'Just a minute.'

I shuffle down the hall, wiping the mascara smears under my eyes.

I should fetch that box down from the spare room and hang all the photos back up. That would show him. As I turn the latch, the thought makes me smile.

The door slams into my face.

I stagger back, cupping my nose.

343

The man drops the package and barges past, his shirt straining against his chest, as if it can barely contain him. I glimpse a tattoo, the length of his forearm. He scans the lounge and marches upstairs.

Red petals spot the carpet.

I need to run, but my legs won't move.

I hear him thudding around, opening all the doors. Adrenaline surges, and I rush to the SmartPod, hit the button and steady my voice to give the command.

'Police emergency. Stream security footage and pet-cam.'

Feet hurtle down the stairs.

I race for the back door, but a hand grips my shoulder and spins me against the wall. Black eyes consume a sharp white face.

I point at my bag on the table. 'Money, cards. Take them.'

His mouth twists. There's a ferocity in those eyes: drugs? Booze?

Something else.

'Where. Is. It?'

My phone starts to ring, its playful chirps now obscene.

'I . . .' I swallow. 'I don't know what you — '

He clamps my neck, stopping my breath like a valve.

'The abomination.' Each syllable, staccato. 'Where is it?'

He leans closer, crushing my arteries. Black discs spin behind my eyes.

And that's when I realise. He's here for Zurel.

I claw at his face, scrabble at his fist, a primal strength eclipsing my fear. The choke releases as he grabs my wrists; breath and blood rush free. His arm wedges into my cheek; there's an inked black cross tapered like a dagger, two words underneath:

Isaiah 64

'Where . . . is . . . it?'

Fingers drill into my neck. The room begins to blur. I hear the ringtone again: faint, like an echo.

My lips make the shape of words. 'Don't . . . know.'

Pain explodes under my ribs. Instinct commands my body to double over, but I am pinned by the throat.

"Know that the Lord Himself is God; it is *He* who has made us, and not we ourselves." His lip curls back in a snarl. "We are the clay, and He is our potter, All of us are the work of His hand' . . .'

Pricks of light detonate in my eyes.

I think of that first scan, her twilight hand lifting in a wave.

He squeezes harder, spit foaming his chin, hot wafts of breath and sweat. 'Children are begotten, not designed. We will purge the rot, and restore Adam's line.'

Darkness swoops. I strain every nerve and muscle to hold on.

I'd give my life for hers, willingly.

But I cannot protect her if I'm dead.

More than 400 children and adults killed and 700 people injured in brutal attacks over Easter weekend.

By Emma Jimenez and Robin Brown, CNN

At least 223 children and 206 adults have been murdered and 761 people injured after a shocking surge in anti-intervention terror that has left twenty-one nations reeling.

The killings are believed to have been coordinated by a right-wing extremist group calling themselves 'Adam's Holy Warriors' (AHW) who planned the deadly attacks across Europe, the US, Australia and South America.

The worst hit city was New York, where there were 35 victims from shootings — twenty-two fatal — including 19 children, 3 of whom were babies, the New York Police Department said. The killers targeted homes, playgrounds and restaurants where families were celebrating the Easter holiday. London suffered the next highest death-toll, with 20 fatalities, including 13 children.

'These murderers deliberately targeted innocent children,' said the UK's top counter-terrorism police officer Miriam Hasan. 'AHW is an extremist far-right group that advocates violence against the providers and users of genetic interventions during pregnancy. Their online radicalisation campaigns foster wild conspiracy theories

346

intended to incite persecution, and now murder.'

AHW claims that gene editing of human embryos is part of a global conspiracy by a wealthy elite who are engineering a 'super-race' to control and ultimately destroy 'unenhanced' humans. Police now believe that AHW have links with those responsible for the illegal hacks and mass dump of fertility patient data two weeks ago.

The Genome Defence Alliance (GDA), which coordinated last week's anti-intervention protests, has strongly denounced the attacks.

The UK's prime minister condemned the attacks as 'appalling and horrific' and said the government will deploy soldiers on Britain's streets after the threat level was raised to critical.

Bram Klopp, INTERPOL secretary general, said: 'These are monstrous, cowardly crimes targeted at defenceless children and their parents. AHW hijacks Christian scriptures to support its hateful ideology and misinformation campaigns. Far-right violent extremists are exploiting Christianity to radicalise the anti-intervention movement, foment divisions and mobilise acts of terror.'

Klopp continued: 'We are working with the global law enforcement community to track down these killers and bring them to justice.'

68

Zurel

I shuffle along in the crowd, my bouquet in one hand, Dad's palm in the other. It's dark now, but not cold; the air smells of matches and flowers. My head is swimming; I couldn't sleep last night. Nor could Dad. I think I heard him, when it was just getting light, on the phone. I think he was crying.

There must be hundreds of us here, but the only sounds are our feet, and hushed whispers, as though people are even afraid to talk. Families hug each other; the group next to us are holding hands in a line, as if they're about to sprint into the sea. The lady nearest me clutches a knitted giraffe, her face wet with tears. I glance up at Dad, but his eyes are fixed straight ahead, like those mothers in China. Staring, but not seeing.

There are police here, too. Lots of them. They're the only reason Dad eventually gave in to my nagging and agreed I could come. Some are wearing bright-yellow jackets, others have bulky black vests and are carrying guns. Dad said two of them are here to look after me.

An image from the news breaks into my head, and I stumble. Dad catches me.

'Zurel, are you sure about this? Maybe we should go back?'

I shake my head. He sighs, and we march on.

We reach a big square of grass, and stop. The cathedral is lit in a golden glow, as if it's Christmas. But it's not Christmas, it's Easter: when Jesus supposedly rose from the dead. My fingers tighten around the flowers. None of those families on the news are coming back.

A platform's been set up in front of the cathedral, with a microphone. I gaze up at the stained-glass window with a star in the middle, surrounded by a circle of smaller windows, like the petals of a flower. People hold up torches. Some have banners: no dishes with knives. Lots of hearts, with names. And pictures of children.

Love, not Hate

God loves us all

'Let the little children come to me'

And what about the mothers? Where are they supposed to go?

Dad squeezes my hand and asks if I'm OK. I wipe my eyes and nod.

A man in a suit with a gold chain across his chest steps up to the microphone. He taps it twice and clears his throat, and the whispering stops. He welcomes us all, and thanks us for coming, as if it's some kind of party. He praises the police and the ambulance service for their bravery. Says how sorry he is for all the children and adults who were hurt or lost their lives; not just here, in Exeter, but all over the world. Then he tells us we mustn't let the terrible people that did this make us afraid. That we should carry on with our lives and help one another, no matter what we believe. Because there is no place in our community for hate and division. Those are the things the terrorists want. Instead, we must come together and forget our differences, to make things right.

As I listen to him, I think of Gary's mum, and the protestors outside the lab; the strangers pushing things through our door. And I wonder if it's possible for people to come together and forget. Because they don't like it if you're different. It frightens them. And everyone's been angry with each other for so long.

And then another man, with a grey beard, steps up to the microphone. A silver cross dangles over his purple shirt. I remember the woman outside school who was horrible to Mum, and my throat tightens.

'Our community is strong,' he says. 'Stronger than those who try to spread their poison of fear and hate.'

There's something about his voice that calms me.

He opens his arms wide. 'Let us come together. People of all faiths and beliefs. To support one another in our grief at these horrific crimes.'

The man in a red turban standing next to him nods.

'Safe in the knowledge that, ultimately, love triumphs over hate. Good over evil.' His words get deeper and slower. 'Life over death.'

Music starts playing — the sad kind that doesn't have words, and the man bends over a big candle. His cross swings forward as he lights it, and I'm worried it's going to knock the candle over, but it doesn't.

'This flame symbolises the light that burns for all eternity in peace and love. Let us honour those who were taken from us.'

Dad slips his arm around my shoulders. The woman next to him starts to cry. I watch the flame flicker and think of Mum.

The man says a prayer for the injured and dead children, then the mums and dads, then the police officers and other brave people who gave their lives. Dad's eyes are shut, but mine stay open. I'm watching the police, who are watching us. My eyes dart across the rows of bowed heads.

I wonder if any of *them* are here.

The ones who want to kill children like me.

Everyone starts clapping; the noise echoes round the cathedral grounds like gunfire, and I suddenly want to leave. Dad and I push our way through the mass of people, back towards the black-and-white houses with small window panes. One of the houses has blue-and-white tape around the front saying:

POLICE LINE DO NOT CROSS

The pavement outside is covered with flowers. There must be hundreds of bunches, so many they spill onto the cobbles below. As we move closer, I see messages written on cards, toy bears and dolls; wiggly drawings of rainbows and butterflies.

And I feel bad, because I didn't bring a painting of my own.

On the kerb, right in the middle, is a tray of sand, filled with tea lights and candles, all lit up like a shrine. I stare at the picture of two girls with pretty brown eyes cuddling a woman with black hair. A brown rabbit with floppy ears sits one side, a white rabbit the other.

Dad pulls me close and I squeeze his hand.

I lay our flowers near the candle box, on the cobbles. Dad let me choose them. I picked the same colours as those cottages on the seafront, at Lyme. The lady in the shop told me the flowers' names.

Mum would have known.

I kneel on the hard stones. A breeze carries wafts of wax and honey.

I screw my eyes shut and say a silent prayer of my own.

69
Susan

Someone touches my arm. I flinch.

'Hey there, soldier. It's me, Carmel. Are you awake?'

My brain fumbles for a response. I probe my mouth with my tongue and swallow.

Big mistake.

I gasp, which is worse.

'Don't try to talk, honey. Just give my hand a little squeeze.'

Magma sears my throat. I try to focus. Blue curtains. White panels.

Each breath is agony. As if my chest's in a vice.

Carmel's face swims into view. 'You're in the hospital, Susan. It's OK, you're safe.'

Memory unlocks. One question consumes me.

I grip her arm.

'Here . . . ' She passes me a screen. 'Use this.'

The pen lumbers over the keys:

— *Zurel?*

'She's safe, Susan, I promise. She has full protection. She's still with Steve.'

Thank God . . .

I clasp the screen.

— *They can't go home.*

'We know. The police are sorting out accommodation, somewhere secure. In the meantime, they're staying put.'

I let my eyes rest for a second. The moment I do,

his face appears.

My fingers slide up to my neck. It's lumpy and swollen.

'That's going to feel tender for a while . . .' Carmel swallows. 'There's quite a lot of bruising . . .'

She leans closer. Tears glisten. 'They got him, Susan,' she whispers. 'That monster's in custody, thanks to you.'

A bitter taste fills my mouth. I remember the hate radiating from him, like a shock wave. The fever in his eyes.

—*Who was he?*

Her face pinches. 'They call themselves 'Adam's Holy Warriors'. They're terrorists.'

It comes in flashes: the tapered cross on his arm. The bible quotes . . .

'It . . . it wasn't just you, Susan.' She hesitates. 'Hundreds of people have been killed, hundreds more injured . . . The whole world is in shock.'

I stare at her.

'And you know, those bastards . . . they targeted the children.'

I grip the sheets and think of Zurel. This is the life I've bequeathed to my daughter. A fanatic's target, constantly having to check her back.

'The government called a COBRA meeting. Things can't be allowed to escalate any further.'

My head sinks into the pillow. It dizzies me: how could anyone do such a thing?

— *Does Zurel know?*

Carmel takes a breath. 'Steve tried to shield her from the news, but . . . it's virtually impossible.' Her gaze lifts to mine. 'I spoke to him, earlier this morn-ing. He wanted to know how you were, if you needed anything. They both did.'

My throat constricts. I welcome the pain.

I was always so obsessed with the dangers to her, on the inside.

— *I want to see her so badly . . .*

'I know, sweetheart, I know.' She sniffs. 'But you need to get better first. Best give yourself some recovery time.'

My eyes meet hers.

— *How bad is it?*

She sucks in her lip. 'Well, put it this way, I won't be entering you for beauty contests any time soon.' She manages a weak smile. 'Your nose is bruised, but not broken. Your eyes are a bit red, but I'm reliably informed that a few burst capillaries are nothing to worry about.' Her gaze drops to my throat. 'They don't think there's lasting damage, but . . . you might want to invest in some scarves.'

She cuffs away a tear.

'The important thing is that the brain scan was clear. Which just leaves your ribs . . . He cracked two of them.'

The punch. That explains it. Why breathing hurts.

Carmel's face crumples. 'I'm so sorry, Susan. So very sorry . . .'

My fingers stretch across the sheet, still rusty with blood. Carmel folds them into hers.

'That call saved your life, the officer said. Just a few minutes later . . .'

A pinging noise starts in the next cubicle. Carmel glances round.

'I should probably fetch one of the nurses. Let them know you're awake.' She nods at me. 'Then the police will want to take a statement from you. If you're up to it.'

I give her a thumbs-up.

'OK.' She pats my arm and smiles. 'Won't be long.'

Carmel scurries off to the nurses' station, and I quickly pull up the news.

My tears slide down the screen.

Shootings, stabbings. Hit-and-runs.

Babies. Toddlers . . . It's a massacre.

I feel a tingling in my hands and feet. As if I'm standing at the edge of a very high cliff.

A few minutes.

A failed connection.

A different answer.

That's how close we came.

70

Zurel

I wander from room to room, Lola trotting behind me, her ears flat, asking: what's wrong? I try the breathing trick the nurse showed me, count my breaths in and out. Lola watches intently; when she catches my eye, her tail gives a low wag.

Mum will be here in ten minutes. It's the first time I've seen her in more than three weeks. She hasn't visited our temporary home before. That's what Dad calls it, because he doesn't know how long we'll be staying. It's a bit like our holiday cottage in Lyme, but without the holiday. Everything's very modern and tidy, but it's not home.

I read Mum's messages again this morning. Afterwards, I played my favourite audio files from Lyme. The waves sucking pebbles and slapping rocks. Gulls squawking round the fish-and-chip stand. Ropes tinkling against masts in the harbour, as if they're desperate to launch back out to sea.

Each night in the cottage, while Dad rattled around downstairs, I'd listen to the waves and try to imagine all the beaches they'd visited. And I'd think about the sand, and the rocks it came from, that were made when dinosaurs were still alive. I pictured those dinosaurs' shells and bones getting squished in the mud, moulding fossils that I would find one day. And it helped me sleep, imagining it all carrying on over millions of years, despite asteroids colliding, and the

356

oceans freezing over. Because, if our world could survive that, then surely, we could survive this?

Dad looked so sad when he left. I felt like I was letting him down. It's as if he's been hit by his own personal meteor: smashed into tiny, icy pieces. And, like Humpty Dumpty, he can't put them back together again.

I wonder if I should tell Mum about how he stays up for hours after he thinks I've gone to sleep. That distant look he gets, like he's not in the same room, when he is.

The way his back goes stiff, sometimes, when I hug him.

The doorbell rings. I check the camera, like Dad said, even though he's just across the street, and the security men are close by.

It's definitely her, but it doesn't look like her. The scarf's new.

Lola barrels past my legs and paws at the door. She's missed her too.

My fingers hover over the bolt as my tummy spins.

The door opens, and Lola nearly knocks Mum flying.

Mum bends down and strokes Lola's head with both hands, her hair blowing. Then she looks at me. And everything I'd planned to ask vanishes.

Susan

My eyes race over her. She looks older. Thinner. As if the little girl I brought home from school that day left for the seaside and didn't come back. There's something so fragile about her. I remember that scan

357

where I saw her bones through her skin. Like those deep-sea creatures: if you shine a light, you can see their organs.

She lets me hold her, and I breathe in her warm, buttery scent, ignoring the ache in my ribs.

I think of those other mothers. And fathers. The daughters and sons.

And I thank God we are here.

Zurel

Mum smells of perfume and arnica. She runs her fingers through my hair as Lola dances round our feet.

I notice the greeny-yellow blotch poking out from her scarf.

'I've missed you so much,' she whispers.

All she can do is whisper. She warned me about that.

Dad didn't tell me, not straight away. After I read the posts, he didn't have much choice. I begged him to take me to that vigil. That was when things changed.

It had been easier to shut her out. As if not seeing her would make things better. But it didn't. And when that man nearly took her from us, for good, I knew. Despite all the hurt.

So my prayer on the pavement outside the cathedral was a promise.

Because I still had my mum. Just. And she still had me.

Mum winces when she stands up and tries to cover it with a smile. I show her the rooms, as if this is my house, and she's just visiting. She nods a lot and says how nice it looks, but when the tour finishes, I know the hard part's coming.

'I've done a lot of thinking, Zurel,' she says, in her whisper. And I wonder how she felt when she couldn't talk at all.

'I imagine you have, too.'

I stare at the beige sofa and nod.

'I'm very sorry about lying to you, and to Dad.' She pauses. 'And Mr Thomson.'

It stings, but fainter now. I can still breathe.

'I'm especially sorry for frightening you, Zurel. Making you worry that something was wrong . . . Putting you in danger . . . ' She takes a deep breath in through her nose. 'If I had my time again, I'd do many things differently.' She bites her lip. 'But there's one thing I wouldn't change. Even now. Do you know what that is?'

I manage to shake my head.

She looks me in the eye. 'The procedure. Do you know why?'

My palms begin to tingle.

'Because, without it, I wouldn't have *you*, Zurel. The magical combination that makes you, who you are.' Her eyes glow as she takes my hands. 'And I'm so very grateful for that.'

Something inside me unfurls. Like one of those sails, in Lyme harbour.

Strapped to its mast for too long.

Susan

We watch the sparrows on the feeder while Lola snores at our feet. They dart on and off, flashing into bushes, always on alert.

359

I've answered Zurel's questions as best I can. It's not been easy, for either of us.

My throat is throbbing. I'm worried my voice will give out entirely, and I'll have to borrow Zurel's screen.

She fixes me with that intense, serious gaze.

— What happens now?

I swallow. 'I don't expect you to forgive me, Zurel. I can't fix the past or make what I did go away.'

Her delicate fingers clench her screen.

'But, I would like the chance to earn a future. Together. To prove to you that . . . ' I falter. ' . . . That I can be a decent mother. Not a perfect one, but better than I was.' My lip trembles. 'Because I do love you, so very much. And, whatever happens . . . Whatever you decide . . . I'll spend the rest of my life loving you.'

Zurel blinks at me and looks away.

I gaze at her screen and box up my hopes until there's room for them.

Like those things, in the loft.

She takes a slow breath: in and out. 'OK.'

It's the most wonderful sound in the world.

71

Susan

Three months later

I wander over to the tombola stall. The usual assortment of recycled, unwanted objects are on display. Wine (the hangover kind). Chocolates (generic, not customised). Last generation earbuds (not imps). I do my bit for school funds, and buy a ticket for five times the value of any prize. I win a talking tablemat.

'That'll come in handy, for dinner parties.' Marty grins at me.

'Ah, Deputy Headmaster; indeed. Not that I'll be throwing any for a while.'

It's the school summer fete. Zurel's last day at primary. I feel a wrench, but she's ready to move on, like the rest of them. Year sixes always outgrow the school.

Marty arches his eyebrows. 'I thought your pariah status had been rescinded?'

'Well, in theory . . . Let's see how long that armistice holds. At least I'll be back in a job, come September.'

'Amen to that.'

Pupils ping from stall to stall like pinballs, clutching lollies and melting ice creams. A pungent smell of charred bio-meat wafts from the barbecue.

'How's Zurel doing?'

'Oh, you know . . . ' I sigh. 'Up and down. This switching homes isn't easy.'

We had to move, for safety reasons. In any case,

we needed to sell the house. All in all, the separation went relatively smoothly; after the attacks, both Steve and I lost the will to fight. Zurel and Lola come to me alternate weekends, and stay with me during the week. We still need security. But we're getting used to that.

'You'd have been proud of her today, Susan.' He nods at me.

'She did it, didn't she?'

'Yup. Belted it out.'

Every summer, the school has a leavers' assembly, where each year six says something about their class and what they'll miss. I'd never have dreamed, last term, that Zurel would be taking part.

I shake my head. 'She's amazing. When you think of all she's had to contend with.'

'Yeah.' Marty slides his hands in his pockets. 'She said some lovely things, too.'

'I know; she showed me.'

It's taking time for Zurel to get past her difficulties with Marty. He understands, but I know he finds her distance hard. She has weekly meetings now with the speech therapist, and they've made good progress. Mrs Crowther was especially pleased when Zurel felt comfortable enough to speak in front of her. The school's been brilliant. If anyone so much as hints at anything, Mrs Crowther's on to them, and so is Tulya. But most of those comments have stopped.

We stroll over to the rides and I spot Zurel, swinging wildly back and forth on a giant panda, her hair streaming out behind.

Marty glances at me. 'There's a post doing the rounds saying they've caught one of the key figures behind that terrorist cell.'

362

I swallow. 'Yeah, I saw.'

'Tracked him down to a shed in Kansas.'

I don't respond. These people are like weeds: you pull them out by the roots, and it may take a while, but they still grow back.

'Any news on court dates?'

I shake my head as screams erupt from the inflatable slide. 'You know how long these things take. Could go on for years.'

Zurel races over, breathless. She sees Marty and reddens.

He smiles. 'Hey, Zurel. Blown all your credits?'

She looks at him sideways and nods.

I roll my eyes and top up her card. 'That's the last time, OK?'

She links arms with Tulya, and they prance over to one of the jewellery stalls. Zurel whispers something in Tulya's ear, and they burst out laughing. What would Stakhovsky say, if he could see her?

Those meetings are on hold. Indefinitely. Zurel's under a local team of clinicians now. She'll have to be monitored for the rest of her life — something both of us will have to live with. While the science world has rallied to reverse the cancer-inducing mutations, the neurological conditions have been much harder to pin down. There have been attempts to hold those who overstepped the mark to account. Professional bodies have condemned institutions who profiteered from 'illicit and unethical' interventions, and many have lost their licences. Some families have already got the courts involved; others are clubbing together to sue the clinics collectively. Governments have been slower to react: differences in law, and patchwork regulation perpetuating the same old problems.

I heard a rumour that Ukraine's Ministry of Health is launching an investigation. I wonder what their golden boy, Stakhovsky, will do about that.

I decide to move to safer ground. 'So, what are your plans, Marty? For the summer?'

He shrugs. 'Maybe Italy for a couple of weeks, with Rowena. Relax, see the family, get some sun. How about you?'

'Zurel and I have talked about hiring a campervan. Doing a road trip, round the coast.' I hesitate. 'Plus, we might be paying someone a visit.'

'Oh, yeah?'

I glance at him. 'I decided to track down my biological father.'

Marty's eyes widen. 'Oh, I . . . I didn't know . . . '

'Neither did I, until I was tested. As part of the whole . . . you know . . . '

My voice trails off. I think of Book Week, yanking out Marty's hair. Sometimes, I can't believe it was me who did those things.

We stare at the bouncy castle. Small bodies catapult up and down like popcorn in a machine. Even the first-aid bots are looking anxious.

Marty clears his throat. 'So, you've managed to find him, then, your father?'

'Yes, I located him easily, through one of the sites. I honestly didn't expect him to reply. But, he did.' I smile. 'Zurel doesn't have any grandparents left, so she's pretty excited. Turns out he was a donor to help put himself through college. And, get this: I'm the fifth one to make contact.'

'You're kidding?'

'Nope. I've been an only child my whole life. It's amazing to think I have four half-brothers or -sisters

364

I might actually get to meet. Zurel, too.'

He looks at me. 'Actually, there might be someone else for you two to meet.'

'Really?'

'Yeah.' He smiles. 'In around five months' time, all being well.'

I gaze at him. 'That's . . . wonderful!' I have an overwhelming urge to hug him, but hold back. 'Congratulations, to both of you. How's Rowena doing?'

'Oh, you know, a bit nauseous, but taking it all in her stride.'

I squeeze his arm. 'I'm so happy for you. Really. You'll be an amazing father.' Our smiles stiffen. 'Correction: you *are* an amazing father.' I ignore the tightening in my chest. 'I mean it, Marty.'

His mouth twitches and he looks away.

I swallow. 'I was thinking . . . Would you and Rowena like to come over one night, for dinner? My cooking may not be up to Sicilian standards, but I do a wicked toad in the hole.' I brandish my talking tablemat. 'I could even try and win a set, for the occasion?'

'Well, when you put it like that, it's hard to resist.' He allows a smile. 'As long as you think Zurel will be OK with it.'

I watch Zurel launch herself onto the slide. She flies down the chute, skirt billowing, her mouth stretched wide: half scream, half laugh.

'Yeah.' I nod. 'I reckon she will.'

Genome Treaty: Campaigners Hail New Era of 'Genetic Disarmament'

Aanya Khatri, BBC World News

Campaigners against the genetic manipulation of embryos claimed 'comprehensive victory' today after the Treaty for the Governance of the Genome came into force, following years of bitter wrangling.

The worldwide treaty became legally binding this morning after the United States became the fiftieth country to ratify the agreement.

The accord was agreed by 125 countries at the UN General Assembly in 2038, but had to be ratified by at least fifty before it could enter into force. Parliament approved the treaty in the UK in 2039 and its legal requirements will become binding later this year, although similar restrictions have long been implemented under UK law.

The treaty commits signatories to 'never under any circumstances engage in heritable human genome editing (HHGE) research or clinical interventions which introduce non-therapeutic enhancements to the human genome'.

Countries must limit the purposes of HHGE to the diagnosis and prevention of an approved list of diseases, and, only in tested and authorised cases, treatment, using gene therapy.

366

Cassandra Myers, chief executive of the Human Fertilisation and Embryology Authority (HFEA), said: 'Today is a victory for human values, equality and scientific rigour, and it promises a better future for our children and our children's children.'

The treaty's enactment was welcomed by protest group Genome Defence Alliance (GDA), which has been fighting genetic interventions for over forty years. Philippa Morris, GDA's London-based head of campaigns said: 'Decades of peaceful activism have paid off and achieved what many said was impossible; we now have a legally binding treaty to enforce genetic disarmament. The treaty will prevent the weaponisation and misuse of this technology so we can finally put an end to the perilous genetics arms race.'

Morris made reference to last month's report in the Guardian about China's development of a genetically enhanced military elite. The Chinese government continues to deny claims that it has used gene editing to engineer 'super soldiers' with higher pain thresholds and increased strength and stamina.

The UN Secretary-General, Joaquin Morales, welcomed the landmark decision by the United States and the enactment of the treaty, which he described as 'a meaningful commitment towards protection of the equal dignity of all human beings, through responsible governance of the human genome'. He urged the remaining signatories who had not yet ratified to do so.

There has been no immediate reaction from the two remaining powerhouses of genetic engineering who are yet to ratify the treaty — Russia and China.

The Inspiration Behind *Off-Target*

I knew long before my first novel, *The Waiting Rooms*, was published that I wanted to write about genetic technologies next. I've been fascinated by the rapid advances that have enabled us to decipher the living world's biological code, helping us tackle new viruses like COVID 19, as well as preventing incurable diseases such as Huntington's.

The idea for *Off-Target* came when I learned how genetics will not only revolutionise medicine and agriculture, but also the way we have babies, and how soon this might happen. Because the science is moving much faster than regulation or public debate.

We are approaching a future where, as Jamie Metzl says in his excellent book, *Hacking Darwin*, we can take active control of our evolutionary process by genetically selecting and altering our offspring. But, when it comes to rewriting our own biological code, even the scientific community is divided.

The desire to reproduce is a primal urge that we share with all creatures: the in-built drive to pass on our genes. And yet infertility levels in men and women are rising, across all continents. This has inspired the development of multiple assisted-reproduction technologies, offering hope for those who are struggling to conceive.

IVF, once seen by some as monstrous, has normalised our views of conception outside the human body. Egg and sperm donation have become routine. Demand for these treatments keeps growing, despite the physical and emotional challenges they present, not to mention the whopping price-tag. Would-be parents are prepared to put themselves through months, and in many cases, years, of gruelling procedures in their quest to have a child.

There are estimated to be over six thousand genetic disorders, with new ones being discovered all the time. Imagine a future where those diseases have been eradicated. Where miscarriage, largely caused by chromosomal abnormalities, becomes a rare occurrence. Genetic testing during IVF currently offers new parents a chance to prevent certain conditions being passed down through generations. Gene editing of embryos, if legalised, could go further.

The trouble is, genetic testing and editing have the potential to do a lot more than control disease. Some fear that such alterations could veer into the realm of non-medical enhancement and eugenics. Intelligence, athletic prowess, beauty, creativity . . . enhanced sensory capabilities or behavioural traits. The sheer pace at which genetic technologies are evolving is breath-taking. But just because we are developing the expertise to make well-intentioned changes to our unborn children, does that mean we should? How do we decide what's ethically acceptable, and how can we regulate and legislate the application of this technology in a way that is fair and equitable to all?

History shows we are often ill-equipped to understand the longer-term consequences of our scientific ambitions or prevent their malevolent exploitation.

It is these unintended impacts and ethical dilemmas that *Off-Target* explores.

You can find more facts behind *Off-Target* and my other books on my website: www.evesmithauthor.com.

I love taking part in book clubs, so do get in touch via the website.

You can also subscribe to a quarterly newsletter that will keep you posted on upcoming events and news. Thank you for reading.

Twitter @evecsmith

Instagram: evesmithauthor

Facebook: EveSmithAuthor

Acknowledgements

I owe many people thanks for their help in bringing my second novel, *Off-Target*, to life.

First and foremost, my publisher, Karen Sullivan and her amazing team at Orenda Books, including the editorial mastery of West Camel, the promotional prowess of Anne Cater, and all the other hard work that goes on behind the scenes by Liz, Cole and Victoria, not forgetting book-jacket design maestro, Mark Swan.

My agent, Harry Illingworth at DHH, who continues to endure my rookie questions, providing advice and guidance, and who keeps me on the straight and narrow.

All the book bloggers, reviewers and bookshop staff who champion our books with such passion, even in the midst of a pandemic. Thank you.

Special thanks must go to my expert readers, whose patience I sorely tested. The scientists and geneticists: Caroline Scott and Lee Carpenter, for not running a mile when I first put the idea to you. Also Chris Murgatroyd and Victoria Doronina: I am so grateful for your detailed feedback and your tolerance.

Next, Anne Watt, for her frank, invaluable insights into the painful world of infertility and the marathon of IVF: you are an inspiration to us all, Anne.

Also thanks to Jack Grimston, who cast his journalistic eye over my press articles, and whose knowledge and flair made them so much better.

Lindsay Hardy-Wood, whose extensive experience

as a speech and language therapist really helped my understanding of selective mutism. Thank you.

Rosie Boyle, Steve Morley and Pip Borrett for their help checking school procedures.

And last, but certainly not least, my alpha reader Bill Hudson, who can still be relied upon to murder unnecessary characters and restore confidence.

A final debt of gratitude rests with my friends and family, whose encouragement never falters, and especially to my husband, Dave, and two daughters (one of whom let me use her poem, HOPE IS . . .). It isn't always fun living with an author. Despite that, my family are still here and smiling.

Well, most of the time. Thank you.

We do hope that you have enjoyed reading this large print book.

Did you know that all of our titles are available for purchase?

We publish a wide range of high quality large print books including:
Romances, Mysteries, Classics
General Fiction
Non Fiction and Westerns

Special interest titles available in large print are:
The Little Oxford Dictionary
Music Book, Song Book
Hymn Book, Service Book

Also available from us courtesy of Oxford University Press:
Young Readers' Dictionary
(large print edition)
Young Readers' Thesaurus
(large print edition)

For further information or a free brochure, please contact us at:
Ulverscroft Large Print Books Ltd.,
The Green, Bradgate Road, Anstey,
Leicester, LE7 7FU, England.
Tel: (00 44) 0116 236 4325
Fax: (00 44) 0116 234 0205

A THREE DOG PROBLEM

S.J. Bennett

Queen Elizabeth II is having a royal nightmare. A referendum divides the nation, a tumultuous election grips the United States — and the body of a staff member is found dead beside Buckingham Palace swimming pool. Is it a tragic accident, as the police think? Or is something more sinister going on?

As Her Majesty looks for answers, her trusted assistant Rozie is on the trail of a treasured painting that once hung outside the Queen's bedroom. But when Rozie receives a threatening anonymous letter, Elizabeth knows dark forces are at work — far too close to home. After all, though the staff and public may not realise it, she is the keenest sleuth among them. Sometimes it takes a Queen's eye to see connections where no one else can . . .